Whippoorwill

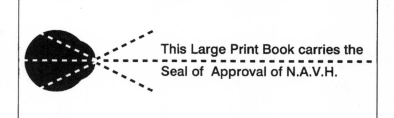

Whippoorwill

Sharon Sala

Thorndike Press • Waterville, Maine

Published in 2005 by arrangement with Loveland Press.

Thorndike Press® Large Print Romance.

The tree indicium is a trademark of Thorndike Press.

The text of this Large Print edition is unabridged.
Other aspects of the book may vary from the original edition.

Set in 16 pt. Plantin by Carleen Stearns.

Printed in the United States on permanent paper.

Library of Congress Cataloging-in-Publication Data

Sala, Sharon.
    Whippoorwill / by Sharon Sala.
        p. cm. — (Thorndike Press large print romance)
    ISBN 0-7862-7461-1 (lg. print : hc : alk. paper)
    1. Prostitutes — Fiction. 2. Kansas — Fiction.
3. Clergy — Fiction. 4. Large type books. I. Title.
II. Thorndike Press large print romance series.
PS3569.A4565W465 2005
813'.54—dc22   2004030427

DEDICATION

Everyone has a gift. Some use it, others are never even aware that it's there. My gift is being a storyteller. And because I feel so blessed by this gift, and because this book is so special to me, I want to dedicate it to the people who are responsible for who I am.

Through my father's people, I am part Cherokee and English, and through my mother, Irish and French, with a sprinkling of more English and German thrown in. While some of my ancestors were native to this wonderful land we now call the United States of America, others came from Ireland, from France, and from England and Germany. They were brave, strong-willed men and women who left the familiarity of one life for the uncertainties of another. Some left willingly. Others were given no choice. They lived and they died, owing no one but God the explanations for the way they did it. Their names are long forgotten, but the paths they struck still guide us from sea to sea.

I am grateful that their journeys all led to me.

As the Founder/CEO of NAVH, the only national health agency solely devoted to those who, although not totally blind, have an eye disease which could lead to serious visual impairment, I am pleased to recognize Thorndike Press* as one of the leading publishers in the large print field.

Founded in 1954 in San Francisco to prepare large print textbooks for partially seeing children, NAVH became the pioneer and standard setting agency in the preparation of large type.

Today, those publishers who meet our standards carry the prestigious "Seal of Approval" indicating high quality large print. We are delighted that Thorndike Press is one of the publishers whose titles meet these standards. We are also pleased to recognize the significant contribution Thorndike Press is making in this important and growing field.

Lorraine H. Marchi, L.H.D.
Founder/CEO
NAVH

* Thorndike Press encompasses the following imprints: Thorndike, Wheeler, Walker and Large Print Press.

FOREWORD

This book represents a departure from the Sharon Sala material you have been accustomed to. It represents a turning point for her in that she was not confined to the formula she has been using for most of her writing career.

Ms. Sala's unique ability to tell a compelling story has been directed mainly toward one kind of genre, which has been the foundation of her writing career. No argument about that. Just ask her loyal fans; they love her books and she loves writing for them.

This book, though a complete departure for her, is a story she wanted to share. Her problem was finding a publishing house to produce it.

Loveland Press provided that place. A place where your favorite authors can also stretch out with new and different material for their readers. Our goal is to provide published authors with an opportunity to produce work that does not fit their usual mold. We ask the authors to throw away the constraints of their normal books. This is the place where their readers can find them "off the leash" so to speak.

Your comments are always welcomed. Is there an author you would like to see break away from his or her normal subject matter and try something different? Let us know, give us a call or mail a card.

We look forward to hearing from you, and in the meantime, we hope you love this new book as much as Ms. Sala loved writing it for you.

PREFACE

Whippoorwill is a new venture for me. I wanted to explain that in advance so that you will not be taken unaware by the change in my usual story line.

I am so excited to be sharing this with you and hope you enjoy reading it as much as I did writing it. I've always wanted to do more than the romance and romantic/mystery/suspense stories, but couldn't seem to convince my current publishers to let me "branch out" so to speak.

However, persistence pays off and this wonderful book is the result. *Whippoorwill* is not a romance, or a historical, or a western, yet it has a little bit of all of the above. I call it a funny, sometimes bawdy romp through the old West and it all starts with the imminent arrival of a "real" preacher from back East.

It's a wonderful, funny story about second chances. I hope you enjoy the book and will recommend it to all your friends.

DREAMS ARE BORN NOT MADE

Sleeping with men for money was not something Leticia Murphy had planned on doing when she grew up, but then, neither had she planned on being orphaned at twelve, or winding up in a godforsaken place in the Kansas Territories like Lizard Flats. But here she was, like most of the other lost souls who'd come West, looking for something better, and in her case, wishing for a second chance. She knew the odds were against her, but it didn't stop her from yearning.

There was a ritual from her childhood that she performed each evening as the sun was going down. She would step out onto the balcony off her bedroom above the saloon, lift her face to the heavens to search for the Evening Star, then stand quietly in the growing shadows and listen for the call of the whippoorwill.

It came from a memory of her mother who had died when she was ten. Always, she was sitting in her mother's lap outside their clapboard house watching night fall across the land. They would sit on the front step with their bare feet planted firmly in the still warm dirt while enjoying the first cool breezes of evening. As they sat, they would search for the first star and wait for the call of the whippoorwill. Her mother had told her the bird was searching for its mate, but Letty had yet to meet a man who was worth the call. However, the memory was one of the few good ones she had left. Two years after her mother's untimely death, her father was killed by a Comanche hunting party. Letty survived by hiding in a hollowed out badger hole. That was the last time fate showed her any kindness. At twenty-seven, she was well past the marrying age and nearly too used up to care. Yet she didn't stop wishing, and she didn't stop dreaming about a different sort of life.

Then one day, something happened in Lizard Flats that had never happened before. Word began to spread throughout the area that a real preacher from back East was coming to perform a wedding. The news set off a whole series of unforeseen events. Caught up in the excitement of the occasion, Letty couldn't help but think that a change was coming for her, too.

A gunshot sounded just outside Letty's window. It wasn't the first time she'd heard that sound in Lizard Flats and she would bet her next year's wages it wouldn't be the last. When the sound of an argument followed, she didn't even bother to get up and look out to see what was going on. Chances were she'd see both of the stupid louts who'd started the fuss before the night was out. Men were always the same. Drink. Fight. Then celebrate their victories or losses by paying for her pleasures. And since her friend, Truly Fine's exit months earlier, Letty was the only woman still working at the White Dove Saloon, which meant she got more than her share of fools in her bed.

Refusing to think about the boredom of her life, she pushed the coal oil lamp a little closer to the mirror and then leaned forward, giving herself a final check before going downstairs.

Her eyes were still blue. Her hair was still brown, but there were fine lines at the corners of her eyes that hadn't been there last year. She pouted her lips to check her lip rouge then gave a stray curl a final tuck. It didn't do to dwell on the inevitable. She was getting older. The day was going to come when she would no longer be able to get a dollar for each man that she laid.

The strange thing was, she had never been able to see beyond that fear. What happened to old whores, she wondered? Did they just dry up and blow away like the earth in Lizard Flats, or was there something worse? Something more sinister than even she could imagine?

She made a face at herself just as Will the Bartender banged on her door.

"Letty! You come on downstairs now. I got customers wanting a little female attention."

"I'm coming! I'm coming!" she yelled. Just before she left her room, she blew out the lamp and then walked to the open door leading out onto her small balcony overlooking main street.

There was a faint breeze blowing, shifting the thin lace panels over her windows in an effort to get inside. She ran her fingers over the lace. Hanging the curtains had been a feeble attempt to give elegance to her life, but they also gave her a sense of satisfaction to know she'd paid for them herself. Her momma would have loved the fine lace, she thought, as she walked out onto the balcony, although she would have heartily disapproved of how Letty had come by the money to pay for them.

Once outside, she looked up. The sky was clear without a cloud in sight — the Evening Star already evident. The air smelled of dust and gunpowder. The thin slice of moon hanging just above the horizon would not cast many shadows upon the darkening land. For Letty, it was a night like so many others, yet she still listened, waiting to hear that call.

"Letty! You get on down here now!" Will the Bartender yelled again.

Letty ignored the call, watching as a half-dozen cowboys from a neighboring ranch came riding into town in a flurry of whoops and shouts. She rolled her eyes, hoping at least half of them got drunk and passed out before they got the notion to take her to bed.

Just as she was about to give up and go inside, she heard the haunting, mournful coo of a lone whippoorwill. Even though it was what she'd been waiting to hear, it brought shivers to her skin. Somewhere beyond the lights of the town, a small brown bird was calling to its mate. The sound was a reminder of who she'd been and not what she'd become, and it gave her enough solace to face the oncoming night. Satisfied, she walked back into her room and closed the door. It was time to get to work.

As she started down the stairs, Pete Fairly started banging on the piano keys. She didn't recognize the song, but it didn't really matter. The noise level inside the White Dove had already reached fever pitch and no one was listening to him play. When one of the cowboys saw Letty coming down the stairs, he let out a whoop.

"There she is!" he hollered, and took off his hat and threw it in the air before yanking her off the last two steps and whirling her around in his arms.

Letty pasted a smile on her face and let her mind wander as the cowboy took her around the room in what passed as a dance. Pretending that she liked it was part of the job. She knew how to laugh and flirt and drink with the best of them.

One hour passed and then another. Letty's toes had been stepped on so many times by so many drunk cowboys that she wanted to cry, and she was wishing for something substantial to eat.

"How about a song?" someone shouted.

Letty sighed with relief. At least while she was singing, they couldn't step on her feet.

"Yeah, sure, cowboy!" Letty said, and sauntered toward the piano when someone picked her up and set her on the end of the bar instead. She threw back her head and laughed and when she did, the men in the room laughed with her. Then she looked over at Pete, who was waiting for her to begin.

Letty cleared her throat. The room began to settle. She had a good voice, but it never occurred to her as she sang that her life was a perfect analogy for the small brown bird she listened for each night. She would never have admitted, not even to herself, that through her songs, she was calling for a mate of her own.

"Mother, oh Mother, where did I go
      wrong?
I was a good boy until I left your sweet
      home.
Now I sleep on the ground and spend
      my days on the run.
With nothing to remind me of you but
      this song."

The poignancy of the words blended with the pure notes of Letty's voice, bringing more than one wild cowboy to tears. Before she was through, the room had gone completely quiet.

Even the gambler at the back of the

room had laid down his cards and was leaning forward, his elbows on the table, his gaze fixed on Letty's face. He'd been at the White Dove for exactly six days now, and each night he found himself drawn to the woman sitting at the end of the bar. He knew her name was Leticia Murphy, but she called herself Letty. In her youth, he figured she must have been quite a looker, but the hard life and the years had etched their own brand of scars on her face. The smile on her lips never quite reached her eyes, and her laugh was too brittle to be believed. Still, there was something about her that drew him. Maybe tonight he'd make it his business to do more than tip his hat.

When she sang the last notes of the song, there was a hush and then a collective indrawn breath from everyone in the room before the men erupted in a chorus of whistles and cheers. Then, to kill the painful memories resurrected by the song, the cowboys immediately began buying more drinks, which suited Will just fine.

"Hey, Eulis," Will shouted to the drunk at the end of the bar. "Go to the storeroom and bring me another crate of whiskey. I'm gettin' low."

Eulis Potter pushed himself from the bar and aimed his feet in the general direction of the back room. Once he'd been a soldier with General LaMoyne's army. The fort was long gone, burned to the ground back in forty-two by a Comanche raiding party. After that he'd quit the service and wandered the Territories until he'd come to Lizard Flats. He'd gotten drunk in the White Dove that night and had yet to sober up long enough to leave, although he did have two jobs that kept him partially occupied. One was doing odd jobs for Will at the White Dove and the other was digging graves on the hill outside of town. He didn't particularly care for either one, but they kept him in drinks.

Letty watched Eulis as he stumbled toward the back room. His clothes were little more than rags that stunk to high heaven and she'd never really seen his face. It was hidden behind a mop of dark, unshorn hair and a thick, greasy beard. But she was a 'live and let live' sort of woman and rarely wasted energy on something that didn't concern her. Thankful that the men were otherwise occupied, she slipped off the end of the bar and nodded to Will. It was her signal that she was going to her room.

He hesitated, as if thinking about calling her back, then saw the look on her face and waved her on.

She started up the stairs, her mind on the warm bath waiting for her in her room, when she heard footsteps behind her. She turned, a ready rejection on her lips, only to realize it was the cardshark who'd been occupying the back table all week.

"I'm done for the night," she said. Then the gambler doffed his hat.

"Miss Murphy, my name is Jim LaSalle. May I buy you a drink?"

His voice was cultured. His fingernails were clean. Despite her weariness, it was enough of an oddity to pique Letty's interest. She hesitated, then shrugged.

"I guess."

She started to go back downstairs with him when he shook his head and cupped her elbow instead.

"Is there somewhere we could go that is a little more private?"

Letty snorted. It was unladylike, but then his last question had been ungentlemanly, and she wasn't in the mood to take another man to bed.

"Speak your mind, mister. I'm too tired for games. You can drink by yourself. If you want to take me to bed, it'll cost you a dollar."

The gambler heard disappointment in her voice and it shamed him. He lifted her hand to his lips and gently kissed it, then fixed her with a dark, secretive gaze.

"I don't want to drink by myself. Besides, I think you sell yourself too cheaply, Letty. You're worth far more than a dollar."

Letty's mouth dropped.

"Now how about that drink?" he asked.

Letty found herself nodding.

LaSalle hurried back down the stairs, talked Will the Bartender out of a fairly decent bottle of wine that he'd been saving for himself and grabbed the cleanest two glasses he could find before joining Letty back on the stairs.

"After you, Miss Murphy," he said.

Letty stared for a moment, then turned and led the way to her room.

Jim didn't know what he'd expected, but clean sheets and lace curtains wasn't it.

"I don't bring my customers here," Letty said, and then wondered why she'd said that.

Ah, so that explains it. "Then I thank you for the courtesy of considering me a friend."

Letty's eyebrows knitted. "I don't know what I consider you, mister, but I wouldn't call you a friend. I don't have any friends."

"My friends call me Gentleman Jim," he

said, "but I would like it if you would call me Jim." The wine and glasses were set on a nearby table. He opened the wine and then looked at Letty. "May I pour?"

She shrugged. "It's why you came. Suit yourself."

He muffled a sigh as he poured the wine. So, she was harder than he would have liked. From her viewpoint, he doubted that his life looked any rosier. As he handed her a glass, he realized that, subconsciously, he had been hoping she would behave as had the women from his past — simpering and flirting while knowing full well that their lush bodies and sweet lips tricked hungry men into vowing words of love and marriage that they didn't really mean.

"To friends," he said gently, and lifted his drink. The distinct clink of glass to glass echoed within the quiet of the room, and he thought as they took their first sip that at least this woman was honest. She didn't pretend. With her, a man knew where he stood.

"To friends," Letty echoed, and then walked out of her room onto the small balcony, knowing the man would follow.

He did.

"Why, this is a wonderful place," Jim said, taking note of the night sky while looking down upon the sprinkling of lamplights throughout the small town.

Letty shrugged. "I guess," she said, and then tossed back the wine in the glass as if it were medicine.

"Would you care for more?"

Letty sneered. "You don't have to get me drunk to do it. Or maybe it's you who has to get drunk before you can lower yourself to use a woman like me."

Jim frowned. "What are you getting at?"

Thankful for the darkness that hid tears in her eyes, Letty handed him the empty glass and then put her hands on her hips in a defiant manner.

"It's obvious you're not like the men around here. You're used to elegant women and nice places. I'm not elegant and the White Dove Saloon isn't much, either."

"I'm afraid you misjudge me, Miss Murphy. What I once was is no longer important. I am nothing more than a man who makes his living at cards. I have no home, no family, nothing but a horse and two suits of clothing. I fail to see where that sets me above you in any way."

Letty's heart started to pound. What was he up to? "Then what is this all about?"

For a moment, he said nothing, and then

he sighed. She heard it from where she was standing.

"I can tell that I've caught you at a bad time," he said gently. "My mistake. Next time we'll do this at the beginning of your day, rather than at the end of it."

He took a step forward, once again lifting Letty's hand to his lips, but this time he pressed a kiss in the center of her palm.

Letty's heart skipped a beat.

"You sing like an angel, Miss Murphy. Maybe tomorrow night when you sing, you might look my way. At least I can pretend that you're singing especially for me."

"Uh, I don't —"

He tipped his hat, lightly vaulted the distance between her balcony and the one on the next building, then took the stairs down to the street. She watched as he sauntered toward the hotel and then disappeared inside.

She couldn't think. She couldn't move. Something wonderful had just happened but she wasn't sure what. Not since her father's death had she been treated so decently. She wanted to laugh and at the same time, felt like crying. In the distance, she heard the sound of horses hooves and then a shout of laughter. Confused by what had transpired, she went back into her room and closed the door.

Wearily, she pulled the curtains shut, took off her clothes, and stepped into the tub of bath water that Will furnished for her each night. As she sank into the depths of the hip bath, relishing the warmth of the water lapping at her thighs, she thought of how many trips Eulis had made up the stairs to fill her bath. If he spent that much time on his own personal hygiene, he wouldn't be so disgusting. Then it dawned on her that judging the town drunk was hardly in her best interests. Even though she hadn't let demon rum get the best of her, they weren't so far removed from each other after all. For three free drinks of liquor each night, Eulis Potter swept the floors of the White Dove Saloon and carried water for Letty's bath. For a roof over her head and food in her belly, Letty let strangers have their way with her body.

Disgusted with the rambling nature of her thoughts, she reached for the washrag and lye soap and began scrubbing the scent of her customers from her skin. A short while later, she turned back the covers on her bed and crawled between the clean sheets. Her head hit the pillow with a weary thump, but just before she closed her eyes, she remembered the gambler and the way his lips felt on her skin. She wouldn't let herself believe that he'd meant anything personal. She couldn't afford to care.

Even though she didn't trust him, the gambler continued to sit at the back table for the next five nights. When he wasn't playing cards, he was listening to her sing. And each night she found herself watching for his smile of approval when the songs were over. On the sixth night he wasn't there, and she learned that he'd picked up his horse from the livery and ridden out around noon. She wouldn't let herself care that he hadn't said goodbye or wonder what the brief moments she'd shared with him had really meant. Instead, she immersed herself in the business of her life and told herself it didn't matter.

A couple of days later, Will was busy closing up for the night. He was polishing the glasses and Eulis was sweeping up the floor for his usual three free drinks as Letty started up the stairs.

"Well, Letty, looks like you had a good night," Will said, as he counted out the coins she'd laid on the bar.

Letty frowned. "Depends on what you call good. I made twelve dollars, half of which is yours, and thanks to the last three cowboys I pleasured, I smell like a horse."

Will frowned. Keeping Letty happy was part of what made his business so good. His other girl, Truly Fine, had been gone for close to a year now and he couldn't afford to have Letty leaving, too. He'd noticed that she'd been sulking some since that fancy gambler had left town. While he wasn't sure what that had to do with anything, he didn't want her leaving him as Truly Fine had done.

"Eulis! When you get through sweeping that floor, you take Letty up some hot water for her bath! Do you hear me?"

Eulis braced himself with both feet apart and leaned on the broom before turning a bleary gaze toward Letty.

"Bats? Letty has bats?"

Will the Bartender cursed and then came out from behind the bar and swatted Eulis on the shoulder.

"No, you old sot. I said, bath! Letty wants her bath."

Eulis reeled back in shock. "I ain't givin' no woman a bath. Not even for a whole bottle of hooch."

Letty clenched her teeth to keep from screaming.

"Eulis!"

He veered his gaze in her general direction.

"What?"

"Go get the hot water and bring it to my room."

Light dawned. "Oh! Right! The hot water."

He dropped the broom where he was standing and headed for the back room.

Letty glared at Will, daring him to argue. When he remained silent, she tossed her head and started up the stairs.

Eulis thumped up the stairs with the two buckets of hot water for Letty's bath only to find her door was ajar. He stumbled in, slopping a goodly portion from one bucket into his shoe before getting it into Letty's tub.

"Tarnation!" he yelped, as the hot water soaked through his threadbare sock onto his skin.

In pain, he quickly dumped the water into the small hip bath, then dropped to the floor. He was in the act of taking off the wet shoe when Letty came in from the balcony.

She saw Eulis on the floor taking off his shoes and thought he was getting undressed.

"Don't even think about it!" she yelled,

and picked up her hairbrush and hit him on the back of the head.

At this time of night, Eulis was always less than steady on his feet. Sitting down made little difference to his equilibrium. The blow from the hairbrush sent him face forward between his outstretched legs. He groaned, both from the shock of the blow and from the pull of unused muscles at the backs of his legs.

"What did you go and do that for?" Eulis cried, then ducked again in fear of a second swing.

"There's only one reason a man ever takes his shoes off in a woman's room and I'm done with that for the night," Letty said.

Eulis groaned. "No. No. I wasn't tryin' for no poke. I swear. I spilt hot water in my shoe. That's all."

Letty frowned. "Oh. Well then. I guess I'm sorry for hitting you."

Eulis shrugged. "It's all right. It didn't hurt none. It just startled me."

He peeled the sock from his foot, then eyed the skin.

"What do you think? Reckon it'll blister?"

Letty snorted. "I reckon it didn't make it past the first two layers of dirt. That's what I reckon."

Now it was Eulis's turn to frown. "It

don't pay to insult the man what brings you your bath every night."

Letty sighed and then sat down on the side of the bed.

"You're right. I'm sorry, Eulis. No hard feelings, okay?"

Eulis waited until she tossed the hairbrush onto the other side of the bed and then he rolled over and dragged himself upright.

"Yeah . . . well . . . just see that it don't happen again," he muttered, and started out the door when Letty called him back.

"Hey, Eulis, do you ever want more in your life than what you got?"

Eulis's head was starting to float right off his shoulders, which always meant he had about five minutes, no more, no less, before he passed out. He preferred passing out on his bed in the back of the saloon, but if Letty didn't stop her yapping, he wasn't going to make it down the stairs. However, he knew women well enough to know that if he didn't answer this question, there would be another and another until they got the answer they wanted, so he shrugged.

"I reckon so."

"Me, too," Letty said. "What do you want?"

"That's easy," Eulis said. "You know that

big fancy bottle of Tennessee bourbon Will has sitting on the back of the bar? The one he's never opened?" He grinned. "That's what I want."

Letty snorted in an unladylike manner and grabbed for the hairbrush again.

"Get out of my room, you old sot, and take your stinkin' shoe with you."

Eulis ducked as she picked up his shoe and sock and flung them past his shoulder and out into the hall. He made it out of her room just as the door hit him in the backside. It sent him staggering even more, but he caught himself on the stair rail and then turned and glared at her closed door.

"I wish she hadn't asked me no question. I knew I wouldn't have the right answer," he grumbled, then rubbed his hands on his face, trying to stimulate blood circulation.

He eyed the shoe that she'd thrown and knew that if he wanted it back, he would have to bend down to pick it up. He also knew that if he did, he'd spend the night on the floor in the hall.

"I reckon I'll get it tomorrow," Eulis said, and started down the back stairs, one shoe lighter than when he'd come up. He made it all the way to his room, but when he turned around to sit down, missed the side of the bed and sat down on the floor.

"Tarnation."

It was his last thought of the night as he rolled over on his side and fell asleep.

Upstairs, Letty was in a similar state of mind, but her fugue was not from drink, it was from the miasma of her life. As she washed the stink of her job from her body, she began to imagine what it would be like not to have to put up with any more men ever again and as she did, Jim LaSalle's image drifted through her mind.

Long after she'd finished her bath and gone to bed, she'd lain awake, thinking of a dark-eyed gambler who'd smiled at her and kissed her hand.

Howe the Mighty Do Fall

Reverend Randall Ward Howe was a sinner. He knew it. He accepted it. He even blamed God for it from time to time, claiming he was nothing more than he'd been born to be. It was true that Randall Howe did everything in extreme — from demanding the best cuts of meat to the richest of desserts. And it was also true that he was more than a little bit vain. His clothes were tailor-made, his bowler hats imported from London, England. His shoes had a perennial shine and the part in his hair was straight down the middle.

Even though he was well over six feet tall, he was more than a little bit pudgy. He accepted the fact that with age, would come corpulence. His father had run to fat. His mother had been Rubenesque in stature as well. Still, at forty-two, he carried himself well, in spite of a growing paunch.

But these were the least of Randall's sins. The one he fought most often — the one that least befitted his role in life — was the sin of lust. It was a sad and truthful fact, but Randall Ward Howe — Reverend of the United Brethren Church in Boston, Massachusetts — lusted after women.

It was also true that as he moved from parish to parish, he left weeping widows in his wake. Lonely women who'd been easy game for the sweet-talking preacher. Women who'd let themselves be swayed by the power of his voice and the caress of his hands. And, because they were widows, he had gotten away with his indiscretions. They were the women who had been relegated to the sidelines of society because they no longer had a gentleman to accompany them. It had been so easy to slide into the role of protector. It had been even easier to become their confidante. After that, bedding them had been simple. The trick was staying on the far side of a wedding ring.

For a while, the joys of being wooed overshadowed the widows' hopes of being wed. But that phase never lasted. Eventually the gullible women would begin to see that their expectations did not coincide with the reverend's intentions.

That was when the hoohaw would begin. It was also the signal for the Bishop of the

34

United Brethren Churches to once again step in, sternly admonish Randall Howe for his sins, and discreetly move him to another city. To Randall's credit, his shame always seemed sincere, and his promises to do better rang true. But there was a limit to everyone's patience and Randall Howe knew that his appointment to the Boston church was his very last chance. In fact, he'd heard it on good authority that had it not been for the fear of public scandal, the bishop would have already stripped him of his collar and shown him the door. Yet he *was* in Boston, and he had *no* intentions of betraying God, or the bishop, or himself again.

But that was before Priscilla Greenspan, widowed daughter of the United Brethren's deacon, Ambrose Tull, sallied into the church. One look at the petulant pout on her lips and he knew his restraint was going to be sorely tried.

By normal standards in any society, Priscilla Greenspan would have been called a fine looking woman. For Randall, who had been abstinent for more than three months, she was a goddess. One look at her burgeoning bosom and trim waist, and his body betrayed him. Only the fact that he was covered by the mantle of his reverendly robes saved him from public humiliation. He took a deep breath and gritted his teeth as he reminded himself it couldn't matter how lovely she was. He was here to spread God's word, not to sow his seed in unhallowed ground. And then she smiled at him. The battle was lost before it began.

Priscilla lay in the jumble of covers with a frown on her forehead and her lips drawn into a pout. This was the fifth time in as many weeks that she had agreed to a secret assignation with the reverend, but her patience was wearing thin. Granted she'd been swayed by his fine figure and pretty ways. And there was the fact that she'd been ripe to be had. A widow for more than two years now, her needs as a woman had been brimming to running over. Randall Howe had taken care of everything, including the brimming needs. And she'd loved it.

But now that Priscilla Greenspan's fire had been dampened, her thoughts had turned to the future — hers and Randall Howe's. The only problem was he'd never even said he loved her. She didn't want to give him up, but playing loose to keep him wasn't in her plan. Last night she'd decided all he needed was a nudge. So she'd agreed to meet him again, telling herself it was to be the last time without benefit of vows.

"Randall, darling, I simply don't understand."

Randall smiled at her as he buttoned his shirt. All rumpled and pink-cheeked from their recent bedding, she was a picture to behold.

"Don't understand what, my dear Priscilla?"

His mind was already moving toward tonight's church council meeting. His conscience pricked as he thought about what he'd been doing, but only slightly. This time he'd convinced himself it was different. This woman was perfect for him. She hadn't demanded a thing from him except more lovemaking. He'd been happy to oblige.

He reached for his pants.

"Why have we yet to speak of our future?" she asked.

At that moment he knew, as surely as he knew his own name, that his days at the United Brethren Church were numbered. He pasted on a sweet, sickly smile and tried to focus on something besides throwing up.

"My goodness, Priscilla, you take me by surprise. I was not expecting such forwardness from a woman of your stature."

Priscilla heaved herself out of bed, unmindful of her naked state or the fact that her breasts were swinging.

"Forward? We've made love, Randall. Several times, in fact. I've risked my reputation to be with you."

She threw herself into his arms, and it has to be said that for a moment, when her bare body pressed against him, Randall did consider the institution of marriage. But the thought left almost as quickly as it had come. All he could do now was placate her until he figured a way out of this mess.

He pressed a nervous kiss to her cheek and then helped her into her wrapper.

"I know, I know," he said quickly. "And I appreciate your feelings. But you must give me time."

Her pout tightened. "I never did like to wait," she muttered. "And my papa would tell you it's true."

The fact that she'd thrown her father's name into the conversation had been no accident. It was a subtle reminder that her father was the deacon of his church. He stifled a curse and took her into his arms.

"My dear, it is with sorrow that I must leave you now. The church council meets tonight. I need to have time to gather my thoughts, both for it, and for the future."

He watched as her face broke into a smile. He'd purposefully misled her into thinking that his future and hers were one and the same. His conscience pricked again. But not enough to make things right. A few minutes later he was in his buggy and leaving the small country inn with haste. Priscilla Greenspan had gotten herself there. She could get herself home. He had plans to make and they did not include the deacon's daughter.

To say that Bishop Hale was surprised by Randall's request was putting it mildly. He still couldn't reconcile himself with the man he'd known, to the man he saw before him now.

"Are you certain this is what you want?" Bishop Hale asked.

Randall nodded solemnly, clutching his Bible close to his chest.

"As I told you before, I believe it to be a revelation from God, Himself."

Bishop Hale frowned. "But the Territories?"

Randall posted his most reverent expression. "Where else is God's word more needed?"

The bishop felt like crying. All these years and it seems that he'd been misjudging this man terribly.

"Then West it shall be! I'll firm up your initial itinerary by the end of the week. In fact, this timing is most opportune. I've had a letter just last week from a friend. It seems there is a need for a man of the cloth in a place called Lizard Flats."

Randall's heart skipped a beat. Lizard Flats? Somehow he doubted that the amenities of civilized society had yet to reach that far. But he pasted on a smile and just nodded as the bishop continued.

"And Randall, after the first month, you will be on your own as to where or how far you travel. As for monies, you understand there won't be a lot. Our missionary budget is slim. You must count on donations for a goodly portion of your livelihood."

At this point, Randall gave himself a mental pinch. Stupid. Stupid. Stupid. He hadn't thought of that. He'd been so set on escaping before everything fell down around his ears that he hadn't taken into consideration his standard of living would suffer as well.

Then he sighed. It was, after all, no more than he deserved.

He sighed. "When I am in need, I'm certain that God will provide."

It was the perfect answer. Bishop Hale beamed.

And while Howe's journey was about to begin, a journey of another kind was already in progress.

Alfonso Worthy was the banker of Lizard Flats. His rise to success had been hard-won. He was not a man given to flights of fancy, and yet because of his adoration for Sophie Hollis, he'd become something of a rake. For the first time in his life he'd fallen in love. Making money no longer gave him the satisfaction it once had, and he had long ago accepted that his physical appearance was less than admirable. He was small and skinny and his white-blond hair had been thinning for years. He feared that openly courting the wealthy widow was out of the question, but his lust and love had overflowed, so he'd begun a rather unique method of gaining Mrs. Hollis's attention.

Several times a week after all others were asleep, he would sneak out of the hotel where he resided and leave small gifts and letters, even poems of adoration and love upon her doorstep. It wasn't gaining him any ground with her, but he was able to pour out his heart just the same.

In effect, he'd become Sophie Mae Hollis's secret admirer.

THE MAN OF HER DREAMS

Sophie Hollis squinted as she peered into the mirror. The faint, but permanent, frown lines between her eyes and across her forehead only deepened her resolve. By her reckoning, she was in full bloom. Very full bloom. If she didn't latch onto another husband within the next couple of years, it would be too late. By then, her looks would be gone and she'd have to spend the rest of her life without a man in her bed. For the lusty and lonely widow, it would be a fate worse than death. While some people refuse to accept certain truths about themselves, Sophie had long ago come to terms with the fact that she didn't like to live alone. Yes, she was a well-to-do widow, but her life was empty without a man.

If Nardin Hollis hadn't happened along twelve years ago and snatched her out of her own bed and into his own, Sophie suspected that her youthful bodily desires would have gotten the best of her. She would have mounted the first man who hadn't smelled like manure, and ended up flat on her back being rode by every other man who did, like that disgusting Letty creature at the White Dove Saloon.

With a heartfelt sigh, she pinched the soft, fleshy parts of her face and bit her lips to the point of pain. When she looked in the mirror again, the pink pout on her mouth and the rose flush on her cheeks sent the frown on her face into hiding.

At this point, she reminded herself that all wasn't lost. For the past six months, small gifts of wildflower bouquets and pretty rocks — even a delicate little bird's nest with three tiny blue feathers interwoven within the grass and twigs — had been appearing on her doorstep. Then the letters began, sometimes just a message relating how fetching she had looked that day, or a bit of poetry that leaned toward love and romance while maintaining decorum. She'd been shocked, excited, and then downright curious to know who in Lizard Flats had become her secret admirer.

Now, six months had passed and the idea of being adored from afar wasn't as enticing as it once had been. Sophie was tired of the secrets. She wanted a flesh and blood companion to grow old with, someone with whom she could share her fears as well as her desires. But as hard as she'd tried, she couldn't figure out who, of the unattached men in Lizard Flats, was eloquent enough to have penned the sweet missives.

She moved to the desk and opened a drawer, taking out a packet of envelopes, then lifted the top one from the stack. She knew what was inside, but she wanted to read it again. Maybe this time she would see a hint of the writer's identity in the lines.

You passed me on the street today and my poor heart went aflutter.
I wanted to tell you how your smile delights me, but all I could do was mutter.
The brief hello I managed to say was pitiful and small,
Dear lady of my heart please know that you're the best of all.

Your ardent admirer

Sophie laid the poem back on top of the stack and closed the drawer.

Dear lady of my heart. He always calls me dear lady of my heart.

"I might be a bit more impressed if he

had the guts to say it to my face," she said under her breath, then tucked her shopping list into her purse, picked up her parasol, and headed for the front door.

She stepped outside, pausing long enough to open the parasol against the blistering heat of the day. Holding it at a stylish tilt, she stepped off the porch and started down the walk then stopped at the gate, looking back at all that was hers.

The two-story clapboard house gleamed white in the sunshine, while the gingerbread decorating the eaves, porch, and posts had been painted a robin's egg blue. Well-kept flower beds overflowing with hollyhock, sweet peas, and asters circled the house from front to back, broken only by the cobblestone walk that Nardin had carefully laid to keep Sophie's feet dry during the rains.

In Savannah, where Sophie had been raised, this small white house would have been nothing to talk about. But in Lizard Flats, where she and Nardin had settled, it was elegance at its finest.

Sighing with satisfaction that all was well in her world, she gave her parasol a quick spin and walked out the gate. Nardin Hollis might have died and left Sophie in heat, but he had not left her penniless. She owned half of Lizard Flats and the connecting stage lines to seven other towns in the Territory.

But while Sophie owned one thing, she wanted another. All the way to the store, she kept thinking of what she'd lost when Nardin had died.

Moments later, with the Territory dust swirling around her head and the parasol threatening to take flight, she turned the corner toward Main Street and stepped onto the uneven planks of the sidewalk. The bell-like skirt of her new yellow dress swayed vigorously with each step that she took. She was a bright flower of womanhood on the verge of shedding.

Inside the Territorial Bank of Lizard Flats, Alfonso Worthy kicked back in his chair, contemplating his worldly goods. It was true that he had accomplished more in his forty-two years than he would ever have believed. As the seventh and last child of a widowed Kentucky dirt farmer, his future had been uncertain until the day his daddy had unexpectedly died. After the bank had reclaimed the land for unpaid debts, the offspring of Conrad Worthy found themselves homeless and scattered to the four winds.

At the age of seventeen, Alfonso hired

himself out as a driver to a sickly couple who were leaving with a wagon train heading West. They died in mid-trip, leaving Alfonso with a wagon full of dry goods. It amounted to the beginnings of a small store that would be his grubstake. After that, it seemed as if his good fortune had all been downhill. It had taken him several years and several Territory towns to get where he was today, but as the only banker in Lizard Flats, he had the world by the tail. Only now and then did he ever wonder what had become of his six brothers and sisters, but the thought never stayed with him long enough to pursue it. Except for the absence of a woman in his life, Alfonso was as satisfied with himself as he knew how to be. He had steak when he wanted it, a bath every other night, and could afford the pleasures of Letty Murphy, the only easy woman within two days' riding distance. But life wasn't perfect. What he wanted but had yet to achieve, was his heart's desire. He was in love with a woman who barely acknowledged his existence.

In the midst of that thought, a flash of yellow caught his eye. He turned to look and then jumped to his feet. He didn't have to look twice to know who he'd seen.

Sophie Hollis stirred his blood. The fact that she begrudged him so much as the time of day hardly mattered. When he thought back to where he'd been and how far he'd come, changing an unwilling widow's mind had become his next and hopefully, last challenge. Determined not to let the opportunity to speak to her go to waste, he took his hat from the hat rack and headed for the front door.

"Greeley, I'll be out for a bit," he told the teller, and hurried out to the street.

He admired Sophie's attributes greatly; those long, blonde curls and that sweet baby-face, her wide blue eyes, and the way she filled out a dress. There was a smile on his face as he called out to her.

"Sophie! I say . . . Sophie Hollis!"

Sophie stopped in mid-step, wondering if it would be possible to ignore him, yet when she heard the rapid beat of his footsteps behind her, she sighed. She knew who it was. She recognized the voice, but ignoring Alfonso Worthy was like trying to ignore a tick stuck fast to your skin. No matter how small and unsightly, the little thing would persist, sucking and chewing and drinking you dry. She stifled a sigh and turned around.

Alfonso swallowed twice in rapid succession as their gazes connected, unaware that his Adam's apple was bobbing on his neck like the float on a line with a fish on the hook.

"Good morning, dear Sophie. I must say, you look positively beautiful."

Sophie twirled her parasol absentmindedly. She would have to speak. He'd put himself directly in her path again. The quick once-over she gave him was out of habit. As often as she looked and as close the inspection, his appearance did not entice her, but she managed a smile in response to his praise.

"Why, thank you, Alfonso."

He shuffled nervously as he stood and manfully tried to lift his gaze above her breasts, but for a man of Alfonso's size, it was nearly impossible. Sophie's bosom was too close to his eye level and she'd left too much of it bare to ignore.

Sophie fanned herself as Alfonso's eyes glazed over. She thought of how long it had been since she'd had a man in her bed and fanned a little faster.

Alfonso frowned. "Sophie dear, are you all right?"

"It's just the heat. I'd best be on my way. I want to finish my errands before the day gets any hotter."

Alfonso offered her his arm, his accounts and his bank quickly forgotten.

"Allow me."

Sophie slipped her hand beneath his elbow. Gentlemen were few and far between in Lizard Flats and manners forbade her to ignore his offer. She stifled a sigh, wishing Alfonso were more of a man. It never entered her mind that he might be her secret admirer. He was the banker who stored her money and nothing more.

Upon entering Goslin's General Store, she released the catch on her parasol, letting it fold like a wounded bird. Inside, the shade was welcome, even if the odors that came with it were not.

Matt Goslin was the size of a buffalo and nearly as wooly. He carried an assortment of goods ranging from asafetida to bear traps and everything in between. Sophie was never sure what it was that smelled the strongest, but the heat of the day and how close she got to the storekeeper seemed to have a lot to do with it.

"Mornin' Miz Sophie," Matt said, eyeing the buxom widow's escort with a baleful glare.

He'd had his sights set on Nardin Hollis's widow since the day of old Nardin's funeral, yet no matter how many overtures toward courtship he had made, she kept turning him down. Finally in desperation, Matt Goslin had turned to Letty Murphy at the White Dove Saloon for relief from his manly needs. What she gave could hardly be called affection, and whatever attention he got cost him a dollar on a regular basis. It was, however, better than nothing, which was exactly what he'd gotten from Sophie Hollis.

Sophie nodded primly at Matt, then laid her list upon the counter for him to fill. She watched as he peered at the scrap of paper, using a grimy finger as a guide while he read it slowly, spelling out the words, item by item. It was all the proof Sophie needed to eliminate Matt Goslin as her admirer. No way could he be the one writing such beautiful missives when he could barely read and write.

Unaware of Sophie's thoughts, Matt was mentally ticking off the items she wished to purchase. When he got to the last one on the list, he suddenly shook his head and looked up.

Frowning, he scratched his belly through a hole in his shirt while surreptitiously measuring the size of Sophie Hollis's breasts in comparison to Letty Murphy's over at the White Dove. They seemed of

52

about the same size, but he knew from experience that one too many men had sucked on that cow's tit. What he'd like was a chance at Sophie Hollis. He'd show her what a real man was all about. Then he remembered what he'd been about to say.

"Ain't got no cinnamon. Shipment's due in next week. Maybe I'll have some by then."

She pouted, aware that both men's eyes went straight to her lips as she'd intended. "And I did so want to make fresh apple pies. My trees are just loaded."

Alfonso almost danced in a circle before he got himself calm enough to speak. "I have cinnamon. Sometimes I use it in my tea. I'd be glad to loan you some. Maybe you could see clear to making me one of your fine pies in return. I hear you're quite a cook."

Sophie flushed. Praise always did go straight to her head.

"Why thank you, Alfonso. I do believe I *will* borrow some. Just until Matt gets in his new shipment, you understand. If you don't mind, you could drop it off at my house tonight. I'd come get it myself, but I wouldn't want people getting the wrong idea." She flushed again. "Coming to your hotel room just wouldn't be proper."

Alfonso grinned. He wouldn't care if the entire population of Lizard Flats got the wrong idea about him and Sophie Hollis.

"Of course, of course. I understand." He looked down his nose at the wooly store-keeper who was turning redder by the minute. The point he'd scored was well worth gloating about. "I'll be over as soon as the bank closes. I don't have anything else to do. I'll just drop it off and then go eat my evening meal at the boarding house — just like always." He paused after the bait that he'd dropped, waiting to see if he got a strike.

Sophie sighed. Alfonso was not a subtle man. That was as blatant a plea for a dinner invitation as she'd ever heard. Every manner her southern-born mother had taught her knocked at the door to her con-science like an undertaker to a wake. She pinched the bridge of her nose, looking ev-erywhere and at everything but Matt Goslin who was now standing in the corner of the store and grinning like a shit-eating dog. Finally she sighed.

"About dinner . . ."

Alfonso held his breath.

"I'll be frying a chicken and making beaten biscuits and cream gravy. If you want to join me, I'd be pleased."

Anxious to pin down the invitation before she reconsidered, Alfonso asked, "What time?"

"I usually eat my evening meal around six. That's when my dear-departed husband always wanted it. I seem to have kept the habit, even though Nardin is no longer with me."

Alfonso's head bobbed up and down in time with the Adam's apple knocking against his throat.

Sophie tried not to stare, but so help her God, the man reminded her of one of the lizards for which Lizard Flats had been named. He was long-necked and skinny and seemed to dart rather than walk.

Matt glared and thrust a sack in between the pair.

"Here's your bait of groceries, Miz Sophie. Wouldja' be needin' any help with it? I could lock up and fetch 'em to your house."

Alfonso snatched the small cloth sack from Matt's hands. "I'll do it. That's why I came."

Matt glared at the scrawny little banker.

Sophie rolled her eyes. She didn't know which was worse — lizard necks or buffalo breath.

Resigned to her fate, Sophie led the way

home with Alfonso and her groceries a step and a half behind. Just as she looked down to brush a fly off her bosom, a man staggered out of an alley and into her arms.

"Unhand me!" she screamed, and stepped backward in haste, brushing at the front of her dress, certain that the grime on Eulis Potter's body had rubbed off on her, instead.

Being the town drunk had its moments, but this was not one of them. Eulis rolled on his heels from the unexpected motion of being responsible for his own mobility. It was instinct that made him reach out to steady himself. But his eyesight was as impaired as his judgement. He caught a handful of Sophie's left breast instead of the side of the building. The last thing he remembered were the spots of high color on Sophie Hollis's cheeks and a bright yellow parasol coming at him in full flight. He hit the sidewalk with a thump and rolled off into the alley in the dust.

Alfonso gasped. "Sophie dear! Are you all right?"

No thanks to you, she thought, as she dug a handkerchief out from between the mounds of her breasts and began to dab at the perspiration on her upper lip.

"The nerve of that man," Sophie said, glaring at Eulis's inert body as if it was something foul. "Come along, Alfonso. I've been out in this heat far too long as it is."

"Certainly, my dear."

Eulis was still reeling from the blow when the pair disappeared. He crawled to his feet and peeked out from the alley. The coast was clear. That damnable woman and her parasol were nowhere in sight. He smoothed a hand over his jacket and lifted his head as he started across the street to the White Dove Saloon, certain that he would be able to con Will the Bartender out of a drink.

Just as he was about to step inside, a flutter of white caught his eye. He turned and squinted, trying to adjust what was left of his vision to the wanted poster flapping in the breeze. It took him a bit to sound out the name, then he staggered backward in shock.

KIOWA BILL

God all mighty! He knew the name, but he hadn't seen the face in more than twenty-five years. Images he'd long ago buried suddenly flashed through his mind.

A squirrel barking at him from a nearby

tree as he knelt at the creek to draw water for his mother's laundry.

The sound of gunfire, then his mother's shrill screams.

The answering belch of his daddy's buffalo gun.

The water he spilled in his shoes as he dropped the bucket and ran up the hill toward the house.

The way the rafters caved in on their home as fire ate through the roof.

His little brother's screams from inside the house, then the deafening silence as the fire continued to consume.

After that came the shock of seeing his mother's blood soaking into the dust and the hard-eyed young man on the Appaloosa horse who'd come riding down on him. The half-breed outlaw they called Kiowa Bill was already responsible for the deaths of six men and three women.

Eulis shuddered, remembering his mad dash for freedom, and then knowing he couldn't get away — of grabbing his daddy's chopping axe and drawing back as far as his reach could go — then flinging it high in the air toward the man who was riding him down.

He grunted, remembering the spurt of blood and the outlaw's wild scream as the axe hit him square in the face, then seeing him fall back off his horse and into the dirt near his mother's foot.

At that point, Eulis had grabbed the horse's reins and vaulted into the saddle.

"I'll make you pay!" he shouted.

But by the time he got back with help, the fire was nothing but smoldering ashes and Kiowa Bill was nowhere to be found.

Eulis shuddered as he touched the poster, tracing the dark line the artist had drawn from the outlaw's right eye, then angling across the bridge of his nose, to the edge of his left cheek. This was the first he'd seen or heard of the man since.

"I put that scar on his face," he muttered, and yanked the poster from the side of the building.

When he turned, Will the Bartender had come outside and was sweeping the sidewalk in front of the White Dove Saloon.

"I put that scar on his face," Eulis shouted, waving the poster under old Will's nose.

Will the Bartender frowned. "Dagnabit, Eulis. The Marshall was just through here putting them up and now you done went and pulled it down."

Eulis smoothed out the paper, pointing

with a shaky finger to the scar on Kiowa Bill's face.

"See that? I done it. I was only twelve years old, but I done it. I put that scar on his face."

His drink forgotten, he clasped the poster to the curve of his belly and walked away, leaving Will the Bartender to make what he chose of Eulis's outburst.

Meanwhile, Alfonso was scurrying to keep up with Sophie's quick steps. He was so close upon her heels that Sophie had no time to fret over the fact that she'd been manhandled, however innocently, by Eulis. She reached the door to her house, paused at the threshold and lifted the sack from Alfonso's hands before he could find an excuse to follow her inside.

"Thank you for your assistance. I'll be seeing you this evening then. Don't forget the cinnamon now, you hear?"

Alfonso's head was still bobbing as Sophie shut the door in his face. He couldn't find it in his heart to be miffed that she hadn't even said goodbye, because he was already planning what he would wear.

In the space of time it took to get back to the bank, he'd gone from conversation to lust. His imagination was running rampant as he pictured her naked. He just bet she would be soft everywhere it counted.

Shame rode his coattails like a leech as he entered the bank. His face was flushed and he was afraid to look at the customers for fear that they could read his lustful thoughts.

That evening, Alfonso stood beside his bed, looking first at the clothes he'd laid out, and then at his own skinny legs beneath the hem of his muslin underdrawers. Shrugging at the hopelessness of making himself into something he was not, he reached for his best suit of clothes and began to dress.

A few minutes later he was standing before the mirror, smiling at the results. So he wasn't the tallest man in Lizard Flats and so what if his shoulders were the tiniest bit slumped. It came from honest work.

The last thing to go on was his coat and hat. As usual, the long tail on the frock coat hung even lower on Alfonso's short frame, bobbing against the back of his knees. With the cinnamon in hand, he headed for the door. Alfonso was ready for Sophie Hollis's fried chicken and apple pies, and anything else she might dish out.

Sophie cursed beneath her breath as she puttered about the kitchen putting finishing touches to the evening meal. If she'd only kept her mouth shut she wouldn't be facing this impossible evening with a man who couldn't fill Nardin Hollis's shoes, let alone his bed.

She dusted flour and kneaded dough, all the while refusing to admit she was actually gaining pleasure from cooking for a man — even if the little sucker only came up to her chin.

Cut, sop, plop. The precision with which Sophie made biscuits would have made a starving man cry. With a crystal drinking glass for a cutter, the thick dough came free in perfect round shapes from the dough slab on the table. The layer of bacon fat coating the bottom of the biscuit pan was just waiting for the flick of Sophie's wrist. She swiped the biscuit into the grease, then turned it over with a plop, leaving the smooth, white orb freshly coated with the last remnants of Porter Griffin's pig. One after the other, she cut, sopped, then plopped, until her dough was gone and the pan was full and ready to bake.

The knock at the door ended her train of

thought. She slid the pan of biscuits into the oven and dusted off her hands. Who would have thought a jar of cinnamon would cost so much?

As she hurried toward the door, her steps were muffled by the fine Persian carpets covering her floors. During their last winter together, Nardin had hauled the carpets overland, traveling north from the eastern coast of Texas to Lizard Flats. Eyeing the fine weave and the colorful red and yellow pattern, Sophie sighed. She would trade a lifetime of warm floors for one good night in a real man's arms.

When she opened the door, Alfonso was standing there with a wide, charming grin.

"Sophie, my dear, you look beautiful."

To her surprise, he winked and entered her home without an invitation.

Stunned by his unusual behavior, Sophie took the spice he handed her, then watched as he tossed his hat onto the hall tree. When it caught and spun on the peg before rocking to a halt, all she could do was stare as Alfonso sauntered about the room, sniffing a bouquet of cut flowers, running his hand lightly across the curve of the vase.

"Thank you for the compliment, and the spice," Sophie muttered, unable to believe

Alfonso Worthy's personality transformation. He seemed almost manly. "Please take a seat in the parlor. Supper will be ready in a few minutes. Oh, and if it seems too warm, feel free to remove your coat. I've had the oven going all afternoon."

Alfonso nodded then unbuttoned his frock coat and swaggered over to the hall tree, hanging it on the peg next to his hat.

Sophie couldn't get over the difference in Alfonso's behavior. He seemed so confident, so at home.

That notion made her heart skip a beat, then told herself she wasn't really interested in the little man, just overheated.

"I'll let you know when supper is ready," Sophie said, and darted toward the kitchen with the cinnamon clasped to her breasts.

He watched her skirt tail swinging to the sway of her hips as she exited the room and then he sat down in the easy chair with a thump. Loaning her cinnamon was hardly a declaration of love and adoration, nor was her invitation to supper anything but a kindness. Still, as he sat within the silence of the room, he couldn't help but wish it were more.

The meal went down in near-silence. Alfonso had never eaten such wonderful food in his life, which reinforced the notion that he would corner Sophie Hollis and marry her, or die trying.

Sophie, on the other hand, was nearly at her wit's end. She could hardly eat for watching the little man chew. He ravished the food from her platters and bowls as if he were starving. Someone had once told her a man who enjoys his food also knows how to enjoy his women. If that someone had been right, then Alfonso's women would be in ecstasy. She thought of that loose woman over at the White Dove. She didn't want for the attentions of a man. Just because this one was smaller than most, didn't have to mean he was worthless in the sack.

As she passed him the potatoes for the third time that night, she reminded herself that she didn't want just any man. She wanted someone who adored her in every way — like her secret admirer.

As the evening progressed, Sophie found herself looking for Alfonso's admirable qualities, when before all she'd done was look for his faults. Granted he was a little skinny, but a good woman's cooking could take care of that. And yes, he was a bit on the short side, but height wasn't everything. By the time they'd gotten around to dessert, Sophie had convinced herself that it was wits, rather than bulk, that made a man, a man. Still, if only —

"Ah, dear lady, that was a very fine meal," Alfonso said, and leaned back in his chair, patting his belly with both hands.

When he reached beneath the table, Sophie inhaled sharply, then began to fan her napkin against her face. Her Nardin had been in the habit of rearranging his own masculinity from time to time when the situation demanded. Sophie was convinced that Alfonso had unwittingly just done the same, and she was certain that her sins were emblazoned upon her face for all to see.

Harlot. Strumpet. Loose woman.

Her father had called her all three. Nardin Hollis had called her his wife. She had a sudden and terrible urge to regain that last title — even if it was with another man — even if he was a little skinny and had bulging green eyes like the lizards of Lizard Flats.

"Would you care for more?" she asked, and tried not to stare at the edge of the table and what lay beyond and below.

Alfonso had been watching her all night. And while he was a skilled businessman, he knew little about the ways of a proper woman. But he hadn't reached the heights of his successes by hesitation. He knew if ever there was going to be a time to make his pitch, it had come. He leaned forward and slipped his hand over hers.

"Ah, dear lady of my heart, I want more, much more. But I'm afraid it has nothing to do with food."

Sophie's heart skipped a beat. *Dear lady of my heart? Had he just said that or did I imagine it?*

Sweat began to pour out of her hair and down the back of her neck as she stared down at his hand. She fluttered her napkin a little faster against her breasts, wondering if she had indeed just spent the evening with her secret admirer? If so, then there was much, much more to this man than she had believed.

"Oh my! Why Alfonso! I am speechless."

Alfonso feared a rejection was coming, and because he did, he began to talk faster.

"Dear, dear Sophie, I know this may be sudden, but I cannot wait any longer to tell you what's in my heart."

"Uh . . . Alfonso, I —"

"No, wait, dear lady," he said quickly. "Please hear me out."

Sophie gasped again. *Dear lady? He said it again. Oh my word! I believe that it's true!*

This sweet little man is the one who's stolen my heart.

"Alfonso! Oh Alfonso!" Sophie gasped, and threw her arms around his waist, burying her face against his shirt somewhere between his belly button and his chest.

Alfonso was stunned. He didn't know what had precipitated the gesture, but he wasn't going to refuse it. He laid his hand on the top of her head, then cupped her cheek, tilting her chin until they were staring into each other's face.

"Sophie, dear. I am overwhelmed by your show of feelings, and since they echo mine, I beg you to please hear me out."

Sophie's heart was pounding. *Say it. For God's sake just say it!*

Alfonso knew that timing was of the utmost. He clasped her hands, then dropped to one knee.

"My dear, dear Sophie. I have long admired you, and feel that a proper time has passed in which you have honored your late husband's name. But you must realize that living does go on. I can't believe that your husband would have wanted you to do without the security and honor that comes with being properly wed."

Then he took a deep, dramatic breath and leaned closer.

"Sophie Hollis, will you marry me?"

She clutched at his hand as joy mingled with relief. "Oh Alfonso! I would be honored."

Unable to believe that it had been this easy after all, he stood abruptly, then leaned forward, pressing his lips exactly and properly against the shocked pout on her mouth before she could change her mind.

"There! Our pledge has been sealed!"

For added measure, he let his hand trail suggestively from her cheek to the upper edge of her bosom. When he might have ventured further, he decided to leave her wanting.

Sophie was in shock. Her pulse was racing, her eyelids fluttering. All this time and she hadn't known he possessed such fire.

"I fear, dear lady of my heart, that I should leave now before I compromise your reputation."

Sophie followed him back into the living room with thoughts in a flutter. Before, his idiosyncrasies had bothered her. Now, they were enticing and intriguing. She pictured them side by side at the altar, and then down through the years, growing old together. She shivered longingly. Thank

God, she would never be lonely again.

Out in the hall, Alfonso was trying to maintain his dignity when in truth he wanted to kneel at her feet and thank her for rescuing him from an empty life. He slipped on his coat and then reached for his hat before turning to her with a smile.

"I have a friend back East. I'll write and ask for a preacher to be sent here immediately. Plan whatever kind of wedding you think proper for a lady of your standing. I will let you know his approximate arrival date."

She simply grinned and nodded, trying not to show her disappointment that he was leaving.

"Until tomorrow, my dear Sophie."

He grasped her cheeks with both hands and sucked a kiss from her face before she knew it was coming. Then, quick as the lizards he so reminded her of, he was gone.

Sophie began to clear the table as visions of bodily satisfaction and earthy pleasures filled her head. Once she'd cleaned up the remnants of their meal, she took all of the letters from her secret admirer and retired to her bed. One after the other, she read them through. This time, picturing dear Alfonso as the author and imagining his feelings and his longings as he put pen to paper for her. She fell asleep with them in her lap, and for the first time since they'd buried Nardin Hollis in his grave, she slept the entire night through without awakening.

The next day, she began to plan for her wedding. Word began to spread of the coming nuptials and the citizens of Lizard Flats began plans of their own for the preacher's arrival.

Letty was trying hard to curb her jealousy, but it wasn't easy. Every time she turned around, someone was talking about that blamed wedding. It wasn't as if she begrudged Sophie Hollis the permanent company of one of her more frequent clients because there was always someone else to take his place. But she couldn't help but remember that handsome gambler who'd treated her special. Every night since he'd disappeared, she'd cursed herself for the way she'd behaved, then cursed herself for thinking that he meant anything by it. She wasn't the kind of woman who had a chance at happy ever after and that was that.

Still, each night as she sang at the bar, she couldn't help but look toward the back of the room, wishing that Gentleman Jim

LaSalle was sitting there.

A few days later, she got up earlier than usual. It was her habit to sleep until after the noon meal, but she'd ordered some things special from Matt Goslin and he'd sent word by Will that they'd come in.

She washed her face and brushed out her hair without bothering to curl it back up on her head. Instead, she pulled it away from her face, securing it with a couple of combs, then took her only decent dress from the armoire and put it on. After fastening her shoes, she stuffed some money into her purse and started down the stairs.

There were two men in the saloon. One was Eulis, who was trying to sober up with his morning whiskey; the other was Will, who was polishing glasses behind the bar.

"Where are you off to?" Will asked.

"The general store."

"Want me to fry you up a steak for when you get back?" Will asked.

She hesitated, then shrugged. Will was going out of his way to make sure she stayed happy.

"Sure. That would be nice," she said. "I won't be long."

She walked out onto the sidewalk, and then had to sidestep a pair of young boys who came running past.

"Look where you're going!" a man yelled at the boys, then realized it was Letty and turned his back to her, as if it no longer mattered that she'd almost been knocked down.

The slight was nothing she hadn't suffered before, but it still made her angry.

Yeah, you pretend you don't know me now, but just wait until you come knockin' on my door again. I might be too busy for your miserable dollar.

She stepped off the sidewalk, ignoring the dust swirling about the hem of her dress and headed for the general store on the other side of the street. Several wagons were parked nearby and she frowned, wishing she'd paid closer attention to how busy he was. She wasn't in the mood for shocked expressions and cold stares from the homesteaders' wives who considered her less than the dust beneath their feet.

Still, she slipped inside without calling attention to herself and began to circle the room, fingering the new shipment of cloth and eyeing the colorful tins and boxes along the shelves as Matt filled orders for customers at the counter.

Just when she thought she was going to escape detection, she heard a muffled gasp and then a snort of disapproval. She looked up and found herself face to face with the one and only Sophie Hollis.

Willing to ignore the fact that they were touching the same bolt of cloth, Letty dropped the fabric she'd been eyeing and turned away, but not before she heard Sophie's indignant hiss.

"How dare you?" Sophie muttered.

Letty turned. "How dare I what?"

Surprised by the harlot's cavalier attitude, Sophie's face reddened. She dropped the other corner of the fabric as if it had become disgusting, but found herself locked into Letty Murphy's stare.

"I do not converse with your sort," Sophie muttered.

It hurt, but Letty would have died before she'd acknowledge the slight. She shrugged.

"If you don't want an answer, then don't ask the question," Letty said. She gave Sophie a slow once-over look before allowing herself a small grin, then lifted her chin and strode directly up to the counter and spoke to Matt.

"Did my order come in?"

Matt eyed the red flush on her cheeks and then the woman in the back of the room and figured the best way to avoid a fire was to remove the tinder before the match was struck.

"Shore did, Letty. I got it all packed up for you here under the counter. It'll be two dollars and thirty-seven cents."

Letty counted out her money, laid it on the counter, then started to pick up her package when she felt a presence behind her. Before she could turn around, a man had reached over her shoulder, lifted the package from the counter, then cupped her elbow.

"Miss Murphy, I hope you will allow me to carry your package for you?"

Even before she turned around, she recognized the voice and her heart began to pound. It was Gentleman Jim. He'd come back.

She turned with a smile, aware that all eyes were on her. "Why, yes, thank you Mr. LaSalle. I would appreciate your help."

LaSalle was wearing a white linen suit and a broad-brimmed Panama hat. He dressed especially for her when he had been told by Will where she'd gone. He'd come into the store just in time to hear the exchange between Letty and the other woman. While there wasn't anything he could do to change the inevitable, he could give her a graceful exit. He tipped his hat to the gawking women and then smiled down at Letty as he led her from the store.

Letty's heart was still pounding and she was starting to feel faint. Maybe she should have eaten that steak before she did her shopping instead of waiting until later. Curious, she glanced up at the gambler and felt her heart skip a beat.

"I figured we'd seen the last of you."

His smile slipped. "I hadn't planned on returning."

"Then why did you?" Letty asked.

"Because of you," he said softly.

They crossed the dusty street in silence. It wasn't until they'd gained the shade in front of the White Dove Saloon that Letty found the nerve to speak.

"What did you mean by what you said?"

LaSalle handed her the package. "You, dear lady, have haunted my dreams. Will you have dinner with me? The hotel fixes a fairly decent meal."

"Now?"

He nodded.

"Why? Why me?"

He shook his head and then smiled. "If I knew the answer to that, I might have kept riding," he said. "So will you?"

"If you'll give me a few minutes to fix myself up. I can't go out with my hair like this."

He fingered the thick brown strands

resting on her shoulders then shook his head.

"Please — leave it. I like it like this."

Will came outside, eyed the couple, then frowned. "Your steak is done, Letty. Ain't you comin' in to eat it?"

Letty thrust her package into his arms.

"Give it to Eulis," she said. "And put this in my room. I'm having dinner with Mr. LaSalle."

"Now Letty. You can't just go and —"

Her eyes went hard. The smile on her lips thinned to nothing.

"I don't work for you until the sun goes down."

Having said her piece, she lifted her chin, thrust her hand beneath the gambler's elbow and followed him down the street.

A Preacher by

Any Other Name

"Good bread. Good meat. Praise the Lord. Time to eat. Amen." The sanctimonious expression on Parson Sutter's face disappeared as he lifted his head, gauging his partner's attention span before aiming for the skillet of fry bread.

Henry Wainwright looked back over the campfire with a warning glance. The last thirty-three years of his existence had been spent with Elmer Sutter. And at each meal, no matter where or what condition they were in, the parson, as his old friends called him, said grace before he ate.

Henry reached for the a'forementioned bread just ahead of his partner's fist, thanking his lucky stars that he got a goodly portion on his plate before Parson got to it. Parson Sutter had an appetite bigger than his feet. And while he was a good man to have at your back in a fight, he was hell to feed behind.

The evening sun was at their backs as they crouched before the campfire. The concoction in the cast iron pot hanging over the flames bubbled slowly from the heat. A day-old jackrabbit, wild onions, and a bit of sage added for flavor, composed the contents of the pot. It was the rabbit's last dance.

Parson lifted a ladle, dripping with stew. "How 'bout another round, Henry?"

Henry nodded. "Don't mind if I do."

He offered his plate as Parson poured an extra-full ladle of rabbit stew onto the battered tin. Overflowing droplets fell into the fire with a hiss, bringing a familiar frown to Parson's brow.

"Waste not, want not," Parson said, and ladled his own helping more carefully.

Henry shook his head as he ate, chewing on one side of his jaw while talking out of the other. It was the same dinner conversation they'd had for the last thirty-three years, but it suited the two old trappers just fine.

"Do you hafta preach at every dang meal?" Henry muttered, sopping at his stew with what was left of his bread.

"A godly man is a decent man," Parson said, then belched and farted at the same time to prove he was also on the same plane as his buddy, Henry.

Henry nodded. "Yeah, and a decent man woulda' died out here long ago and you know it."

Parson shook his head in disgust at his partner's lack of reverence. He leaned against the tree at his back, smoothed a hand over his long gray hair, and then did the same for his beard.

"When I die —"

Henry spit into the fire and then interrupted. "Hells bells, Elmer, as if I ain't already heard this a thousand times. When you die, you want proper words spoke over your body a'fore you're planted in the ground. Not by just anyone, but by a real man of the cloth. Right?"

Parson's expression brightened. "By a real preacher. Not some old coot who got religion after the shit was scared out of him. I'm talking about the real thing. That's what I want."

"And ain't I been telling you ever night for thirty-odd years that I'd find you one?" He waited until Parson nodded. Satisfied that he had his attention, he finished off the conversation and the last of his bread at the same time. "Well, I ain't had no reason to change my mind. If I said I'll do it, then I'll do it."

Having said that, Henry glared at the rapt expression on his partner's face. Parson was like a gnat buzzing on a sore. When he got to talking religion, he didn't know when to stop.

In the midst of a sigh, Parson paused, giving Henry a long, hard look. "You promise?"

The conversation had taken a change from the norm and it startled Henry enough that he answered without rancor. "Well shore I promise. I'm your partner ain't I? If you can't trust your partner, who the hell can you trust?"

"Then that's that," Parson mumbled.

Henry frowned, then scratched at his privates out of habit. Except for that time last year when they'd gotten stranded in Lizard Flats and he'd visited the White Dove Saloon, it had been years since he'd used them for anything other than relieving himself, but it still felt manly to shift them from side to side now and then.

"What's the big deal, Parson? You act like you're about to cross over any minute, gettin' all serious like that on me, and all."

"You never know when your time is coming," Parson said. Then he shook his head and tilted it sideways before he belched. There was too much sage in the stew for his liking. "You just never know."

"Hey, Parson, what was that pretty little woman's name at the White Dove Saloon?"

Parson frowned. "Lord have mercy, Henry Wainwright. I told you then and I'm tellin' you now, you're too old for such foolin' around."

Henry snorted. "A man is too old for foolin' only after he's been planted six feet under. Besides, I didn't say I was gonna go see her. I was just tryin' to remember her name."

Parson swatted at a stray spark from the fire that had come too close to his beard, then leaned against the tree at his back and looked up at the night sky.

"As I recall, I believe her name was Leticia."

Henry shook his head. "No, that weren't it."

Parson's frown deepened. "Yes, it was. I remember because I had an aunt named Leticia. She always smelled like mothballs and licorice." Then he added, "I'm speakin' of my aunt . . . not the saloon girl. However, I may have heard that bartender call her Letty."

Henry's eyes widened. "That's it! Letty!

Everyone was calling her Letty." He leaned over and pointed a finger in Parson's face. "By golly, the only way you would have knowed that about her name is if you visited her, too."

Parson glared. "Personal matters are best left unspoken," he said shortly.

Henry slapped his leg and whooped so loud it spooked the horses tied nearby.

"By golly, you old fart! You gave her a poke, too."

Parson's mouth pursed angrily, but he refused to comment further. Instead, he emptied the contents of the coffeepot into his cup and sloshed it around for effect. It was useless. No amount of stirring would thin down Henry Wainwright's coffee. It was dark and bitter, but in a pinch, was a fairly good substitute for an antiseptic, should one be needed. He took a long swig of the black drink, coughing once before it slid on down his throat. Substantial. That's what Henry's coffee was. Substantial.

Unexpectedly, Parson shuddered. The action came upon him without warning, like the time he'd sensed the blue norther of '44 that froze the ears off his mule. Without thinking, he looked up from his cup and out into the darkness beyond Henry's shoulder, as if he expected something, or someone, to materialize before them.

At that moment, firelight reflected off of Parson's eyes, giving them a strange god-like appearance. Had flames suddenly shot out of Parson's mouth, Henry would not have been surprised. Startled by the image, he flinched, and in doing so, forgot all about the whore at the White Dove Saloon and spilled what was left of his stew into his lap.

"Shit!" he shouted, and began brushing at the hot stew he'd inadvertently dumped on his britches before it boiled his balls.

Parson frowned. "Profanity is the curse of —"

"Dammit, Parson. Just shut the hell up, all right? That stuff was hot, that's all."

Parson grinned. He loved to get Henry's dander up. It was Parson's private opinion that it kept the blood flowing in the old bastard.

"Better get some sleep soon," Parson said, scraping what was left of the rabbit stew into the fire. "These Rockies are higher than they used to be."

Henry snorted.

Before long, the two old men had fallen sound asleep, each lost in similar dreams of times gone by, of valleys where rivers flowed swift and sure, where game was rich and the only sounds of humanity were the sounds of a man's own voice.

By daybreak they were gone.

Just before nightfall on the seventh day into their trek, they entered a canyon they'd never traversed before, following it to the face of a mountain and then packing up through the gap Henry found in the rocks. It took the better part of a day to move through the pass. They emerged to find themselves several hundred yards from a towering precipice. Henry yanked his hat from his head and slapped it against his leg in disgust.

"All this way and it warn't nothin' but a dead end."

Parson dismounted, relishing the opportunity to stretch his legs. "Maybe so, maybe not," he said, then walked toward the edge of the cliff.

The closer he got, the wider his eyes became. When he was standing on the edge, he took off his hat and held it against his breast in a gesture of respect for the wonder of God's creation.

"Praise the Lord," he said softly, then started to grin. He jammed his hat back on his head and began frantically waving for Henry to come see. "Praise the Lord! Praise the Lord!"

Henry started to run. His reaction was

less fervent, but he felt no less joy. A look of disbelief came and went as a gap-toothed smile broke the somberness of his face. In mutual silence, they gazed into the valley below.

It was deep and wide, and cut in two by a swiftly flowing river. To the north, a herd of elk was moving through a clearing. Overhead, a pair of eagles circled the sky, as if keeping watch over their domain. Off to the left of where the trappers were standing, the land began to slope downward in a perfect access into the valley.

Parson looked at Henry as Henry looked at him. A wide grin broke across both their faces and almost simultaneously, they let loose a shout. Within moments they were mounted. They kicked their horses in the flanks and down through the trees they rode, ducking low branches and laughing and whooping as they went. Startled by the unaccustomed sounds, rabbits darted into thickets and birds took sudden flight.

By the time they reined to a halt, the horses were winded and Henry's hat was hanging beneath his chin like a bib. He straightened the leather string and slapped it back in place, then looked up at the way that they'd come. Even though he was stunned by the foolishness of their stunt, he would have done it all over again. He looked at his partner and grinned.

"Hell of a ride, Parson."

"It was at that," Parson said.

They dismounted then, letting the reins trail to the ground as they quickly removed their packs and saddles. The horses began to graze, their heads almost out of sight in the knee-high grass.

Henry shook his head. "This is it, ain't it, Parson?"

Elmer Sutter shoved his hat to the back of his head and squinted. There was green as far as the eye could see.

And there was the quiet.

He held his breath for the moment, unwilling to sully the silence with sound. Finally, he exhaled slowly.

"Yep, Henry, I reckon it is."

Henry's fingers were already itching to get to his traps. "I reckon we could winter here."

Parson nodded. "That sounds like a plan."

Henry sighed with satisfaction and then picked up his rifle. "Reckon I'll go see about fetchin' us some supper."

"I'll set up camp," Parson offered.

And so it began.

They named the place Plenty Valley, because it was. There was plenty of everything, from fish in the river to game on the ground. And the old trappers knew that when the seasons changed and the animals put on winter pelts, that trapping would be plentiful, too. One day moved into the next and then the next until before either knew it, a month had passed.

And then as one might have expected, perfection slipped. But only a little. Not enough to ruin their vision of Eden. Just enough to make them remember that they were still at the mercy of the Almighty and His whims.

Rain poured off the leaves, onto the top of their lean-to, and down the back of Parson's shirt. He sat beneath their makeshift shelter with his rifle across his lap, his gaze fixed on the gap between the place they had named Three Pines. By his estimation, more than four hours had passed since Henry had left to go hunting. In this downpour, anything worth eating would have long since taken to its own sort of shelter. Parson couldn't quit thinking that Henry should have come back. And then he would remind himself that Henry Wainwright didn't need a keeper. He had been taking care of himself for the better part of sixty-three years. But when another hour had passed and the rain was still falling and the thunder still rolling, Elmer Sutter could not rid himself of a growing anxiety.

A bolt of lightning came out of the clouds, piercing a nearby peak. The crack of sound seemed to solidify some purpose that Elmer had been contemplating. Suddenly he was on his feet. Ignoring his stiffened joints and aching knees, he tossed his blanket aside and started toward the gap in Three Pines. He would at least go that far. After that, he'd see.

Henry was in trouble. If only he'd paid more attention to the clouds than to that deer he'd been tracking. It wasn't until he'd felt the wind shift in his face that he'd thought to look up — straight into the underside of a mixture of dark, boiling clouds. Now, thunder was rumbling overhead and while he watched, a shaft of lightning streaked across the sky. He shivered. He hated storms, and on a mountain, they were dangerous as hell. He remembered a cave about a mile or so back and turned, heading for it on the run. Halfway there, it started to rain. Nothing subtle. Just an immediate downpour. Staggered by a sudden lack of visibility, he stopped to take stock of his location. The best he could figure, he had another fifteen minutes before he got to the cave, but the raindrops were peppering his shoulders and hat like bullets. He pulled his hat low upon his forehead, leaned into the wind, and started to walk. Other than the fact that he was getting cold and wet, he thought nothing of it. He'd lived his entire adult life at the mercy of the elements. It wasn't the first time he'd been rained on. It wouldn't be the last.

But in his haste to reach shelter, he took a wrong turn. On the mountains, in a storm, with visibility less than ten yards, it was understandable. It came close to being fatal.

One minute Henry was on solid ground and running and the next thing he knew the ground had disappeared from beneath his feet. In the space of time it took for one breath to come and another to leave, he'd fallen off the mountain. And when he hit the first tree, he knew the fall would be bad. Instinctively, he tightened his grip on his gun. Later it would occur to him that he should have let it go and grabbed at a tree. But it was too late. Everything had been set in motion. Down, down, down, he fell, bouncing from bush to tree to rock, every jolt racking his body with pain.

And then as suddenly as it had begun, it was over. The cessation of motion was almost as startling as the fall had been. He lay for a moment, shivering from shock and assessing his injuries. Rain hammered upon his head. He groaned and tried to move. The motion was agonizing. Blessedly, he passed out from the pain.

Much later, it was the sound of rushing water that brought him to his senses. This time when he opened his eyes, the thought crossed his mind that, if he could have reached his rifle, he might have given some thought to shooting himself now to get it over with.

The best that he could tell, he'd gone feet first into a deadfall, and was now wedged between it and some rocks, sort of like forcing a square peg into a round hole. One arm was folded up beneath him while the other was over his head and caught between the space in two rocks. The weight of his body and the momentum of the fall had driven him deep into the morass. One leg pained him terribly, the other he couldn't feel or move at all. His rifle was underneath him and the water in the nearby creek was only a couple of yards from where he was trapped. And it was rising. By his reckoning, he had an hour, maybe two before he drowned.

Henry hadn't planned on dying today, but unless a miracle occurred, it was going to happen. He kept telling himself that he'd lived a full life and that if he had to die someplace, then Plenty Valley was the place it should be. He'd been happier here than anywhere he could remember.

But he also hadn't lived to be sixty-three years old by being a quitter. He began to struggle. Yet no matter how hard he tried, he couldn't pull himself free. It crossed his mind then how sad old Parson would be when he found his body.

A shaft of lightning cracked nearby, followed by the scent of sulphur and something burning. The fire soon went out, but in spite of the rain, the scent stayed with Henry. He thought then he might be sniffing sulphur *and* brimstone where he was going.

An hour passed, maybe more, but it was hard for him to tell. All he knew was that his right ear was full of rainwater and it was getting on his nerves. And though the horror of the rising creek became more and more apparent, the continual downpour had offered Henry an opportunity that hadn't been there before. The deadfall beneath him was getting looser by the minute, so loose that he'd been able to reach far enough to make some space beneath his own body. He wiggled a bit, squirming and reaching, ignoring the pain until he could feel the sight on his gun. With a little more effort, he moved his hand along the barrel until he could get a good grip, then he pulled. At first, the gun wouldn't budge. He pulled again, then felt it give. He continued to pull, easing the barrel up out of the limbs until the trigger was beneath his fingers. While he didn't know how this would help him, he felt better for it all the same.

But the sense of satisfaction was short lived. When water began lapping at his moccasins, he started to curse. By God, he wasn't ready to die after all. In a sudden fit of rage, he screamed Parson's name.

Parson hadn't stopped at Three Pines. Even as he was telling himself that he'd never find Henry in all this rain, he was moving through the trees and up the trail he knew Henry favored. Within seconds, the rain became a blinding downpour, each raindrop splattering like a rifle shot on the canopy of leaves about his head before catapulting to the ground. The sound was deafening. Over and over, he called Henry's name as he went, but the words were thrown back in his face. A verse from an old church song popped into his head. Something about being lost and then found. He started to pray.

"God, one of yore sheep is lost. I'm a tryin' as hard as I know how to bring him in, but I reckon I could use yore help."

Less than a hundred yards in front of him, a bolt of lightning suddenly struck a tree, shattering it into thousands of pieces. Parson dropped to the ground on his knees, his eyes wide and filled with awe.

"Oh Lord, oh Lord," he moaned, trembling in every muscle of his body. "I heard you, I just ain't sure what you meant."

But the evidence of the splintered tree was impossible to ignore. Shaking in every muscle, he got to his feet. Maybe God was telling him not to go any further. Then he nodded his head. Yes, that made sense. He picked up his gun and started retracing his steps. He walked and walked until he'd lost all sense of direction, and still couldn't bring himself to stop.

Just when his hopes were all but gone, he heard a cry through the storm, like a ghostly wail coming up from the depths of hell. He stopped, then yanked off his hat so that the splatter of raindrops upon the leather would not detract from what he heard. It could have been anything, but every instinct he had told him it was Henry. He stood without moving, straining to hear, praying it would come again.

And it did.

At that moment, hope sprung, bringing with it a new set of fears. Even though he could hear Henry's voice, it was impossible to tell the direction from which it was coming.

He shouted with rage, shaking his fist at the elements that were tearing through the mountains. Rain plastered his long, graying hair to the shirt on his back and matting his beard to his chest like a tattered lace veil. His eyes glittered with anger as he fought back a sense of frustration. Somewhere out there his partner was hurting. That made Parson hurt, too.

He turned in a circle, listening, listening, trying to get a fix on the direction, and in doing so, his rifle bumped against the trunk of a nearby tree. To him, it was like God giving him a quick thump on the shoulder to remind him it was there.

He stared down at the rifle, then started to grin. Without hesitation, he lifted it to the sky and fired off a round. Although the sound was muffled by the rain, he knew it would carry far better than his voice.

A few moments later, he heard what sounded like an echo of his own shot off to his right. He started to run.

It wasn't until Henry heard the shot that he started to laugh. He shouted at the mountain, and the storm, and at fate.

"By God, ain't none of you gonna get old Henry yet!" He started to yell then, knowing that Elmer would follow the sound of his voice. "Here! I am here! I am here!"

Water was up to his waist and rising and he knew now why the deadfall was so large. The curve in the creek was a natural snare for anything caught in a flood. Already a new batch of debris was being added to what was already here. But he needed to be found before his bones were added to the pile.

Time passed and Henry had shouted until he was hoarse. Still he wouldn't quit. Water was up to his chest now and licking at his chin like the cold, taunting tongue of a woman. He stifled his fear and turned it all into rage. With one last monumental effort, he let out a roar.

"Noooo!"

Water tugged at his legs, at his shirt, yanking and pulling with the force of the flow. An eddy of foam swirled into his line of vision and then up his nose. Startled by the sudden and uninvited intrusion, he gasped and then choked when a mouthful of water went down his throat.

"Sweet Jesus," he moaned, wildly eyeing the rising flood. It was going to be too late after all.

And then he heard Parson shouting his name and he started to cry, his tears mingling with the rain as it fell.

"Here!" he shouted, laughing and spitting as water lapped at his cheeks. "I'm here!"

Moments later, Parson was above him, hacking at limbs with the hatchet he wore at his waist as he shouted Henry's name.

"It's me, Henry, it's me! You hold on now, old friend, you hold on."

Henry choked and spit and then did as Parson suggested. But it wasn't faith that he was holding onto just then, it was life. Completely submerged now, he was holding his breath.

Parson was shaking with rage. He hadn't come all this way to be too late. He chopped and hacked like a man gone mad, tossing away limbs, digging through the submerged deadfall and praying as he'd never prayed before. Just when as he thought it was all over, he felt buckskin beneath his fingers. With a mighty grip, he braced his feet against the limbs on which he was standing and pulled. Henry gave. But not enough to come free. Parson groaned and then took a deep breath as he went under water, frantically shoving and pulling at the limbs still holding Henry down. When his lungs were full to bursting, he came up then, sputtering and gasping and fighting for air. His hair was in his face and his beard was wrapped around his neck as he took another deep breath and went back for more. This time when he grabbed hold of Henry, his grip was solid.

God help me.

Parson pulled. Moments later Henry gave, popping free of the debris like a cork in a bottle, and bobbing to the surface of the flood. Parson's jubilation foundered at the sight of Henry's pale and waxen face.

"No, no, no," he moaned, and began thrashing through the water and limbs, dragging Henry's inert body as he went.

When there was nothing but hard ground at their feet, Parson flopped Henry onto his belly and started pounding on

Henry's back. Over and over, harder and harder, he pushed and he pummeled while the rain continued to fall. A minute passed, and then another and Parson never knew when he started to cry.

"Wake up, Henry Wainwright, wake up! You can't go and leave me like this."

Henry came to just as Parson's fist hit the middle of his back. One minute he was spitting up water and the next he was gasping for air.

When Parson saw Henry kick and then vomit, he leaned back on his heels and smiled. There in the rain, on the banks of a flood, he gave thanks to the Lord on whom he'd called.

When Henry could breathe without panic, he rolled over, relishing the feel of rain on his face. There wasn't a place on his body that didn't hurt, and he was pretty sure he'd busted some ribs. But he was breathing and for now it was enough. He looked over at Parson who was still in the throes of a prayer.

"Damn it all, Elmer, save that for when we ain't got nothin' better to do. I got water in my ear. I busted some ribs. And I might never take a bath again. Let's find us a place to get dry."

Parson stood then, his eyes aglow with a

passion that Henry wished he could share.

"Can you stand, Henry?"

Henry groaned. "I ain't for sure, but I'm ready to try."

Parson held out his hand and Henry grabbed it. Moments later, he was on his feet and fighting a wave of nausea.

Parson put a sheltering arm around Henry's shoulders. "Lean on me, old man. With God's help, we'll find a way."

Henry leaned, telling himself all the way up the mountain that he was leaning only because he was weak in body and not in spirit.

Within days, the episode had become a thing of the past. Henry's ribs soon healed and their lives slipped back into the same old routine, and they began to fell trees in preparation for building their winter cabin. They cut mountains of firewood, then stacked it to cure. It was nothing they hadn't done every year for as long as either man could remember, but in their joy, they became complacent. It was a luxury they couldn't afford.

A Promise Made Is
a Promise Kept

The moon was at twelve o'clock high and the two old trappers were snoring in their bedrolls when a sound came out of the forest that sent them scrambling to their feet and tossing wood on the dying embers of the fire in wild abandon. It was a sound to put the most experienced of woodsmen on the alert, and it set the horses into a frenzy. Their two geldings whinnied in fear, snorting and pawing at the ground as they tried to escape that, which now stood at the edge of their fire.

Henry ran to steady the horses as a low whine, accompanied by a belly-deep grunt, drifted through the darkness. Something was disturbing the carpet of rotting leaves beneath the trees, sending the musty scent of decay and danger into the air along with a keening roar.

Bear!

Henry's belly rolled with fear. "Oh shit," he muttered, and tied the horses' leads a little tighter as Parson began flinging all their kindling onto the fire at once. "Where the hell did he come from? I ain't once seen bear sign this far down."

"Tell that to the bear," Parson grumbled, as he began searching his pack for extra ammunition. Henry quickly did the same.

They smelled him before they saw him. By the time he shuffled into the light of their fire, they had their guns in hand and were aiming at the ready.

"Think we oughta make a run for it?" Henry asked.

Parson studied on the idea about a second too long. "I think we shoulda' done that when we heard him, not after we saw the whites of his eyes."

Henry cursed and spit. "Them damned eyes don't look none too white to me. They're burnin' red as the devil, or I'm a son-of-a-gun."

The bear rose on his hind legs, swaying back and forth like a drunken sailor unaccustomed to land, and at that moment, Henry spied a dark, patchy stain running down the big bear's belly. "Looky there, Parson. He's done been shot and ain't figgered out how to die. No wonder he come in on us like that. Ain't no tellin' how long it's been since he ate."

Parson shivered. "Is there any of that stew left? Maybe we could pitch it over to him and change his plans a mite."

Henry had a sudden urge to pee. "Hell no. There ain't never any leftovers around here. You eat ever dang thing that ain't bitin' back, and you know it."

Parson inhaled slowly and took aim. The bear was coming in. "Henry, if we don't get out of this one, it's been a hell of a ride."

"Same here, old pard. Aim for his head."

Parson shifted the rifle onto his shoulder and squinted his right eye. "Remember your promise. Don't plant me 'til the proper words have been said over my body."

"Shut up you crazy preacher and take aim a'fore you talk the bear to death."

Seconds later a single shot rang out. It was Parson's gun that belched, then kicked. Smoke from the campfire blew across his face. The wind had changed. When his vision cleared, he had a momentary glimpse of Henry frantically pounding at his gun which seemed to have jammed, before the paw came out of nowhere and removed most of the hair he had left on his head.

It was as skillful a scalping as any Crow warrior could have done. But the deed was wasted motion. Parson's neck had already snapped. It was just as well. Being disemboweled, which came next, would have hurt like hell.

"No! Oh no! Oh goddamn!"

Henry didn't hear himself screaming. Adrenalin shot through him, swift and painful as a rattler's strike. He took one look at his partner's body and began to shiver with rage. Without thought for his own safety, he grabbed a blazing stick from the edge of the fire and ran toward the mortally wounded bear who was now on all fours, trying to feed on Parson's remains.

"You hairy bastard!"

His shriek tore through the night as he thrust the fire onto the animal's pelt. It caught like dry grass on a flat plain.

The bear roared and then reared up on its back legs, pawing first at Henry, then at itself as the fire spread. As Henry watched, it fell to the ground, a burning pyre of pain-filled rage. After that, the horror of the night became a series of sensations Henry would take to his grave.

The scent of scorched and burning hair.

The vibration of the ground beneath his

feet as the horses stomped nervously at his back.

The warmth of Parson's blood as he tried, without success, to shove the loops of entrails back into his old friend's body.

When the guts slid through his fingers for the tenth time in as many seconds, he leaned back on his heels, his voice thick with tears.

"Hell and damnation, Parson. You always were a slippery old cuss. I just didn't know you was slick clear through."

But there was no critical comment from Parson to chide Henry for the curse words, or the fact that he'd been unjustly maligned. Only the stench of burning animal hair and flesh, and the sounds of his own sobs tearing up his throat and out into the night.

Remember your promise.

It came to Henry as suddenly as the bear had come upon them. He bowed his head, his shoulders shaking with grief as he gave up trying to reassemble his friend.

"I remember, Elmer. And I swear to that God you was always a'talkin' to that I will find you a true man of the cloth, or die tryin'."

They'd been traveling with him for days,

running parallel, yet never coming close enough for a rifle shot. Big gray shadows on long skinny legs. Yellow-eyed timber wolves with a mouthful of teeth and nothing to show for their trouble but ribs sadly lacking in flesh. It had been a hard year for man and beast out on the prairie. As best Henry could count, the pack ranged in count on a day-to-day basis from ten to thirteen.

It was getting dark and time to make camp again. The plains that seemed so flat in the daylight now started to take on shape and shadows, hiding things in the belly-high grass that could take a man's breath and life away in nothing flat.

Henry swiveled around in his saddle, looking beyond the horse and travois that was pulling Parson's body. They were no closer. But they also had not given up. He sighed. He hadn't expected them to.

Parson had been dead for five and a half days now and was riper than persimmons after a hard frost. And while Henry had done his best to put Parson back together, he knew that his best had not been good enough. There was no way he'd ever be able to unwrap Parson and bury him decent in a suit of clothes.

And yet it didn't seem to matter. In fact,

the old trapper would have laughed with glee knowing that Henry had been forced to use their best buffalo robe as a shroud just to keep from stringing what was left of his mortal self all over the mountains and out onto the great Kansas plains.

"Oowee, Parson. You smell like you ate your best friend and done forgot to swallow."

And then his gut drew, but not from the smell. It was the entire situation that he hated.

A lone howl split the air, and a second followed. He drew his gun, aimed and fired. It did no good. They were out of range and seemed to know it. It pissed him off royally to know that dumb animals were smart enough to outwit him. It didn't seem quite right or fair.

"One more night, old friend, and we'll be at the fort. There's bound to be a preacher there. He'll know the words to say that'll give your heart ease."

But it was Henry whose heart was in pain, not Elmer Sutter's. Pain was, for him, a thing of the past.

"Horseshoe Creek, dead ahead. Yore favorite campsite, remember?"

Henry didn't think it strange that he was talking to Parson as if he still rode beside him, instead of persistently rotting behind. Solitude was something each man had been familiar with, even comfortable with. Henry just hadn't faced the fact that Parson was gone. That would come when the last shovel of dirt went on top of his grave and he was forced to ride out alone.

There was a deep overhang of rock and earth near the north side of the creek bank where the water ran cool and swift. It would be a good place to park Parson's body. He could tether the horses close to him and build a ring of fires around them all. He'd been doing it now for three nights. A fourth couldn't be that much more difficult. The main thing would be to put Parson downwind. It was nothing personal, just a matter of convenience.

By the time darkness came to the prairie, Henry was ready. Surrounded by a ring of fires with a pile of brush ready to add to them at a moment's notice, he settled down to wait out the night with his rifle in his lap and his finger on the trigger.

"Cold camp tonight, old friend," Henry muttered. "Cain't cook and stand watch at the same time."

He tore off a chew of jerky, sliding it to the side of his jaw to soften, like a plug of tobacco.

The horses neighed softly, one to the other, aware of the wolves' presence as no man could ever be. Henry tilted his canteen, letting the fresh creek water slide down his dry, burning throat. Quietly, methodically, he began to chew and listen and watch.

They came. Standing just outside the ring of fires like ghostly shadows. Only now and then did Henry catch a glimpse of yellow eyes. But the snarls and the yips, the growls and the howls were still there, then gone far too swiftly for him to do anything more than fire his rifle at the place they'd last been.

"You ain't gettin' nothin' to eat here, you mangy sons-a-bitches. You cain't eat me, I'm too damned tough. And you cain't eat Parson cause there ain't no one here to say the blessin' a'fore you do."

The laughter caught at the back of his throat. It felt like a sob. Henry snorted, a bit disgusted with himself at the constant emotion he couldn't seem to lose. He pinched his nose through his thumb and forefinger and blew snot on the ground. This was no time to go all weak and sissy. If he didn't pay attention, he'd wind up like old Parson, rotting in the sun and gathering flies.

Only twice did Henry succumb to bone-deep weariness and nod off to sleep. But each time he did, the nervous snorts of his horses were as good as a kick in the pants. Every so often he would fire off a shot into the darkness. It served no purpose other than to remind Henry he was still the one in charge. Only once did he hear a yelp of pain, but it was enough to send the wolves back into the shadows.

Hours later, when the breeze picked up and a flash of lightning on the far horizon lit up the sky, Henry prayed for daylight to beat the approaching storm. The last thing he needed was a rain to put out his fires before he could see what the hell was out there on the prairie.

Daylight and a gray pall of rain came within the same breath. Henry could have cared less. It was light enough to see, and wet enough to dampen the smell of Parson's carcass. By noon he'd be at the fort.

The ordeal of the bear and the years of abuse he'd put himself through were telling on Henry Wainwright. It was all he could do to mount up. But mount he did. Aiming his horse east, he wrapped the other horse's lead around his saddle horn and kicked him in the flanks. As the horse began to move, Henry settled easy in the saddle. It was, he hoped, his last night on the prairie.

The weight of the travois cut a trail through the wet grass. Water ran from the brim of Henry's hat and down onto his knobby nose. Every now and then, a lightning bolt would hit the ground close enough that his horse would shy. At those times, he wished he was not the highest target in sight. Once he looked back, searching behind him for the latest location of the pack. For the first time in days, the wolves were nowhere in sight. He glanced back at the travois and grinned.

"Well I'll be damned, Parson. The furry buggers lit a shuck. Guess they don't like this lightnin' any better than me."

An hour later, he'd ridden out of the storm and into the tail winds that were sweeping over the prairie. By the time he topped the knoll overlooking the fort, he was nearly dry.

He started to tease Parson about the floozy at the cantina and ask him if he knew her name, too, when it dawned on him that Parson couldn't hear.

"Well, hell." He situated his hat a little tighter upon his head and ignored the lump in the back of his throat. "I don't know as how I'm gonna adjust to this situation, old friend. I don't rightly know at all."

He kicked the horse in the flanks and started down the rolling hillside toward the gaping doors of the fort. It would be the last time Parson Sutter covered his back.

"Hey, Wainwright! Aren't you a little early this year? Don't look like you got many furs to trade. And they got wet to boot. What were you thinking?"

Henry ignored the smart-ass sentry at the gate and kept on riding. By the time he got to the adjutant's office, it was obvious to anyone within fifteen feet that Henry was hauling something foul.

A sergeant Henry had known for years held his nose as he walked past.

"Damn, Wainwright, I thought you knew better than to bring green skins like that in to trade. The sutler won't give you shit for them."

Henry glared as he dismounted and tied his horse to the hitching post. He didn't take kindly to anyone maligning his friend, even if it was true. But he wasn't ready to admit that it was Parson, and not a load of green skins, that was stinking up the fort.

"Dang smart-mouth," he muttered, and

yanked his pants up over his stomach as he started inside.

The commander was coming out just then, and the smile on Jack Robie's face withered to a gasp of disgust.

"My God, Wainwright! What on earth are you packing?"

"Elmer Sutter."

It was enough to stop Robie's next remark. He'd known the two old trappers for years and couldn't remember ever seeing one without the other. No matter how bad the smell, Wainwright must be suffering highly from the loss of his partner.

"What happened?" Robie asked. "And pardon me for asking, but why the hell are you hauling him around like that? Why don't you do the decent thing and bury the poor man before he pops?"

"He ain't gonna blow," Henry muttered. "Bear done ripped out all the parts that tend toward that condition. Besides, I cain't plant Parson until I find a preacher to say words over his body. I promised."

Robie rolled his eyes and tried not to gag. "I'd be glad to read the Bible over your friend's grave. But we need to cover him up first, I think."

Henry shook his head. "Nope. Parson wanted a real preacher. I promised." He ducked his head and then looked up. "No offense and all, Commander, but a promise is a promise. And I don't suppose you're a *real* man of the cloth?"

Robie shook his head, and then his expression lightened. "No. But I heard that a preacher is coming to Lizard Flats. Some banker is getting married and they've sent back East for the real thing. Maybe you could try there."

Henry's eyes widened. Lizard Flats was less than a two-day ride. And in a way, it seemed provident that they go back to the place where they'd last shared a woman to share their last moments together, as well.

"That's real good news," he said. "But I've got to get me some sleep a'fore I go anywhere."

Jack Robie frowned as he gazed at the flies and the lump beneath the buffalo robe. "I guess it's been rough losing your partner like this. As time passes, you will find it easier to sleep."

Henry shrugged. "Oh hell, it wasn't losin' Parson that kept me outa my bed. It was a damned pack of wolves. They followed me nigh onto four days and nights, trying to eat old Elmer, there." Henry lifted his hat to wipe sweat from his brow, relishing the faint wash of air that tunneled through his sparse growth of hair. "It's bad enough that the bear gutted him right a'fore my eyes. I wasn't havin' no damned four-legged fur-balls eat what was left, by God! Now I'm goin' to get me some sleep. And when I come out, Parson better be right where I left him. Do I make myself clear?"

Jack Robie nodded his assent as the gaggle of soldiers around the building began to disperse. It made sense to them. They just didn't want to be in on the downwind side of Elmer Sutter while it happened.

It was nearing sundown when Henry pulled two travel-weary horses to a halt just outside of Lizard Flats, surveying the town from the hilltop. As he'd predicted, it had taken him two days to get here, but from what he could see, it was time well spent. Someone was putting up some sort of shelter. The poles had already been planted into the ground and the workers were near to done with the latticework roof. Piles of brush and leafy limbs lay in bunches around the area, ready to be woven into the framework of the roof as a makeshift shade. And with the thought came the realization that this must be where the preacher would hold his sermons.

"By God, Parson. We did it. Before you know it, there'll be a real preacher-man sayin' sweet words over your stinkin' hide."

He could almost hear Parson saying, *Cursing is the handiwork of the devil.*

He sighed, then kicked his horse forward, confident that Parson wasn't far behind.

Letty was out on the balcony, enjoying her evening ritual when she saw the rider on the hill. At first, she thought nothing of it. Word had gotten around that a preacher was coming to Lizard Flats. It had brought all kinds of newcomers into town for the event. So many in fact that Gentleman Jim was at the card table day and night, plying his trade. They'd shared several dinners and once he'd rented a buggy and taken her for an afternoon drive, but he had yet to make a pass, which, considering Letty's occupation, had her completely confused.

Even though the sun was almost gone, the heat of the day still lingered. She lifted the weight of her hair from her neck while wishing for a breeze or maybe a good rain. But it was August, and rain came rarely to the Territory this time of year.

A loud shout sounded from the hilltop where the brush arbor was going up. She turned and frowned, wishing she could tell them to be quiet. How was she to ever hear her whippoorwill call with all that noise?

Then Will the Bartender walked off the sidewalk in front of the White Dove and turned around and looked up at the balcony.

"Letty! Are you comin'?"

She rolled her eyes and then leaned over the railing.

"Don't I always?"

Will smoothed his hands down the front of his apron and hurried back into the bar. Ever since Letty had heard about the wedding, she'd been acting like a bear. He didn't know whether to scold her or ignore her. Instinct warned him that if he pushed too hard, she'd leave him, too, so he tried to give her some space. Still, his clientele demanded more than a fair game of cards and some drinks. He just hoped she hurried on down before someone got antsy and started a fight in lieu of a good bedding. He couldn't afford any more broken chairs and glasses.

While Will was worrying about the cost of running his business, Letty was staring at the rider who'd been on the hill. He was a wooly-looking old man and looked familiar, but then all men looked familiar to her. She leaned over the railing, watching as he passed by, then wrinkled her nose as she smelled something foul.

People began calling out to the man as he passed, yelling at him to get rid of the stink, but he kept on riding and didn't stop until he'd reached the livery.

When he dismounted, she saw that he walked with a limp. He untied the horse he'd been leading then spoke briefly with the man at the stable. She watched as he left his own horse and led the other one with the travois away.

It wasn't until later that night when he came into the White Dove that she learned who he was and why he'd come. After he'd walked out of the White Dove, she'd excused herself on the pretext of using the chamber pot, when in reality, she'd wanted to cry, but not because an old man was dead. Life was hard out here. People died every day. What had undone her was the affection in the old trapper's voice as he'd spoken of his promise to find a preacher to bury his friend. Unless something changed in her life, there wasn't a person on this earth who would care if she were dead.

As she was passing an open window next

to the stairs, she felt a shift in the air. She paused to enjoy the brief breeze, and as she did, heard the whippoorwill call that she'd waited all day to hear. Her voice was low as she stood in a posture of abject misery.

"Yes, Mama, I hear it, but it doesn't call for me."

Westward Howe

Unaware of the building turmoil in Lizard Flats, Randall Howe was suffering some doubts of his own. Between the heat and the coal dust and the squalling child in the seat across the aisle, he thought he might lose his mind. And that was only within the first three hours after boarding this train. It was his second on the way to the Territories, and he was already sorry about his decision. Maybe he should have stayed and married after all. It wasn't the worst fate he could imagine. As soon as he was allowed, he retired to the sleeper car and crawled into his bunk, morose, and full of self-pity. Foregoing his noon meal, he continued to mope, and sometime during the heat of the day, fell asleep.

He woke just as the sun was beginning to set. His stomach growled as he rolled onto his back, and he wondered if it was too late to get something to eat. Just as he was considering the wisdom of heading for the dining car, the train suddenly ground to a halt. Were it not for his quick reflexes, he would have fallen out of his bunk and into the aisle.

Muttering to himself about the carelessness of the engineer, he looked out the window, expecting to see some sort of town, or at least a depot. Instead, he saw nothing but a vast, rolling prairie. With a disgusted shrug, he thought again of the dining car. Just as he was about to get up, he heard a woman's high-pitched scream. He sat up again, peering nervously out the window, and again, saw nothing.

Carefully, he parted the curtains of his bunk and looked out into the aisle. All he could see were the curtained compartments of the other bunks.

"I say," he called out. "What's going on?"

Someone muttered a curse from a bed close by, but it was the only answer he received. Weary to his bones and missing his clean, soft bed in the Boston rectory, he closed his eyes, contemplating the sins that had brought him to this fate.

It occurred to him then to just get off the train. It would be a long trek back to the next town, but it would be worth it. With a little luck, he could be in Boston tomorrow. He thought of his clothes, stashed somewhere in the baggage car, and the blisters he might get on his feet. Then he thought of the Bishop's anger and Priscilla Greenspan's outrage — and not the least of it all, her father's indignation, so he rolled back into the bunk and closed his eyes, the food forgotten.

A few minutes passed, and Randall began to doze. On the verge of a snore, a gunshot suddenly sounded at close range, followed by another. He choked as his eyes popped open. Again, a woman screamed, but this time close by. He froze.

"This is a stick up! Don't nobody move!" a man yelled.

Holdup? Dear Lord! Money! His money. They would take it all. Unless. . . .

With shaking hands, he ripped his wallet from his coat, removing all but a few dollars, and then frantically stuffed the money between the wall and his bunk. Desperate to finish the deed before he was discovered, he shoved his wallet back in his pocket and reached for his Bible, praying as he'd never prayed before.

He could hear them now, laughing and yelling as they tore through the sleeping compartments, taking jewelry and money from the terrified passengers. A woman began to cry, begging for them not to take her wedding ring. Randall leaned against the wall of the compartment, taking comfort in the knowledge that most of his money had been secured.

They were closer to him now — just across the aisle — then the compartment above him. He held his breath. Suddenly the curtains of his sleeping compartment were ripped open. Randall found himself staring into the barrel of a gun.

"Hand over yore stuff!"

Randall's hands were trembling as he began to fumble in the pocket of his coat.

"Well, well, what we got here?" the outlaw drawled, as he grabbed up Randall's Bible and began waving it over his head. "Lookee here, boys. We got ourselves a preacher man."

Randall's first impression of the outlaw was of filth — from the brown crust on his knuckles to the stains on the outlaw's clothes. His second impression was the stench. His nostrils flared. Had the man *ever* bathed?

The outlaw stared at Randall over the top of his mask and then tossed the Bible aside and held out the bag.

"Gimmee your valuables," he growled. "And be quick about it."

"Take it and begone," Randall said, as he

dropped his wallet and pocket watch into the bag. Then he took out his handkerchief and covered his nose, trying hard not to gag from the outlaw's breath.

The outlaw wagged his gun under Randall's nose. "What's a matter mister? Ain't you never smelled a real man a'fore?"

Fear disappeared as a wave of disdain reconstructed Randall's expression. "Oh, is that what you are?"

The man spit in Randall's face.

They were gone as abruptly as they'd arrived. Outside, the outlaws mounted up and rode off into the setting sun as Randall threw up in the aisle. While it was some consolation that he'd saved the bulk of his money, at that moment, he would have traded it all for a bath.

The next day, they finally rolled into Feeney. It was to be the first place on his missionary journey where he would preach the word of God. His anticipation of the upcoming event had helped him get past the trauma of yesterday's robbery. Here was where his new life was destined to begin.

He stepped off the train with his head held high, his Bible in one hand and his bag in the other. His stride was filled with purpose as he moved across the platform and into the street. Seconds later, the distinct odor of manure drifted up his nostrils. He looked down and groaned. He was standing in shit-horse to be exact.

"Reverend Howe?"

Randall forced a smile and looked up, finding himself eye to eye with, quite possibly, the tallest, homeliest, woman he'd ever seen. She was wearing a pair of men's pants, as well as a man's shirt and jacket. Her brown, shoulder-length hair was pulled away from her face, and tied at the back of her neck, elongating her features even more. The wide-brimmed hat she wore low on her forehead shaded her eyes, as well as most of her face, and still she squinted, more from habit than any nearby glare. By his best guess, she was in her late thirties. Put off by her appearance, as well as her manly attire, it was all he could do not to stare.

"Yes, I'm Reverend Howe."

"Welcome to Feeney."

She extended her hand to him as one man would have to another. There was something commanding about her presence. He took it without hesitation.

"Name's Mehitable Doone. I own the biggest spread in these parts. You'll be stayin' at my house until you're ready to leave."

Randall beamed. At last. A semblance of normalcy had returned to his life. He tipped his hat.

"I appreciate your kindness, and that of your husband," he said.

"Ain't got one," Mehitable announced, and yanked his bag from his hand. "Follow me. I'll show you the church on the way out of town."

Stunned that he'd allowed a woman to carry his bag, he began to run along behind, trying to catch up and rectify his social faux pas.

"Uh, I say, Mrs . . . uh, Miss. . . ."

"Hellsfire, preacher. Just call me Hetty, ever'one does."

He flushed. "Well then, Hetty . . . about the church."

She pointed off to her left. "There it be."

He looked. His steps slowed and then he stopped.

"Where?" he asked.

"There," she said, pointing to a vacant space between a saloon and a livery stable. "We'll be settin' up some benches."

"You mean I'm to speak without . . . uh . . . you mean there isn't a real —"

Mehitable snorted. "Oh hell no, there ain't no church. The town ain't but five years old." Then she added. "But everyone is fired up about your comin' and all. You'll probably draw a good crowd."

Randall took a deep breath, reminding himself that of course things would be different out here. It wasn't that he minded preaching outdoors, in fact, now that he thought about it, it seemed fitting. He would be like Moses who'd wandered in the wilderness before bringing his children to God. And the mention of a crowd didn't hurt. Randall liked to preach to a crowd almost as much as he liked lifting women's skirts.

"That's fine, just fine," he said, then resumed his sprint to catch up with his hostess.

Their ride to the ranch was long, but without fault, and for the first time since leaving Boston, Randall began to have hope. He glanced up at the sky. It was cloudless. Good. That meant no rain. He glanced at the woman beside him. Her eyes were still squinting against the glare of the sun, and the hair hanging out from beneath her hat was whipping wildly about her face as the buggy sped along the road.

"Have you lived here long?" Randall asked.

"Born here," she said, and flicked her whip across the backs of her team, spurring them on to greater speed.

Randall tightened his grip on the seat to keep from being pitched out and searched for another vein of conversation that might not play out as fast.

"So, your family was here before the town of Feeney, right?"

She looked at him then as she might have a simpleton, with pity and patience. "Yeah, that would figure now, wouldn't it?"

He flushed. Damnable woman. If he'd met more like her in his past, he wouldn't be where he was now.

"So when do we get to your ranch?" he asked.

She tightened her grip on the reins and pointed with her chin. "We been on it ever since we left town and we'd still be on it if we kept drivin' till tomorrow."

Randall's eyes widened as he looked at his hostess with renewed respect.

"You own the town of Feeney?"

"In a manner of speakin'."

"Then was it you who requested the presence of a minister here?"

She threw back her head and laughed and Randall had a fleeting impression of a horse whinnying. Added to that, he wasn't sure, but he might have just been insulted.

"If not you, then who?" he asked.

"My sister. She thinks she wants to be a nun."

It was all he could do not to gawk. "But I'm not Catholic."

Hetty shrugged. "It don't hardly matter. Neither is she."

Charity Doone was on her knees in prayer when she heard the buggy. It had to be Hetty. She always drove as if she were in a constant race with herself. Her pulse accelerated as she jumped to her feet and dashed to the window. This was the third time in as many days that Hetty had gone to town to meet the train, and each time she'd come home alone. She peeked through the curtains, her expression fixed, her lower lip caught between the edges of her teeth.

Please God, let this be the day. Please let the preacher be here. At the age of twenty-three, Charity needed some answers to the dilemmas overruling her life. Hetty had been after her for more than five years to pick a man and get married. But somehow the thought had seemed foreign. Hetty had followed her own inclinations rather than those of society. No one had forced her into something she didn't want. Charity couldn't see why she had to be the one to make all the sacrifices. There were things that she wanted to do. Places she wanted to see. And marrying some rancher who cared more for his cows than he did her wasn't high on her list of importance.

And then there was the dream. She'd had it a total of seventeen times now. Of standing naked before God in a pale white light and pledging her life to him always. At least she thought it was God to whom she kept making the promises. In her dream, the man was tall and strong and cloaked in the light shining down upon her, and she'd wept with joy as he reached out his hand. In the dream she kept feeling his fingers curling around her hand, and every time she would get to the point of seeing his face, the dream would end. But Charity had deduced that was because no one on earth had looked upon the face of God.

Her fervor to follow the dream was about to begin as she gazed out upon the man getting out of the buggy. Her pulse kicked. The preacher! He was here!

She needed guidance and answers, and who better suited than a man of God? She held her breath, waiting, willing him to turn around. When he did, she exhaled on a sigh. His countenance was glorious, just as she had expected it to be.

She dashed to the mirror and fussed with her hair, poking loose ends into place and pinching her cheeks until they were a deep, rosy pink. Smoothing her hands down the front of her dress, she stepped into the hall and made her way to the drawing room at the front of the house. Already she could hear Hetty's loud, booming voice and winced, hoping the preacher would not be put off by her sister's strange ways. A few moments later, she entered the room, pausing in the doorway and allowing herself a final moment to collect her thoughts.

And then Hetty turned around and Charity's thoughts were no longer her own.

"Here's Charity now," she said. "Reverend Howe, this here's my sister, Charity Doone."

Charity gave herself permission for an humble smile.

"Reverend Howe, it is an honor, I'm sure."

To say Randall was stunned would be putting it mildly. He kept staring from Hetty, to Charity, and back again. When he could speak, the best he could say was, "You don't look anything alike."

Hetty snorted. Charity blushed. At four inches over five feet tall, and with her baby doll face and womanly shape, she was the antithesis of Mehitable Doone.

"Same sire, different dams," Hetty said.

It took Randall a moment to decipher the animal references to their parentage. Finally he deduced that they'd had the same father, but different mothers.

"It's a pleasure to be here. I hope I can be of some service," Randall said.

Impulsively, Charity reached for his hand. "Oh yes, Reverend, you certainly can! I have been suffering these many months now, puzzling to discern the message God has been sending me. I know you will have the answers I need."

Randall nodded, trying to concentrate on something beside the softness of her skin and the length of her lashes.

"It has been difficult trying to live with all this confusion. I long to soothe the ravages of my soul," she murmured, then blessed him with a bashful smile.

He bit the inside of his cheek to keep from laughing. Ravages of her soul, indeed. If this fine figure of a woman became a nun, it would be the greatest waste of femininity ever known to man. He patted her hand and then took a step back, hoping to maintain a proper distance between them. Yet even after she'd moved away, he could still feel her touch, hear her voice, smell the scent of verbena on her person. She was woman personified. But a nun? He thought not. He cleared his throat.

"Sometimes we misinterpret God's messages."

Hetty laughed out loud. "That's what I been a'tellin' her all along. I ain't never heard tell of anyone becoming a nun after dreaming they was naked."

Randall's mouth dropped.

Charity glared at her sister, the flush high on her face. "You hush now, Sister. I won't be made fun of."

"Is this true?" Randall asked.

Charity shrugged. "Only in a manner of speaking."

"You dreamed you were naked?"

Her lower lip jutted, not enough for a pout, just enough to show her disapproval. "Well . . . yes."

"And this was the sign that said you must be a nun?"

"It's a bit more involved than that," Charity said.

Randall smiled benevolently because he couldn't think of a single comment that wouldn't be misconstrued.

"You know," he said, "it's been a long trip. If you would be so kind as to show me to my room, I'd like to rest before my sermon."

"Shore," Hetty said. "Charity, you show him the way. I got things to do."

Charity nodded, pleased that she would have the preacher all to herself. She could explain about her dream. Then he would understand.

Randall grabbed his bag and started to follow the wannabe nun when he remembered something he'd been going to ask.

"Oh Hetty, I forgot to ask you something."

She was already buckling on a gun and holster and swapping hats.

"Like what?" she asked.

"What time did you schedule my sermon?"

"Ask Charity, she's the one who's in charge of all that. All I did was promise to pick you up at the station. You and Sister Bare Ass there are on your own."

She strode out the door, ignoring Charity's indignant glare and leaving the unlikely duo alone. Randall licked his lips and then turned.

"My sermon," he prompted. "What time?"

Charity beamed. "Why, you're giving it tonight, under a full moon."

The benches were full to overflowing as Randall gazed out across his new congregation. He would have been disappointed to know that they'd come out of curiosity, more than a desire to be saved. Life was difficult enough out here without worrying about a few measly sins. A couple of torches had been stuck into the ground on either side of his pulpit. Their fires burned hot, sending sparks and smoke spiraling up into the night sky. A lantern hung on a nail outside the livery, its flame weak, the wick in need of a trim. Lights from the bar next door spilled out of dirty windows and onto the ground.

After the dusty ride from the train station to the ranch, Randall had brought his bag into town, deciding to change into clean clothes after their arrival back in town, rather than before they'd left the ranch. He wanted to be as fresh and dust-free as possible. And now he stood silently in the midst of the smoke and flames, his clerical robes billowing out about his feet and his Bible held close to his chest.

More than one person in the congregation took note of his holy appearance and commented upon it to a neighbor. But none was as taken as Charity Doone. She sat loose-lipped and silent, staring up at the man who would help seal her fate. Transfixed by his demeanor, she watched as he stepped up to the pulpit.

When he opened the Bible, she took a deep breath. Then his magnificent voice spilled out across the gathering like water over a dam, cleansing lost souls and healing weary bodies. She shivered where she sat.

"Judge not, lest ye also be judged," he began.

Within moments, Charity had become motionless. Her gaze darted from his lips, to the Good Book, to the breadth of his shoulders beneath his robes. Her thighs began to quiver. Her heart began to pound. When he shouted, "Praise the Lord," she broke out into a sweat. Something was happening to her. Something she didn't understand.

He moved away from the pulpit and stepped into the aisle, pausing less than a yard from where Charity sat. Anxious not to miss a nuance of this wonderful night, she tilted her head for a better view. Within seconds, she started to shake.

Silhouetted against the back light from

the torch, Randall Howe looked as if he, too, were on fire. And in that moment he became the figure from her dream. The man surrounded by a bright, burning light. The man who had reached out to her. It was all she could do to stay still.

She never knew when the sermon ended, but her mind was racing. She'd been given a sign. But it wasn't what she'd expected. It hadn't been God in her dream; it had been the preacher. She sighed, telling herself that it wasn't so far off. Randall Howe was God's representative, wasn't he? She'd just misunderstood.

She kept remembering her dream, but this time there would be no mistaking the path she must take. By the time the last buggy had pulled off into the night, Charity was wound as tight as a top. To add to the turmoil in her soul, it had started to rain.

Randall was beside himself with glee. In spite of its inauspicious beginning, his first sermon on his missionary trail had been a resounding success. The collection money was jingling in his pockets and his fervor was at an all-time high. If only his colleagues could know this sensation, there would be an exodus of preachers out of the cities and into the wilderness. And then he felt the raindrops upon his face and turned with quick concern.

"Miss Doone, it's starting to rain. I fear it would not be wise to journey back to your ranch tonight. Is there a hotel nearby?"

Still speechless by her revelation, she pointed toward a building across the street. There was no name on the front, only a sign in the window.

Rooms.

"Our horse and buggy are already in the livery. Under the circumstances, I think it would be wise if we stayed in town."

Charity's fingers knotted. This was it! She'd been right!

"Will your sister worry if we don't come home?"

Charity tried not to giggle. "No. She would expect us to stay. After all, she owns the hotel as well."

Randall thought of his bag in the back of the buggy. It should be safe in the livery for the night.

The sky belched fire. The rumble of thunder put them in flight. They ran, but not soon enough. By the time they'd gained entrance into the hotel, they were drenched.

The desk was vacant. Only a single lantern burned nearby.

"Oh no. There's nobody on duty. What shall we do?" Randall asked.

Charity slipped behind the desk and pulled keys to adjoining rooms out of their slots.

"The last man who worked here died," Charity said. "People just choose a room and leave their dollar on the desk when they leave."

Randall shook his head in disbelief. Despite the lack of amenities, this lawless country had some intriguing ways.

"Here," Charity said, handing Randall the lantern. "You lead the way. I'll follow with the keys."

He did as she asked. Only after they started up the stairs did he realize that he was about to spend the night in an empty hotel with an unattended female. A loud crack of thunder, followed by a bright-white streak of lightning broke the darkness on the staircase.

He looked down at her then and shuddered at the thought of her womanly flesh. His gaze moved from her body to her face and to the rapt expression that she wore. It was then he knew a moment of fear. He couldn't do this — shouldn't do this. She was an innocent, not a widow well versed in the ways of a man.

Then she touched his arm. Her voice was low and trembling.

"Randall, please hurry."

He swallowed suddenly. Randall? Her familiarity was unlikely for a woman who dreamed of being a nun, but the darkness was a blanket to his conscience. He dashed up the steps ahead of her, then stood aside as she unlocked each of their doors. He escorted her inside the room that was to be hers, staying until the lamp had been lit. When he looked at her again, she was shivering.

Concern overrode lust.

"Miss Doone, you should get out of your wet clothes and into a warm bed immediately, or I fear you shall catch your death."

Charity swayed toward the resonance of his voice. She looked at him then. The image of him surrounded by light was burned in her brain. Do it! Do it now, a voice said. Her hands moved to the long row of buttons that ran down the front of her dress. Her eyes were wide and fixed upon his face as she began to undo her clothes.

Frozen to the spot, Randall stared. There was no mistaking her intent.

"Miss Charity . . . what are you doing?"

"The dream. I have to fulfill the dream."

He knew he should look at her face, but he couldn't. His gaze was fixed upon the revelation of her pale, creamy skin, as one by one, the buttons came undone. His tongue felt thick, almost as thick as the member that was swelling inside his pants.

"Dream? What dream?" he muttered.

"My dream of becoming a nun. It wasn't God I was standing naked before." Suddenly she threw herself into Randall Howe's arms. "Oh Randall, it was you."

It should be stated on Randall's behalf he did think about resisting. But it should also be mentioned that the thought came and went as fast as a fart. Within the space of time it takes to take off one's shoes, they were lying together in bed. Highlighted by the flickering light from her lamp, their naked bodies seemed to be writhing upon the covers.

Caught up in a passion of which she would never have believed, Charity Doone lost her virginity, and what she thought was her heart, to a man she'd known less than a day.

Randall's lust was easily overwhelmed by what little conscience he had. It wasn't until he'd shot his own wad that it began to dawn on him just what he'd done, and by then it was too late to take anything back.

Charity was in convulsions of rapture and moaning words of happy ever after in his ear. He waited with his heart in his mouth until she'd fallen asleep before he'd crept to his own room.

From there, he watched the storm until it had passed, and then he watched for the first signs of gray to break the bleakness of night. This wasn't Boston and there was no bishop to stand between him and what he'd just done. Out here, people made their own laws and he shuddered to think what kind of retribution a woman like Mehitable Doone might take on a man such as he.

He dropped to his knees then by the side of the bed and began to pray, making promises to God from the depths of his heart, swearing that he would never, as long as he lived, take advantage of a woman again. From this moment on he would be celibate, even if it drove him mad.

At daybreak, he tiptoed to her door and looked in. She was sprawled out across her bed, her nudity all the more blatant for her lack of covers. He shuddered, silently cursing himself for his weaknesses and slipped back to his room.

As he stood beside the window, he heard a sound that gave him some hope. It was the distant whistle of a westbound train. In that moment, his decision was made. Without a backward glance, he grabbed his coat and robes and his Bible and headed for the stairs at a lope. Out the door he ran, then toward the livery to recover his bag.

Just this once. Just this once, let me please get away and I'll never do it again.

Charity came awake within seconds, and as she did, the memory of last night came crashing down upon her.

"Randall," she gasped, and then bounced out of bed, grabbing clothes as she went.

Haste made her nervous. She giggled girlishly as she tried to force buttons into holes, all the while planning the next fifty years of her life. And it was comforting to know what that would be. She shook her head as she thought of the dream and her own misconceptions. A nun. How silly. She couldn't be a nun, not now. Not when she'd experienced the wonders of being a real woman. Finally she was dressed. She dashed next door, knocking lightly upon Randall's door. He didn't answer. She knocked again, thinking to herself that he was just sleeping in. After all, the rigors of last night had been strenuous indeed. But still he didn't come. She frowned and then tried the knob. When it turned, she peeked inside. The room was empty. His clerical robes were gone, as was his Bible. Her heart gave a funny twitch, but she ignored it.

Outside, she heard the loud, mournful wail of the train whistle as it began to leave. She turned and walked to the window, absently watching the smoke billowing from the smokestack and the slow flow of people and horses moving about in the street.

The train whistled again, and as it did, a sudden panic came on her. She spun around, gazing frantically at the closed door.

"No," she moaned, and clutched at her stomach. "He wouldn't," she whispered, and ran for the door.

Out into the street she ran, heading for the livery with single-minded intent. Once inside, her worst fears were revealed. His bag was gone, too. She stood then, listening to the beat of her heart and hearing the last mournful call of the train as it disappeared into the distance.

Without speaking, she hitched up her horses and climbed up in the buggy. A few minutes later, she started home. Back to Mehitable. Back to her shame.

At first she was numb. But as the miles sped away, her emotions began to kick in. She went from heartbreak to humiliation and back again. By the time she topped the rise leading down to the ranch, she was sobbing hysterically and the horses had begun to stampede. The reins slipped from her fingers and she fell back in the seat, hoping that she would die before her shame could ever be revealed.

Near the barn, a young wrangler named Wade James was the first to hear the commotion. When he looked up and saw the runaway buggy, his heart skipped a beat. He'd long been an admirer of Mehitable's sister, and the knowledge that she was in danger sent him running for his mount.

His race from the barnyard brought the others out to see. Mehitable cried in alarm and jumped on her horse as she, too, gave chase.

But it was Wade who got there first. Riding at full gallop, he leaned sideways and grabbed the lead horse's reins. With every ounce of his strength, he began to pull back. Moments later it was over. The team had stopped. He leaped from his horse and dashed to the buggy.

"Miss Charity! Miss Charity! Are you all right?"

She took one look at the tenderness and concern on his face and fell forward into his arms.

It has to be said now, that at that moment, Wade James fell the rest of the way in love. With her warm body against his and her soft hair tumbling around his face, it was all he could do not to cry. As for Charity, the knowledge that she had even failed at dying sent her into a new spasm of sobs.

Wade's heart twisted with panic as he looked back over his shoulder to his boss who was bearing down upon them at a fast pace. He didn't know what to do except hold her.

Moments later, Mehitable was on the ground running. "My God!" she yelled. "What happened Charity, what happened? And where is the Reverend? Why did you come back alone?"

Just the mention of his name was enough to send Charity into new fits of sorrow. She forgot Wade James was holding her. All she could think was to tell Sister. She would know what to do.

"The preacher," she sobbed. "He's gone."

"Gone! Already? But why? What happened?"

"It's ruined," Charity sobbed. "Everything's ruined . . . including me. I thought he was . . . I trusted him to. . . ." She swallowed, unable to hear the truth of her horror said aloud.

Mehitable's face turned a dark, angry red as she reached for her gun.

"Are you a'sayin' that he had his way with you and then skipped out of town?"

Charity swayed on her feet. "I want to die," she whispered. "I just want to die," then she fainted in Wade James's arms.

A rage unlike any he'd ever known began to fill young Wade's heart. His Charity — his love — had been ruined by the lies of a stranger. And as he gazed at her tear-ravaged face, he knew what he had to do. His eyes were hard; his lips grim with anger as he turned to Mehitable Doone.

"Miss Hetty, I reckon I'll be turnin' in my notice and leavin' you now. There's somethin' that has to be done."

Mehitable's own ire was rising with every breath that she took. She looked deep into the young wrangler's eyes and saw something she hadn't known was there. The man was in love with her sister. And now it was too late.

"Put Charity in the buggy and drive it back to the house, then help me get her inside. And you ain't goin' nowhere. It'll be me that puts the bullet in that fat bastard's belly."

Wade did as he'd been told, but what she'd said had not changed his mind. A few minutes later he carried Charity into the house with Mehitable right at his heels. When he laid her down on her bed, her head lolled limply on the pillow. He kept hearing Charity's words. She wanted to die from her shame. When he stepped back, the anger in him was palpable.

"Miss Hetty, I reckon if you're goin' after the bastard, I'll be goin' along with you. With or without your permission."

Hetty looked at Wade and then down at Charity and sighed.

"So it's like that, is it?"

"Yes ma'am, I reckon it is."

She nodded. "So be it, then. And it's probably just as well. I'll need someone to help me look after Charity."

Wade's eyes widened. "You're takin' her with you?" he asked.

Hetty frowned. "Hell yes. You heard her. She wants to die. It would be just like her to do something foolish to herself before I got back."

Fear swamped him as he turned to look at her. The thought of that beautiful face and sweet laugh buried beneath six feet of Territory dust made him sick. His voice shook.

"There ain't nothin' wrong with her. Any man would be proud to call her his wife." Then he flushed, realizing he'd gotten too familiar with his boss. "When you plan on leavin'?"

Hetty glanced down at her sister. "I'd like to say now, but I reckon we'd better give her a day." Then she nodded, her mind made up. "We'll leave first thing tomorrow." She gave Wade a hard look. "It may take a while. I ain't got no idea where he was goin' from here."

Wade pulled his hat down low on his head. "Don't matter," he said. "I got as long as it takes."

One day passed into another as Randall Howe traveled farther and farther away from his shame. But the distance in miles did not lessen his guilt. He'd done the unthinkable and taken a virgin — a young, helpless woman who'd been caught up in the throes of her own passion. He should have known better. They'd sent for him to counsel with her. He bedded her instead.

He stared at the changing landscape without seeing the green give way to a flat, open plain. Heat intensified. And for the first time in his life, Randall let his personal hygiene slide. When it came time to embark upon the next leg of his journey, he was sporting a three-day growth of whiskers and his suit was covered with dust. Considering himself unworthy to even read holy words, he'd buried his Bible in the bottom of his bag.

And when he got off the train and discovered that the next leg of his journey would be by stagecoach, he decided it just punishment for what he'd done. The next day he boarded the stage bound for a place called Lizard Flats.

THE QUEST FOR TRULY FINE

Gentleman Jim poured a dollop of Witch Hazel into the palm of his hand and then rubbed his hands together before patting his freshly shaved face. The sharp, spicy scent made his eyes water and his cheeks burn, but the sensations soon passed, leaving a clean and pleasant aroma about his person.

He'd made up his mind that tonight he was going to confess to Letty his growing admiration for her. He knew it was a long shot, but lately he'd been hungering for a different kind of life and hoped that Letty would, too. Will the Bartender had told him a little about Letty's childhood and when questioned, she'd told him the rest. Jim understood all too well how a woman could come to the place in which Letty now found herself and held none of it against her. The way he looked at it, everyone sinned. It was the ones who didn't regret it who were the losers, and he knew that Letty hated her life. He heard the longing for something better when she sang of sadness and retribution.

He glanced out the window and noticed the setting sun. Within a few minutes, Will would be calling up the stairs for Letty to come down and he wanted to talk to her first before she re-entered that world. Smiling to himself, he reached for his hat, settled it on his neatly combed hair and started out the door of his hotel room when he realized his derringer was still on the bed. He slipped it in the pocket of his jacket and then hurried down the stairs and out of the hotel, suddenly anxious to get to the White Dove.

As usual, Letty was out on the balcony, girding herself for another night of drink and debauchery and waiting to hear the call of her good luck bird when she saw Jim LaSalle exit the hotel. An ache rose in her throat as she watched him start across the street. The past few days with him had been heaven on earth for her. He had yet to take her to bed, although his goodnight kisses on the hand had progressed to tender kisses on her lips. Each night when she went to sleep, his face was in her dreams, and each day when she awoke, thoughts of seeing him that night were all that got her through the days. She didn't want to think of the day when she'd awaken and once again, find him gone, although she knew that it could happen.

In her eagerness to see him, she forgot about the bird and leaned over the balcony to call down to him.

"Jim!"

He stopped in the street and looked up with a smile of delight on his face.

"Letty, dear Letty. I need to talk to you. May I come up?"

"Yes, of course," she said. "But hurry. Will has already yelled at me once."

"Will can bide his time," Jim said. "This is important."

Letty nodded and then raced back into her room as Will stepped up onto the sidewalk. She was checking her appearance in the mirror when she heard the gunshots — two — in rapid succession. After that, there was a rush of running feet and loud shouting, and then everything went still.

She stood in the middle of her room without moving, staring toward her doorway with her heart in her throat, listening for the sounds of footsteps on the stairs that would tell her Jim was on his way. But the longer she stood, the more certain she became that she would never hear them again.

Finally, when she could move without falling, she made her way to the door and then started down the stairs. The room downstairs was full of people, but all she could see was a sea of dusty hats. From where she was standing, she couldn't tell one man from another.

Then she saw Eulis come out of the back room carrying the mop and a bucket of water. She flinched, and as she did, he caught the movement and looked up. The expression on his face made her sick. It was pity, pure and simple. And the only reason he would need to feel pity for her was if —

Then, as if on signal, the crowd below where she was standing suddenly parted and she could see the body stretched out on the floor. It was Jim. Even in death, he was still a beautiful man. Blood had blossomed upon the front of his white suit, like a red rose pinned on his lapel, but what had run out beneath him was pooling on the floor.

"No," she moaned, and started to moan. "Not him! Not him! Damn you, God, why do they all have to die?"

Heads turned at the sound of her voice and then the men quickly looked away, as if ashamed to have seen her grief.

Helpless to move, she sat down on the fifth stair from the top and started to shake as what was left of Jim LaSalle was carried out of the room.

Will hurried up to her.

Letty grabbed his arm, unable to speak.

He patted her shoulder. "Sorry you had to see that," he said. "But the man came out of nowhere. Said Gentleman Jim had cheated him the other night in a game of five-card stud. Shot him square in the chest, he did, then yelled out, he wasn't gonna hang, and shot himself before anyone could stop him."

"Who was it?" Letty asked. "Who killed my Jim?"

Will missed the personal reference as he glanced back down at the floor, making sure that Eulis was doing what he'd been told.

"Some drover from the Lipton ranch. Old man Lipton's foreman has done carted him off." Then he urged her to her feet.

"Come on down, will you, honey? Liven up the place for me. Pete's gonna play that new song you like and Eulis is almost done mopping up the mess. It'll be like old times in nothin' flat. You'll see."

Letty stared at him as if he'd just lost his mind.

"Liven up the place? Just like old times? Have you no heart? For God's sake, Will, a man is dead."

Will frowned. "Well, hell, Letty, he was just some deadbeat gambler. Besides, it ain't like you never saw a dead man before."

Letty drew back her hand and slapped him. He staggered backward from the impact, more stunned that she'd done it than from the force of the blow.

"He wasn't a deadbeat. He was my . . . my. . . ." Her voice broke. "Friend. He was my friend. As for livening up the crowd, I'd sooner set myself on fire. You want songs . . . sing them yourself."

Then she ran down the stairs and out the back way into the night, sobbing as she ran. She ran until the tinny sounds of Pete's piano were nothing but a memory, and the lights of Lizard Flats were barely faint pinpricks of illumination in the dark.

It wasn't until a horse and rider almost downed her in the dark that she realized where she was at. The rider dismounted on the run, certain that he'd run her over in the dark. To say he was surprised to find her standing was putting it mildly.

"Lady? Are you all right?"

Letty smelled the scent of sweat and

horse upon the man's body and wanted to die.

"No. I will never be all right again," she said, and fainted in his arms.

It was then that he realized who she was and that he had paid a dollar for her services only a week or so ago. While he didn't know what had happened to her, he knew where she belonged.

With little effort, he slung her unconscious body across the back of his horse as he mounted, then started back to town.

Eulis was dumping out the mop water when the cowboy rode up at the back of the saloon.

"Uh, hey, Eulis! Miss Letty has taken ill, I think. Reckon you could help me get her to bed?"

For Eulis, the shock of seeing Letty draped across the saddle was like cold water in the face. He took one look at her and then pointed to the door.

"Bring her in here," he said, and held the door as the cowboy carried her inside.

It was morning before Letty woke. She rolled over on her back, staring at the dusty, cobwebbed ceiling, trying to figure out where she was and how she'd gotten there. Then she heard a muffled snore and leaned over the side of the bed. That was when she realized she was sleeping on a bug-infested cot only three feet from Eulis Potter's unconscious body.

She bailed out of bed with a shriek.

Eulis had been dreaming and Letty's shriek settled into the dream with such reality that he sat up with a jerk before he was truly awake. All he saw were flaring nostrils and the flash of a red dress before he realized it was Letty who was wearing both.

"Letty, I —"

"Why am I in your bed?"

The shock in her voice was turning to fury. He could hear it coming and started to talk before she got the wrong idea.

"Some cowboy brung you back to town. And don't go bein' all mad at me. I ain't the one who shot your friend and I ain't the one who ran off onto the plains."

It was then she remembered, and with the memory came the pain.

"Where is he?" she whispered.

Eulis shrugged. "At the undertakers, I reckon. I got to dig me a grave before noon. It's too hot to let him wait."

Letty's eyes were glittering with unshed tears, but her voice was cold, her words hard.

"You do it right, you hear me? You dig it neat and you dig it deep. And you tell me when they take his body up to the hill."

Eulis nodded. "Yeah, all right. I'll let you know, right enough. Just don't scream like that no more. My head's killing me."

"No, Eulis. Your headache won't kill you, but I might if I find any bed bugs in my hair. Why the hell you didn't take me upstairs to my own bed is beyond me."

Letty swiped her hands across her eyes, dashing away the tears before they could fall. *Damn the world and everyone in it. I will never — for as long as I live — care for anyone else again.* Then she added, "Bring some hot water to my room. I need to get clean."

Eulis scrambled to his feet, eyeing his mattress as he looked for his shoes. There weren't any bed bugs on his mattress. If there had been, they would surely have been chewing on him all this time. Then he looked down at the skin on his arms and amended the thought. When all was said and done, he did look a bit on the charred side, himself. Maybe in a week or two he'd take a bath, just for a change of pace.

"Eulis!"

The screech in her voice set him on the run, his own bath forgotten.

Sweetgrass Junction was an odd name for a town that couldn't grow weeds, let alone prairie grass. But the name was no more out of place than the people who inhabited it.

At the beginning of the small town's inception, someone had decided to set the first building on a knob of red clay that was so barren it didn't even throw a shadow. That building became the way station for the westbound route of Hollis Freight Line that ran out of Lizard Flats.

When the second building went up, which happened to be a saloon — aptly named the Sweetgrass Saloon — it only stood to reason it would be built near the first. A saloon was a necessity in a land where the population of varmits outnumbered the population of man. It was the ultimate proof that man was never far from beast. Man needed a drink now and then, if for no other purpose than to howl at the moon.

As is usually the case, people followed industry. A house or two was built. The owner of the saloon needed a place to sleep and Nardin Hollis, who owned the freight lines, had been farsighted enough to make certain that his horses had fine and proper care. Thus, a livery was erected on the spot nearest the freight line office. And so it went until Sweetgrass Junction boasted a population of sixty-five, except once every two or three months, when Miles Crutchaw, a miner, came down out of the mountains. Then there were sixty-six.

Only now, Miles' visits were more frequent. He could have waited a lot longer than a month before restocking his provisions, but it wasn't food that brought him down out of the Rockies and east across the prairie to Sweetgrass Junction. It was the recent acquisition this past year of a new female named Truly Fine, formerly of Lizard Flats, and now residing at the Sweetgrass Saloon while taking nightly appointments for her favors.

At forty-four, Miles Crutchaw had a commanding presence and an abundant head of curly, brown hair. His features were far from being handsome, yet manly. His face more nearly resembled a half-finished bust that some sculptor had abandoned in favor of a different project. It was craggy, all angles and planes set off by a pair of clear blue eyes and a beard that grew as wild as the man who wore it.

With a bath, he would have been as fine

an escort as Miss Truly Fine ever saw, except for one undeniable defect. Miles, "Snag" to all his friends, had less than half a dozen teeth left in his head. Four to be exact. It was the one small flaw that Truly Fine could not ignore.

And so it was on a hot day in June while sitting in the lap of a gambler who was fresh from Dodge City, Truly happened to look up and saw Miles coming through the door of the saloon for his monthly visit.

"Oh no."

It was the way she said it that stilled the gambler's hand upon her breast. And it was unfortunate for the gambler that it was his dealing hand with which he was playing fast and loose upon Miss Truly Fine, because it was the first thing Miles grabbed.

"Christ all mighty!" the gambler yelped, and broke out in a sudden sweat as the mountain man forced his hand to bend in the wrong direction. "Let go, you ox! You're gonna break it."

"Maybe if I do, you'll remember next time not to put it upon a lady in such a disrespectful manner," Miles growled.

In spite of the pain, the gambler stared. First at the mountain man, then back at the woman in red. Lady? Not where he came from she wasn't.

Truly shrugged at the gambler, as if to say, 'it's out of my hands,' and as she did, the blue-black feathers around the neck of her dress fluttered against her pearly-white skin like the tail feathers of a pissed-off rooster.

Miles glared, his eyes burning with a sense of injustice that Truly Fine seemed incapable of feeling.

The way Truly looked at it, so many men had put themselves inside of her, that in her estimation, one more feel was hardly worth noting. But she couldn't ignore the fact that Miles had taken it upon himself to right her wrongs and save her from herself, even if it was only for his own selfish reasons.

Miles wanted a wife. He'd chosen Truly Fine. All he had to do was convince her that it was not only for her own good, but also her pleasure. Truly did not understand that concept. She wasn't like her old friend, Letty Murphy, back at the White Dove Saloon. Letty was a dreamer, always listening for the call of some bird, as if it would turn her life into something other than a woman who got paid for a poke. Truly was practical. She got paid to *give* pleasure, not *receive it*.

"That's no lady," the gambler groaned.

"And let go of my hand before I'm forced to shoot."

Considering the condition in which Miles held him hostage, it was an odd and impotent threat that landed the gambler nothing but a trip out the door.

Seconds later, the gambler was face down in the street, licking dirt from his lips and trying to remember where he'd tied his horse. He had a sudden desire to get the hell out of town while he still had all his fingers and toes and everything in between.

"Dammit, Snag, you hadn't oughta done that," Truly grumbled. "He was gonna pay me good. Real good."

Miles frowned and ran his tongue over his teeth. He hated his nickname, but coming from her, it was the ultimate insult.

"I don't call you names, Miss Truly. I wish you would return the honor by using my given name instead."

Truly pouted and flounced toward the bar, her henna-red curls bouncing with every step.

"Moose! I need a drink." She leaned against the bar while the bartender sloshed watered-down whiskey into a less than clean glass.

Miles followed her to the bar and caught the drink before she did. His hands curled around the glass and then shoved it back at Moose before she could set up a fuss.

"What you need is a man, Miss Truly, not a drink."

She rolled her eyes. "I had one. You threw him out into the street."

Miles shrugged. "Not that kind of man. I mean a man like me."

She turned. The appraisal she gave him was suggestively slow. It was to Miles' credit that he did not "rise" to the occasion when her gaze lingered longer than necessary below his belt buckle.

"I don't mind," she finally said. "As long as you keep your mouth closed, that is. One man's money is as good as another's."

Miles gritted all four teeth and tried not to shake her. "I ain't gonna pay to sleep with you, Truly. That would make me no better than the rest. I'm askin' you. Just like I do every time I come to town. Would you be my wife?"

She winced. In spite of his missing teeth. In spite of her bone-weary soul, she was tempted. But the pain in her heart just wouldn't go away. It was an impossible situation. She didn't want to live from hand to mouth, traveling by foot, or straddling the ridgeback of some mule while this fool kept moving dirt from one place to another, trying to strike it rich.

"Snag?"

"Miles," he corrected her.

She rolled her eyes. "Miles, I'll tell you now, like I tell you every time you ask. You go find that gold you keep searchin' for. When you've got the money to take care of me proper, then teeth or no teeth, you've got yourself a wife."

Miles sighed. It was the same answer he'd been getting for two and a half years, right down to the jut of her chin and the stomp of her little foot when she was finished.

"But, Truly, that could take years! By the time I'm rich, I'll be too old to make you happy."

Truly batted her eyes and pursed her lips in a tawdry display of affection. "Oh no, Miles, honey. Money doesn't get old. Only men. If you've got enough money, it don't matter a whit to me whether you can get it up or not."

He growled and spun, knocking chairs and tables asunder as he pointed a long, brown finger in her face.

"One day, Truly, I swear on your good name that I will find that gold and then you'll have to keep your promise."

Truly sighed as he disappeared through

the swinging doors.

"I don't have a good name," she muttered, and hitched at the neckline of her dress. Because she felt so lost inside, she ran to the door and yelled out into the street.

"And you can't find your butt with both hands, Snag Crutchaw. What makes you think you'll find gold?"

"Want another drink, Truly?" Moose the Bartender asked.

She stuck out her tongue and flounced upstairs, not for the first time wondering if she'd made the wrong choice. Her heartstrings pulled as she entered the room and closed the door.

Hell yes, I made the wrong choice. I've been doing it since the day I was born. Why should I suddenly become careful and wise?

Miles rode west.

Out of Sweetgrass Junction.

Back toward the mountains.

With fire in his heart and tears in his eyes.

He'd find gold or die trying, or his name wasn't Miles Crutchaw. This time not even God Himself could have deterred Miles from his quest. He would find gold and he would marry Truly Fine. And he would not return to Sweetgrass Junction until he could claim her.

On the seventh day out of Sweetgrass Junction, he entered his camp, glad that the ride was over. He stored his provisions in the usual places, taking care to secure them against the marauding bears and other varmits that seemed to have a sixth sense about Miles' periodic trips.

Before he'd been mildly irked, allowing them their ravaging for no other reason than because they'd been here first. But this trip was different. When this was gone, there would be no more sugar. No more salt. No more anything bought from Sweetgrass Junction until he'd struck it rich. He'd lived off the land most of his life and would do it again for as long as it took. But what he wanted most was what lay beneath it.

With dogged determination and the spirit of a gambler who believes mightily in the next deal of the cards, he took up his lantern and pickaxe and headed up the mountain above his camp.

The location of his mine was a secret, but one not hard to keep. Except for an occasional Shoshone on a hunting expedition, there was no one around for miles. And the Shoshone gave the big miner a wide berth. No Indian would have anything to do with a man who talked to himself as Miles often did. A man with a "disturbed spirit" was a man to leave alone.

Hours later, and deep inside the heart of the mine, Miles dug and cursed, picked and shoveled, his back jolting from the shock of pick against stone. Dirt splattered and chips flew as he swore beneath his breath.

"I'll find your gold, Truly Fine. And when I do, you'll have to be my bride. You promised."

Slowly, but surely, his wheelbarrow filled. And when it was overflowing, he began the long trek out of the mountain's belly toward the mouth of the mine where he would empty it into the sluice he'd built by a high mountain spring.

Behind him the mountain rumbled, like the guts of a man who's eaten too many green apples. Miles paused, listening.

"Fart and get it over with," he warned the mountain. "I ain't finished with you yet. Not by a long shot."

And so the days passed into weeks, and then months. And before he knew it, the sugar was gone, as was the last of his salt. When he boiled the empty salt sack with last night's squirrel in hopes of soaking some flavor from the cloth, it hadn't tasted bad, but he'd been forced to sort thread, as well as bones, from his meal. Both the squirrel and the sack had come apart at the seams.

That night, wrapped snug in his blankets and sheltered by the lean-to he'd grafted into the side of the mountain, he slept hard and deep, unaware that things were happening inside his mine that were beyond his control.

This particular year in the mountains, the late summer weather was unusually wet. Day after day the rains pounded the earth, running downward in swift, red rivulets between trees and rocks toward the river below, like blood pouring out of a wound. Unbeknownst to Miles, the water wasn't just running over the land, but was pouring inside as well, filtering down into the cracks and crevices of the mountain that housed his wormhole mine, carrying away more dirt than he'd planned, and weakening the tunnel on a daily basis.

Miles began to worry about the constant dampness inside the hole. The walls wept continually. Day after day he noticed that the puddles inside the mountain no longer drained away.

He knew that his first breaths of life had been taken while floating inside his mama's belly. But he'd willingly sucked his last lung full of liquid just before he'd been born. He had no desire to die by drowning inside this mountain's womb.

Even with all the warnings, he had still not prepared for the internal devastation, or the fact that Mother Nature was about to reveal on her own what he'd been unable to find.

Morning dawned wet and gray. The air was thick with mist that hadn't decided whether to fall or hang loose. But for Miles, it was a day like any other day. Whether it rained, snowed, or burned hot with overhead sun, he still spent his days in the dark, in a hole in the ground.

He lifted his head, sniffing the air as he stepped outside the lean-to, letting the mist settle his sleep-ruffled hair and beard in lieu of grooming. Relishing the cool dampness, he combed his fingers through his wild curls, then tied them away from his face with a thin strip of leather.

A slight breeze lifted his beard, stirring the singed scent from yesterday when it had come too close to a lantern's flame. He tugged at its weight, thinking that the last thing he needed was to set himself afire.

Yanking his skinning knife from its sheath, he began to hack at the thick growth upon his chin, wincing as it pulled against the tender skin beneath. A while later, he was finished. The dark, springy pelt covering the lower half of his face was now only a mere six or so inches in length, and as shaggy as a molting wolf. Far off in the next valley he heard the rumble of thunder, but it did not deter him from heading up the slick, mud-covered path toward the mouth of his mine.

Swirls of mist hovered just above his feet, moving slightly as he passed like bashful ghosts. Water dripping from the leaves along the trail fell on top of his hat, splattering upon the heavy leather with intermittent plops. He ignored the discomfort as he continued on, his long legs carrying his mighty weight as if it were of no consequence.

The toothless mouth of the mine gaped similar to that of his own, and as he entered, he had the unusual impression of having been suddenly swallowed whole. His stomach lurched anxiously. This sensation was not normal. The skin crawled on the back of his neck and he even considered not going inside. Then he thought of his Truly and shook off the thought.

Just inside the opening, he paused to light the lantern he'd carried with him from camp. The scent of coal oil and smoke hung heavy in the damp air, stinging his eyes and nose as he adjusted the flame.

Where there had been darkness, now there was light, small, but persistently yellow. He started down the corridor, pushing the empty wheelbarrow through the darkness, and as he did, the rest of the world fell away. The deeper into the mountain he went, the quieter and colder it became, until finally the only sounds he heard were those of his own making.

The squeak of the wood wheel on the barrow.

The splat of his boots as he walked through water.

The soft gasp and hiss of his own breath as it clouded before his face.

The reverberating hammer of his heartbeat thundering in his ears.

When the tunnel ended as suddenly as it had begun, he hung the lantern on a peg. Then, as he'd done every day for the last seven years, he ran his hand along the wet, seeping walls, stroking it like a lover, searching for the perfect place to plunge himself into her depths.

He lifted his pick, squinting just a bit as he aimed for a small seam in the wall that hadn't been there the day before. He inhaled and swung, and the moment of connection coincided with a belch and a roar from the mountain that sent a fresh fall of earth and rocks tumbling down upon him.

Oh hell!

It was Miles first and last thought as everything went dark. At first, he had no way of knowing whether he was dead, or just buried alive. But slowly, pain became the focus of his existence and he decided on the latter.

His face hurt. Everywhere he touched, it felt wet. The morbid scent of blood was thick in his nostrils and salty against his lips. He spit, and teeth fell out into his palm. He fingered them in the dark. Counting. There were four to be exact.

"Christ all mighty!" he groaned. "Everyone's a critic. Even this dad-blamed mountain didn't like my looks."

Miles tossed the snags into the rubble around his feet. Spitting blood and cursing the pain upon his face and mouth, he levered himself to an upright position and began feeling around the walls for the lantern, praying it had not been broken.

His luck held. The lantern was still hanging from its peg on the wall. The draft of air from the falling debris had simply snuffed out the light.

Fumbling in the dark, he fished out the sulphur matches he carried in his vest and relit the wick. Light flared, and for a moment, Miles went blind again, only this time from the light. He looked away, blinking rapidly to readjust his eyes to the sudden change. When he could see, he began to survey the damage. It didn't take long to see that the tunnel had suffered less than he had. Judging from the blood on his shirt and hands, the mountain had worked him over good.

Again, pain wracked his body and his stomach rolled. The cavity inside the mountain began to tilt, and the motion sent Miles to his knees. When the earth had stopped spinning, and he could blink without wanting to puke, he looked up.

Instead of the solid wall he expected to see, there was a wide rift in the surface that had not been there before. And something else shown from deep within, revealing itself in the crack like a woman spreading her legs for her man to come in.

Miles thrust his fingers into the crevice,

feeling along the crack and testing the differences in texture of the light and the dark before his eyes, praying that the blow to his head was not making him see things that weren't really there.

It wasn't his imagination. There was a color far different from the dark obsidian and rich chocolate soil that he'd been carrying out by the barrows full for years. He lifted the lantern from its peg, holding it close, peering into the crack and blinking back tears. Not only was the color still there, but it was brighter — and richer — and it ran long and deep up the wall.

"Thank you, Jesus." He spit blood and grinned. "Truly, darlin', if you only knew. Yore days are numbered."

He hung the lantern back on its peg, his pulse racing as he lifted the pickaxe and started to dig. The first strike was solid with the second coming swiftly behind the first. Like a man gone mad, he began hammering at the wall with the tip of his pick, shattering chunk after chunk from the vein of gold that the cave-in had revealed.

Hours later, he stopped. But only because the coal oil in his lantern was nearly gone. And because the chunks of color that he'd hammered out of the vein were overflowing in the wheelbarrow at his knees.

His eyes were mere slits in a face swollen beyond belief. Yet if Miles could have seen himself, he would have laughed and thumbed his nose at the sight. A rich man could stand to be a little ugly.

It was dark when he exited. Suddenly every tree hid a would-be claim jumper. Every shadow was a Shoshone come to lift his scalp and leave his body for the buzzards. He had a sudden fear that while he had made his find, he would never get out alive to tell the tale. It was strange how instant wealth could change a man's outlook on life. Getting the ore assayed and putting his money in a safe place became all important, and Dodge City offered everything he would need.

An assay office.

Several banks to transfer money back East.

And a dentist.

When he went to Sweetgrass Junction after Truly Fine, he wasn't giving her any room to back out of her promises. The better he looked, the better his chances.

And then he looked down at the gold and grinned. It wouldn't matter what he looked like. If he knew Truly like he thought he knew Truly, she wouldn't see anything but the money.

But by the time he reached the cabin, he'd come to another conclusion. He had some cleaning up to do before he started off the mountain. If he didn't get himself healed, he might die from blood poisoning before he reached Dodge City. And to doctor his wounds meant cutting off the rest of his beard. Just consideration of the feat was daunting. Without a looking glass to see by, he could cut his own throat and never know it until it was too late.

Much later after he'd hidden his find, he dropped onto his bunk with a heartfelt sigh and touched his face, instantly groaning from the pain. It would have to be doctored and that was a fact. But he was too sore and weary to deal with it tonight. The wounds would have to wait.

The next day the sun was already up and shining in a bright, clear sky when he woke. He stretched and then gasped. The act was a painful reminder of yesterday. He looked down at himself, at his arms and his chest and frowned at the mass of bruises. His mouth and gums ached and it hurt to swallow spit. But the necessity of cleaning his wounds was upon him. With a heartfelt moan, he got up and hobbled outside to wash his face. When he leaned over the wash basin, the standing rainwater threw back a wavy reflection of his battered features. The sight made him shudder, but it had also provided a much-needed view of his face. He reached for his knife with a grimace. At least he wouldn't cut his throat when he shaved.

Daily, Truly Fine fielded the rude, sexual innuendoes with a skill born of long years at the task. And every day that came and went past Miles Crutchaw's usual time of arrival made her nervous. For the first time since he'd started their odd courtship, Truly began to realize that she'd been existing for those fleeting moments in her life when a man had pretended to care.

But Miles Crutchaw hadn't come back to Sweetgrass Junction. Truly went to bed each night praying that she'd be given one more chance. Wishing that the wild, bushy miner would come bursting through the swinging doors of the Sweetwater Saloon and yank her out of some man's lap before it was too late.

This time she wouldn't tell him no. This time when he came, she'd willingly ride a mule for the rest of her life rather than ride one more man and pretend he was the best ever to come her way. Even if she didn't have a roof over her head. Even if Miles didn't have many teeth. Even if he never struck it rich.

It was a sad and unavoidable fact, but Truly Fine had realized too late that wealth lay not in the money in a bank, but in the arms of a man who cared.

And so the days passed, and Truly believed that she'd told him 'no' once too often. It broke her heart to think of never seeing him again.

A dog barked outside the Sweetgrass Saloon as the squeak and rumble of wagon wheels drifted through the open door. Truly didn't bother to look up from her game of solitaire. She'd know soon enough who it was. Sooner or later, everyone who came to Sweetgrass Junction came into the saloon.

As she'd expected, someone did come through the swinging doors. Moose the Bartender was the first to look up. The glass he was drying fell out of his hands, shattering on the floor at his feet. Shock spread over his face as he started to grin.

Without looking up, Truly slapped a red Jack on a black Queen. "Dang it Moose, you break many more like that and you'll be sending back East for a new set."

Moose didn't answer. He was too busy

staring at the man who'd come through the doors.

"Truly Fine, are you a woman of your word?"

Startled by the question, Truly looked up. The cards she'd been holding fluttered to the floor. The voice was familiar, but not the man. He didn't look like anyone she knew.

"I don't get it," she snapped, then narrowed her eyes as the tall, clean-shaven man started toward her from across the room. His suit of clothes fit him to perfection and his boots were shining like new. And then he grinned, revealing a set of fine, white teeth in a nearly healed face and something clicked inside her heart as he yanked her out of her chair and began to spin her around.

"Yes, you do. You get it all, just like I promised, Truly darlin'."

By now, the skirt of her yellow satin dress was flying above her waist. Her henna-red curls were bobbing against her cheeks as her eyes widened in shock. She didn't know the man, but those blue eyes looked an awful lot like —

"Miles?"

He whooped with laughter and set her down on her feet.

"I'm askin' you again, Truly Fine. Will you marry me?"

"Yes."

"Consider your choices, now," Miles argued, unaware that she'd already buckled easier than an old belt. "You're not getting any younger, although to my eyes you're still as pretty as a peach."

"Yes," she repeated and clasped her hands together to keep from shaking.

"Remember your promise," he added, having practiced his speech for so long that he'd completely tuned her and her answers out.

"Yes."

"You can't go back on. . . ." His eyes widened. The last thing she said was finally soaking in. "Yes? You said yes?"

She nodded and tried not to cry. She looked like hell when she cried. It made her nose all red and her eyes swelled shut like a horny toad. If he saw her like that, he might change his mind.

"Oh, Truly! You will marry me? Without the gold? Without the riches?"

"Yes, Miles, yes."

She threw her arms around his neck and knew that she'd found her place in life.

"That's good, Truly darlin'." He stole a kiss before she could change her mind. "I promise you won't regret it. When can you leave?"

She started out the door.

He stared at the low-cut dress and the length of leg showing from beneath the skirt and tried to imagine her on the road in an outfit like that. "Don't you want to change and pack your belongings?"

"There's not a damned thing here that I want, Miles Crutchaw, except you, and I didn't think you were coming back to ask ever again."

A wide grin spread across his face. While he'd come to grips with getting Truly on any terms, it felt good, damned good, to know that she came without knowledge of what he'd gained except, the obvious — his mouthful of teeth.

Miles followed her out the door and lifted her into the wagon. "When we get to Lizard Flats, I'll buy you some new clothes."

She frowned as he climbed into the seat beside her. "I've already been to Lizard Flats. I can promise you there's no gold there, and we can't afford to buy clothes. Neither one of us has two dimes to rub together."

He grinned and stole one more kiss before he broke his news.

"I'm not lookin' for gold in Lizard Flats.

We're going there to get married. While I was down in Dodge City, I heard tell that a real preacher is on his way there to marry the town banker. As for money —"

Truly frowned. *He went to Dodge? So that's where he's been all this time.*

He grinned. There was something about the way she kept looking at him that told him she still didn't get it.

Truly stared at his smirk. The longer she stared, the more certain she was that he had a secret he still hadn't told.

"Miles?"

He grinned again.

"I'd like to know what's so funny."

His grin widened even further.

She looked past the mouthful of pearly-white teeth to the cut of his suit, the clean-shaven face, the new, nearly healed wounds, and the twinkle in his eyes. There was something about the way he carried himself that had nothing to do with promises and everything to do with pride.

It hit her then. Her mouth dropped and she pressed both hands to her lips.

The twinkle in his eyes deepened. It was almost as if he had read her mind. It was then that she gasped.

"Oh! Miles!"

"What is it, Truly dear?"

"You didn't . . . did you?"

He started to laugh.

Truly began to hug herself in disbelief! He'd actually found wealth and still came back for her, a woman who'd soiled her body as well as her soul.

"Oh, but I did, Truly darlin'. I found a mother lode." He flipped the reins across the back of his team. "Giddyup," he shouted, and melted as Truly leaned her head against his arm and started to cry.

"I thought you'd be happy."

"You're the first man who ever kept his promise to me."

Miles shifted in the seat as he looked down at the top of her head. "And I'll be the last, too. As soon as we can find that preacher, you'll be as honest as any woman on the street. I don't want you to ever have to turn your head away in shame again. Not from any man, woman, or child. And especially not from yourself. Do you hear me, Truly Fine?"

She batted her eyes, her breasts bouncing lightly with the sway of the wagon as the wheels slipped in and out of hard dry ruts.

"I hear you, Miles darling. Truly I do."

Things Are Not Always
as They Seem

It was Sunday when they laid Jim LaSalle to rest, although the day of the week hardly mattered. Letty was the only mourner, except for Eulis, who was horribly hung over and was leaning on his shovel to keep from falling into the open hole.

The scent of new wood drifted up from the grave as Letty bent down and picked up a handful of dirt. She walked to the mouth of the grave and looked down. There was a large, dirty handprint on the top of the makeshift casket where the maker had held it in place as he'd hammered in the nails. The urge to jump down in that hole and scrub off the mark was overwhelming. To Letty, it was a slap in the face reminder that he mattered so little to the people of Lizard Flats. Then she reminded herself that there was about to be six more feet of dirt that would cover up the mark and everything beneath it.

There was a pain in her chest that made it difficult to breathe as she opened her hand and turned it upside down. Wind caught the dirt she had been holding, scattering it in a wayward pattern on the top of the coffin. She stood without moving, blind to everything but the emptiness of her life.

Eulis began to fidget. His head was hurting and his legs were weak. He needed a drink and a place to sit down, but out here there was neither. He waited, watching for a sign that Letty was finished, but saw nothing that he could interpret as an ending to what was turning out to be a very bad day. Finally, his misery overcame his reticence.

"Uh . . . if you was a mind to say some words now . . . or maybe sing one of your songs, this would be the time to do it," he said.

Letty lifted her head, and although Eulis didn't move, he had the urge to take several steps back. She almost looked vicious. He reckoned it was a good thing that the man who'd shot the gambler had gone and killed himself, too, or Letty would be doin' it for him.

Then something happened that sent

chills through Eulis's body. Letty laughed.

"Sing? You want me to sing?"

Eulis's stomach rolled.

"I only thought you might?"

"I don't do anything for free, Eulis Potter, and don't you forget it. You want a song? It'll cost you. You want to take me to bed? It'll cost you. You want to dance with me? It'll cost you. I get paid for my services. I don't do anything for free."

There was anger in her stride as she stomped down the hill. Eulis watched her go, making sure that she didn't decide to turn around and attack him when his back was turned. She was already pissed that she'd found bugs in her hair. He'd heard about that more than once. When she was little more than a speck in the distance, he started to fill in the hole, putting back the dirt that he'd removed earlier. And, as always, there was dirt left over, displaced by the single pine box at the bottom of the grave. He mounded it up nice and neat, then took the small plain cross that Letty had carried up the hill, tapped it into the dirt at the head of the grave, and followed Letty back to town.

The wind began to pick up as he walked away, scattering loose dirt and dry grass as it moved across the land. A short while later, a meadowlark landed on the newly planted cross, waiting out the wind gusts before taking back to the skies. As it perched precariously on the crosspiece, it started to sing. It was the only song to be sung over Jim LaSalle's passing.

Other things were brewing in the Territory beside Leticia Murphy's rage. A three day ride away, a pair of would-be outlaws named Milt and Art Bolin were brewing up their own concoction of trouble. As always with the Bolins and their plans, whatever they started, someone else would have to finish.

"I tell ya', Milt, that ain't no boy. 'At's a girl, so hep me God."

Milt Bolin sneered. Art, his one and only brother, was peering through a crack in the stable wall at the redheaded youth who was forking hay. The observation he'd just made was almost too far-fetched to swallow. No self-respecting female would cut off her hair, or for that matter, be caught dead in a pair of men's pants, but the idea of starting a little trouble was too good to ignore.

"There's one sure way to find out," Milt said. He pushed his brother aside and swaggered through the door of the livery as if he owned it and Mudhen Crossing as well.

If it hadn't been for the dust in the hay she was forking, Caitlin O'Shea might have seen them coming. But she sneezed, and when she did, her eyes went shut. When she opened them, Milt and Art Bolin were standing between her and the door.

"I don't know," Milt said. "He don't fill out those pants enough to be a she."

Caitie's heart sank. It was all over now. What, she wondered, had given her away?

"Yeah. And he's wearin' his hair shorter than any girl I ever seen," Art added, ready to deny the theory, although it was his suspicions that had started the conversation to begin with.

"Speak up, boy! What's your name?" Milt asked, and poked Caitie roughly on the arm.

Caitie aimed her pitchfork at the men to punctuate her warning. "Leave me the hell alone, ye sneakin' bastards."

Milt grinned. "Oowee. He's a feisty one, now, ain't he? And damned if he don't talk funny. I don't know as how I much care whether he's a *he* or a *she*. I might be tempted to try a little of that anyways. Where are you from boy? Are you one a them English dudes? I might like to try out a tea-sipper."

Rage at being unjustly accused of belonging to the hated English race made her shake. But at this moment, keeping quiet was a wiser decision than arguing in the tongue of her native country.

Art frowned. His older brother's tastes were definitely not his own.

"Oh hell, Milt, give it a rest. That's plumb indecent and you know it. If Mamma could hear you she'd —"

Milt slapped him up aside the head. "Mamma's dead. And you're gonna be too, if you keep tellin' me what to do all the time. Got that?"

Art flushed. Fury mingled with fear. Fear won out. He glared at the stable boy and stepped aside. He lived for the day when someone, even his brother, would give him the respect he believed he deserved. Unfortunately, it was unlikely to happen.

The Bolin Brothers' undistinguished reputation had earned them nothing but ridicule throughout the Territory. No matter what crime they attempted to commit, it either went awry or fell short of their expectations. They were so unimportant in the scheme of things in Mudhen Crossing that they didn't even have a price on their heads. It was a constant matter of great discussion between them as to how that might be rectified. And while they were always planning on bigger and better things, it never hurt to keep the waters muddied, which was what they were about right now.

Milt glanced at Art, then back at the kid, squinting his eyes against the light. "We could kidnap him and trade him for ransom."

Caitie laughed aloud. "And who the bleedin' hell would be payin' a plug nickel for me hide?"

It was a mistake. They'd been laughed at all their lives. Having a snot-nosed boy laugh at one of their plans wasn't going to be tolerated.

"Get him!" Milt yelled, and lunged for the pitchfork as Art went for Caitie's feet.

Two against one was nothing for a girl who'd raised herself on the streets of Dublin. She threw the pitchfork like a spear, nimbly dodging their attack. It sailed through the air with unerring aim, pinning Art's hands to the stable floor just as he tripped and fell.

"Aagh! Milt! Milt! Gawdalmighty! Help me! He's gone and kilt me and that's for sure!"

Milt had trouble all his own. While the boy's initial maneuver to escape had been successful, Milt wasn't ready to give up. He pivoted, scattering dust and hay as he lunged for another try, catching the boy on the run, shoulder high. They crashed to the floor in a tangle of arms and legs. It was, however, a move Milt would soon regret.

Sharp, deadly jabs from the stable boy's knees hit the tender territory hanging low between Milt's legs. Milt grabbed at himself and groaned, certain his manhood would no longer be swinging as God intended and he would be forced to carry his balls out of the stable in his pockets.

"I'll be killin' ye both," Caitie shrieked, windmilling her arms and fists like a madman and nailing Milt with a random assortment of blows that kept him too busy to do anything but dodge.

Meanwhile, Art continued to shriek and moan as he tried to get free. It was no use. One of the tines from the pitchfork had gone through his hand and into the floor. Certain that he was dying, Art lay with his face in the dirt and hay, crying like a baby.

Disgusted with his brother's lack of help, Milt could do nothing but defend himself. And in the midst of it all, Caitie suddenly rolled free. Jumping to her feet, she yanked the pitchfork from Art's hands and aimed it at Milt.

The pitchfork had hurt like hell going in. Coming out, the shock and the pain were too much for old Art to bear. A new set of tears sprang to his eyes as he filled his britches like a diapered baby.

Milt staggered to his feet only to come face to face with the boy and his pitchfork — aimed at him — balls high.

Milt took several steps back then pulled his gun and waved it in Caitie's face.

"It's all over kid."

She paled as Milt yelled at his brother.

"Draw your gun, Art. We got him cornered now. He can't fork both of us at once."

Art's hat fell back as he lifted his head, revealing a shiny bald spot in a circle of ratty, brown hair. "That's easy for you to say. He's done forked me. I couldn't draw a bucket of water, let alone my piece. 'Sides, he made me shit my pants."

Milt made a face. "Well, my Lord a'mercy. If you ain't the sorriest excuse for a —"

"Fun's over boys."

Caitie jerked at the sound. Another man had come in behind her when she wasn't looking. Fear gripped her as she shifted her position, trying to decide which man now posed the worst threat. Two she could handle, but three, she wasn't so sure. In spite of her indecision, she stood her ground with a bloody nose and a busted lip, daring one of them to make a move.

Milt's confusion matched Caitie's. He didn't know who to shoot first, the stable boy, the stranger, or his brother, who was beginning to stink.

"Who the hell are you?" Milt growled.

The stranger's stare never wavered. "Joe Redhawk. Now you get your brother and get the hell out of the stable before I shoot you both and come up with a reason later on."

Caitie shivered. The ominous tone in the big man's voice held more than a warning. There was menace even in the way he slouched against the wall, holding that blue-black pistol aimed straight into Milt Bolin's face.

At the name, Milt paled.

Art moaned louder. "Gawdamn, Milt. Help me up. That there's Breed, one of the fastest guns in the Territory. He'll kill you a'fore you can blink."

Milt holstered his gun with fake bravado. "I know who he is. Now listen here, Breed.

There's no hard feelins' between us, okay? We was just havin' ourselves a little fun with the kid. Didn't mean him no harm or nothin'. Why don't you let me get my shitty brother and leave before someone makes a mistake they can't fix."

Joe gave the stable boy a telling glance, and when the boy finally nodded his acceptance, he took one step to the side. But only one.

Milt bolted for Art and helped him up, cursing him all the way out the door for stinking himself up. There was no way they'd get a reputation when Art kept humiliating them like this.

Caitie poked the pitchfork into the ground and fought back tears as she used it for a leaning post to steady her shaking legs. She couldn't let herself cry. She'd forgone that luxury when she'd lopped off her hair and put on men's pants.

Joe took his time about holstering his gun because the Bolin Brothers weren't known for keeping their word. When he was convinced that the two were really gone, he turned.

"You all right, kid?"

Caitie nodded and looked away. This was the kind of man who would see straight through a short haircut and a pair of man's breeches to the woman beneath.

"I had them cold, I did," she muttered. And then felt obliged to add out of courtesy, "But I'll be thankin' ye just the same."

Joe's eyebrows arched. The lilt to the kid's voice was unmistakable. He'd known men like him before from the country of Ireland they called it. Only they hadn't been as small as this one. And not nearly as pretty.

His eyes narrowed thoughtfully. The thought had come out of nowhere, and it shouldn't have. The kid was a kid. He could be sissy. He could be tough. But he shouldn't have been pretty!

Joe looked closer. Red-gold eyelashes as long as butterfly wings shaded the upper portion of the kid's cheeks. His nose was too turned-up. His chin too shapely. A thought occurred. If he could only see the rest of his face.

"Hey!" Joe yelled.

His sudden shout made Caitie look up.

He'd seen a lot of things in his twenty-nine winters, but never a boy with a mouth like that. He considered calling her hand and then shrugged. Her deception was ludicrous, but Joe Redhawk was a man who minded his own business until someone minded it for him. After that, it was a different story. The kid — *girl* — obviously had her reasons.

Caitie pulled the pitchfork out of the ground, suddenly afraid she'd be needing it again. "And why would ye be yellin' at me now?"

The corner of his mouth tilted. Just a little. Just once.

"Just checking your hearing, I reckon."

Caitie started to roll her eyes, and then caught herself. That was not a manly behavior.

Joe turned away to hide his grin. *Yep. I was right. This here's a girl and that's a fact.*

"Better watch your back for a day or two," he warned. "That pair hasn't got sense enough to pound sand in a rat hole, but that don't mean they aren't dangerous, just the same."

"I'll be knowin' that," she muttered. "I've been takin' care of me'self since I was seven. Swill rats like that can't be hurtin' the likes of me."

Joe's eyes narrowed. Her defiance touched a long forgotten chord of memory from his own childhood. He'd done all right, up until the day two men had called him a half-breed then beat the hell out of him to see if he bled two different colors.

Years later, they were the first two men he ever killed.

He shook off the memory. It was time to move on.

"I'm staying at the hotel a couple more days. If you need help, you know where to find me."

Before she could answer, he had disappeared as quietly as he'd come.

Caitie swiped blood from her nose with the sleeve of her shirt and glared after the man who just left.

"May they all be damned," she muttered. "I'll not be needin' any man's help. I can take care of me'self, just like Paddy taught me."

That night when she went to bed in the loft overlooking the horse stalls, she pulled the ladder up behind her. No one would be sneaking up on her in her sleep unless they could fly. Meanwhile, Art Bolin sat immersed in a tub of hot water, compliments of Shirley at the boarding house, while his only change of clothes hung outside the window, drying in the cool night air. Every time Milt came into the room he would look at his brother, then spit and curse and walk away. Art didn't know what hurt worse, his hands, his ass, or his pride.

And the more Art dwelled on his misery,

the more certain he was that they'd been bested by a girl. He didn't care what old Milt said. He knew a girl when he saw one. And dadgum it all, he was going to prove it. In the morning, when his clothes were dry and his hands didn't hurt so much, he was going to go back to that stable and show them all.

Down on the street, Joe Redhawk leaned against the post outside the saloon and stared into the darkness toward the livery.

Are you asleep, little one? Or are you lying in the dark alone, afraid to close your eyes?

A loud shout, accompanied by a round of gunfire, echoed behind him in the saloon. He looked back at the ongoing scuffle inside, then stepped off the sidewalk. He had no desire to die backshot, no matter how accidental it might be. Moments later the night had swallowed him whole.

It was just shy of sunrise when Caitie bolted for the outhouse. Minutes later she exited, again on the fly. She would have the horses fed and watered before the stable owner showed up, or know the reason why. She wasn't giving any man a reason to fire her. The security of a regular job at Mudhen Crossing was the first real job she'd had since landing in New York City almost a year ago.

America, land of the free, had not proven to be the place she had dreamed it to be. When she'd gotten off the boat from Ireland, New York City was ankle deep in snow. Within three days of her arrival she'd discovered that women alone in America had the same opportunities as women alone anywhere. Basically, there were two options to keep from starving. Scrubbing floors or fucking for money. That's when she'd cut off her hair and donned the men's pants. A week later she'd hopped a train, bedded down in an empty boxcar and rode it west until they reached something called the Mississippi River and ran out of track. She made do by her wits until the weather warmed and was on the first wagon train headed west. After that, she'd seen nothing to remember except weird little towns with even stranger sounding names.

She remembered making camp near a small town called Feeny, because she'd once known a green grocer in Dublin by the same name. After that had been Lizard Flats, then Sweetgrass Junction. By the time they'd stopped near Mudhen Crossing, she was sick of wagons and making dry camps. When they moved on, she'd stayed behind. Now here she was, in the middle of nowhere, in constant fear of being found out, and living a lie.

Caitie cleaned up the stalls, unaware that Art Bolin was back at the same knothole, peering through the opening, watching the stable boy hard at work. Art was a lot cleaner than when he'd left yesterday and only a little bit damp, but this time he'd come alone. Milt had a way of belittling everything he did, so he'd have the facts before he made any more accusations.

Caitie hefted the last forkful of straw into the last stall, sighing with relief. Everything was ready and waiting for the next customer to ride in. Edward Pevehouse, the owner of the stable, had already come and gone, pronouncing everything fit before adjourning to Shirley's Boarding House for breakfast. He hadn't bothered to offer the stable boy a meal. It didn't matter. The stable boy would not have accepted the offer if he had.

Caitie stabbed the fork into the haystack, then looked around once more to make certain she hadn't left a chore undone. Her back ached and she would have killed for an all-over bath. Bits of straw tickled and poked at the tender skin on her neck and itched something awful around her waist. The bath she would have to forego, but she could at least shake out her shirt before getting herself some food.

With one last glance toward the open doorway, she darted into an empty stall at the back of the stable and yanked her shirt over her head. The breeze coming through the open windows was cool against her skin. Her nipples pearled as air brushed over them.

She shook out the shirt, popping it twice in rapid succession before pulling it back over her head. Satisfied for the moment that she'd eased her discomfort, she darted across the street toward the saloon to settle the hungry growl in her stomach. She couldn't afford Boarding House Shirley's prices, but the bartender always had cold biscuits on hand. It wouldn't take much to talk him into frying up an egg. She'd slap it between that biscuit and have herself a fine meal.

Meanwhile, Art Bolin was caught between happy and a hard-on. Watching her strip down had been fine. But there was a time for everything, and right now he had a point to prove to his smart-ass brother.

Once the girl disappeared into the saloon, Art set off in the opposite direction to find Milt. His swollen hands and damp pants were forgotten in the delight of being right. A short time later, he burst into the room of Boarding House Shirley and caught his brother and Shirley in bed.

"Oh, my gawd," Shirley screeched.

Art stood in the doorway with a grin on his face as wide as his butt. Shirley began grabbing at the sheets, trying to cover up her abundance and her shame. It was no use. Milt wasn't through pumping.

"Hey, Milt!"

Milt grunted and cursed, then collapsed upon Shirley with a hump and a thump.

"Ain't you got no damned sense at all?" Milt groaned, and rolled buck-naked off of the shrieking woman. "I was busy."

Art grinned at his brother's limp state. "You ain't no more," he chuckled. "Besides, you're gonna love what I got to say."

Milt grabbed for his pants. "Start talking."

"I was right."

Milt snickered. "You ain't never been right."

Art scratched his balls and considered the possibility of asking Shirley for a turn. But the state she was in and the look on Milt's face told him he'd best get on to what he'd come to say.

"I was right yesterday," Art said. "He's a she."

Milt went still. Anger over their rousting still rankled. "How do you know?"

Art sucked on a tooth, savoring the thrust of his news before he sent it home.

"I seen her without a shirt. She's got tits just like old Shirley there." And then he peered a little closer at the wailing woman's body and recanted. "Well, not exactly like Shirley's. They don't swing near that low."

Shirley buried her face in the sheet. She'd been forced to endure this private moment with an audience, and now, to have her womanly body belittled in such a manner was too much to endure.

"Get out!" she shrieked, and threw a shoe at Milt. "You, too," she said, and hefted the other one at Art.

The brothers turned and ducked, heading for the door. Once outside they stopped and grinned.

"I think she was mad," Art said.

Milt shrugged. "For a dollar, old Shirley can get in a real good mood." Then his thoughts switched from one woman to the next as he fingered his gun. "Let's go get that short-haired bitch. By gawd, she owes us big!"

Art strutted. He loved to be right. Later when it counted, he would remind old Milt that this had been his idea from the start.

Replete from her first food of the day and unaware of what lie in wait, Caitie wiped her hands on her pants as she headed back toward the livery. The empty feeling in the pit of her stomach was gone. And to her dismay, so was the horse at the far end of the stalls. Her heart lurched.

"Oh no! It's for certain that Mr. Pevehouse will be firin' me. Either it's been heisted, or the owner's gone off without the leavin' of pay. Whichever it is, I'm done."

While she was considering the benefits of making herself scarce, the lights went out. Before she could cry for help, someone had stuffed a rag in her mouth and bagged her with an empty gunny sack like so much feed.

Her feet went out from under her, and seconds later she felt them being tied. She was capable of nothing more than grunted curses and frantic squeals as a rope was tied around the sack, pinning her arms to her body and rendering her helpless to fight back.

She heard an ugly snicker and kicked as

hard as she could. When the toe of her boot connected on bone, she knew she'd hit a target. Someone groaned and then cursed and her heart almost stopped. That sounded like the Bolin Brothers!

Merciful God, don't let me be right.

But when one of the men suddenly grabbed at her crotch, she knew her worst fears were realized.

"By damn, Art, you were right. There ain't nothing there but air." Milt pinched her once, his laugh little more than a gurgle. "Make sure you get all of her stuff. They'll think she went and stole a horse, then lit a shuck for parts unknown. We'll be long gone before anyone knows different."

Her stomach lurched, and it was all she could do to keep her egg and biscuit down. Bound and gagged as she was, if she threw up now, she'd choke on her own spit.

"Tie her on that horse," Milt growled, and tossed Art the other end of the rope dangling from the girl's body.

Art quickly complied. A few minutes later they rode out, using the back alleys to get to the edge of Mudhen Crossing.

Only one person saw them leave, and that was Boarding House Shirley. She was none too glad to see the backside of the

Bolins and their horses, and paid no attention to what they were packing.

Caitie had been missing for more than an hour when Edward Pevehouse came back to the stables to find his employee gone, as well as a customer's horse. Certain that the youth had committed a theft, he ran toward the sheriff's office to make a report.

As he came up Main Street, Pevehouse saw the sheriff in front of the saloon with that gunslinger, Breed. He paused, but only briefly. Whatever they were discussing could not be as important as what he had to say.

"Sheriff! I say, Sheriff!" Fully aware of the imperious quality in his voice, he narrowed the distance between them, complaining with every step. "I want to report a crime."

Bud Williams turned, staring intently at the portly man heading his way. "Well, hell," he muttered.

Joe Redhawk grinned. "You're the man who wanted this job."

Bud rolled his eyes. "Why didn't you just shoot me then and put me out of my misery?"

Joe's grin widened.

Pevehouse gave Joe a look of dismissal

while apologizing for his interruption.

"Sheriff! I want to report a crime."

"What crime?" Bud asked.

"My stable boy has stolen a horse. I want a posse formed and I want him brought back and hanged."

Bud frowned. He'd seen the kid around town and was vaguely surprised by the accusation.

"Are you sure it was him?" he asked. "Maybe he fell asleep on the job and someone just rode out without paying."

"No! He's missing, as are his belongings and one of my horses. I want a posse formed now."

Joe was in doubt from the first words out of Pevehouse's mouth, and the more the man talked, the angrier he became. He kept thinking of yesterday's incident with the Bolin Brothers and suspected there was more to her disappearance than a stolen horse.

When Pevehouse finally paused to take a breath, Joe chose the moment to interrupt. "Hey, Bud. Before you go off half-cocked, you might want to check and see if Milt and Art Bolin are still in town."

Bud looked surprised. "Why?"

"I ain't tellin' you how to do your job, but I pissed the Bolins off real big yesterday while they were in the act of trying to mess with the kid. Could be they decided they needed revenge."

Pevehouse poked at the star on Bud Williams' shirt. "Now see here, I helped put you in office. You can go out the same!"

Bud grabbed his finger, warning thick in his voice. "Don't remind me. And I'll do this my way," he added. "If Joe thinks there's more to this, I believe him."

Pevehouse yanked his hand out of the sheriff's grasp. "Damn half-breed. How can he know anything, when he doesn't even know who his own father was?"

Joe's hand was on his gun before he had time to think. But a quiet warning from Bud made him turn and walk away.

Bud frowned. When he could trust himself to talk without cursing the man, he gave Pevehouse a cold, blue stare.

"You know, Pevehouse, if you choose to judge a man by something as insignificant as his birth, then I guess in your eyes, Joe has an excuse. What the hell is yours?"

He left before Pevehouse could answer. The way he was feeling, it wasn't safe to stay and say any more. He caught up with Joe at the hitching post where his horse was tied.

"Hey, Joe!"

Redhawk paused in the act of tightening the girth and looked up.

"Sorry about that," Bud said.

Joe shrugged. His eyes were dark with anger, but his voice was low and even. "You got nothing to apologize for."

"Then why are you leaving? I thought we were going hunting tonight."

"I'm still gonna hunt. Just not for deer."

Bud frowned. "What are you getting at?"

Joe swung a leg up and over his horse, sliding the toe of his boots in the stirrups and testing them for length. "That stable boy is no boy. She's a girl."

Bud's mouth went slack. "The hell you say!"

Joe yanked his hat down low until nothing was visible but the lower half of his face. If his hunch was right, he'd be riding straight into a setting sun.

"If the Bolins have discovered her secret, she's in for real trouble and I've got to find her. I walked away yesterday knowing I should have stayed. It don't pay to think about what they'll do to her."

Bud paled and then turned red in anger. Mistreating a woman was something a real man did not abide. He shook his head in disbelief. "Are you sure she's a girl?"

Joe grinned. "Since when have I missed

something like that?"

He rode out at a trot. A few minutes later, he was galloping across the prairie with the memory of her face for company.

"Better untie her," Art said. "She ain't moved since you pulled her off that horse. What if she's smothered?"

Milt grinned and spit. "Then it means she won't fight none when I have my way with her, don't it?"

Art blanched. It was his opinion that his brother was sick. Plumb sick.

"I still say you need to untie her."

Milt grinned. "You untie her if you're so damned worried."

Art began to look nervous. "I cain't untie nothing. My hands are too sore and swole up."

Milt frowned. "Next thing you're gonna be telling me that I got to pull it out for you so you can take a pee."

"Just shut the hell up and let her get some air," Art said, then stomped toward the campfire. In his opinion, less danger lay in the darkness outside the fire. This girl was hell on wheels.

Their camp had been hasty, and as usual, poorly thought out. They'd made camp in a blind canyon. One way in. One way out. Just like the sack they'd put over Caitie's head.

She was lying on the ground right where they'd dumped her. She could hear Milt circling her sacked body like a dog circles a skunk. She bunched her muscles, waiting for the opportunity to strike.

Remembering the near thrashing she'd given him yesterday, Milt wasn't sure whether he wanted to let her go or just run like hell. In a flash of inspiration, he slashed the ropes around the sack that bound her arms to her body, then jumped back on the defensive.

She didn't move.

Game to go one step further, he grabbed for the sack and yanked. With two hard jerks, it came off of her body.

Seemingly lifeless, she rolled onto her side, as limp as an old man's cock.

Milt nudged her with the toe of his boot. She didn't even moan. He stuffed his hands in his pockets and stared at the situation for a bit before he realized she was still bound and gagged. He bent down to cut the ropes and just as he started to untie the rag around her mouth, Art walked up behind him.

"Is she dead?"

Startled by the sound of his brother's

voice, Milt's gaze shifted. It was the opportunity Caitie had been waiting for. She came up kicking and swinging, although her arms were so numb she had to look to see if she'd made a fist.

"Gawdalmighty!" Art shrieked, and started to run. He'd already had more than his share of this shorn witch.

"Get back here, you dog!" Milt yelled, and then went to his knees, retching from the damage her boot had done to his crotch and certain if he sneezed, his balls would come out his nose.

Art hollered at Milt from behind a bush. "Just let her go! For gawd's sake, let her go!"

"Hell no!" Milt said, then rolled on his back, his knees drawn up under his chin as he rocked in pain. "Shoot her before she gets away."

Art shivered as he pulled his gun. He'd never shot at a woman before.

Caitie yanked at the rag covering her mouth, then stumbled in the dark. As she did, she fell flat on her face. The swift taste of salt and a jolting pain was a good sign that she'd be sucking, instead of chewing, her meals for a while. Her tongue was on fire. But it was fortune — or fate — that made her fall. Art's shot went wild, whizzing over her head and hitting the tree in front of her with a splat. The gunshot echoed within the canyon walls.

She was long gone before the last echo died.

THERE ARE NONE SO BLIND

AS THOSE WHO WILL NOT SEE

Sunrise came without warning. One minute Caitie was walking through grass and trees with moonlight for a guide, and the next thing she knew, the sun was in her eyes. It was the first time since her escape that she'd known what direction she was going.

And while one direction was as good as another so long as the Bolins were somewhere else, Caitie would rather not have been in full view of the world with no place to hide. She paused on a rise and shaded her eyes with her hand, squinting them just enough against the new sun to get her bearings.

To her left, a low line of blue-gray mountains broke the flat horizon. The distance, she knew, was deceiving. It would take days, not hours to reach the foothills. With no food or water, that way was out of the question. To her right, the ground rolled

216

before her, falling away into an undulating sea of grass. A black mass moved upon it like a shadow upon the land. Caitie's heart leaped in her breast. Buffalo, and ranging as far as the eye could see! She'd seen them before, but safely from the seat of a wagon and didn't want to be on foot anywhere near a herd that size.

That left two options. What was before her; and what was behind. She'd escaped the Bolins twice now. Once, thanks to a gunslinger with a sense of fair play, and the second time, pure luck. Having another run-in with them was more than she cared to risk.

Caitie looked intently at the landscape before her. The unknown held new appeal. Without hesitation, she started forward. The sun cooked her face, burning her mouth inside and out and adding to the misery of an empty belly, and still she walked.

It was hours later before she would top a rise that gave her hope. Legs shaking from exertion and hunger, she paused at the crest of a hill and looked down at the valley below. Trees dotted the landscape. Beyond the tops of the farthest trees, Caitie thought she saw —

"Water! Thank you, Jesus!"

She crossed herself out of habit although she'd long since given up counting on anybody but herself, and started forward at a brisk walk. The impetus of moving downhill shifted the walk to a trot, and by the time she'd gained the level floor of the valley, Caitie O'Shea was in an all-out run. Still several hundred yards from the river, the smell of the water was already in her nose.

Eyes Like Mole saw the white man. Several hundred yards away. Running toward him like a madman.

And man is what he thought Caitie to be. Part of his misconception rested upon the fact that she wore the pants of a white man and had chopped off her hair to match. The rest of his mistaken identification was due to the fact that Eyes Like Mole couldn't see his hand in front of his face.

At a distance, his vision was fine. From where he sat upon his horse, he could see for miles in every direction. But up close to his prey, or his enemies, where survival often counted the most, navigation was accomplished with a combination of blurry images and keen ears, and the fact that his horse knew the way home.

A squat man of little import within his people, the Arapaho, Eyes Like Mole had yet to take a wife when some of his friends had already taken a second.

For the last three days he'd been on a vision quest, fasting and meditating, hoping that during his cleansing the spirits of his ancestors would guide him on the right path. Now he wondered what this intrusion into his purpose would mean. So he sat and watched.

The sun was hot upon Eyes Like Mole's bare shoulders. Sweat ran beneath his deerskin leggings and down into his moccasins. It did not matter. Soon a breeze would come by and he would be cool. Personal comfort was a small thing to consider for a man who could not see all that he should.

His horse neighed softly as it, too, saw the oncoming stranger. Eyes Like Mole sat motionless, watching, considering the stupidity of white man in general. An Arapaho child of four winters would know better than to wander away from camp, and yet as far as he could tell, the white man was alone.

As the man came closer, Eyes Like Mole was forced to squint to adjust his eyesight, trying to distinguish between blowing bush and running man. When the man suddenly fell into the water and began flopping like a land-bound fish, Eyes Like Mole grunted. He'd located the white man's new position by sound alone. He kicked his heels against the horse's flanks and rode forward.

Caitie fell to her belly on the river bank, thrusting her hands and arms into the water and then splashing her hot, burning face. With a sigh of relief, she dipped her head and drank long and deep, teasing an empty stomach into thinking it was full. And when she had slaked her thirst, she jumped into the water, clothes and all, sluicing her hot, dusty body in an effort to wash away the grime.

"Ah," she moaned. "What I wouldn't be givin' fer a sliver of soap."

She'd never known it could feel so good to be wet. The current beneath the surface of the water was swift, but she felt no fear. And because she dared to let the river have its way, she missed seeing the Indian on the rise just above the bank. With a gentle kick, she bent her knees and sighed as the river flow carried her out from the bank and into its depths.

Then out of nowhere, pain ripped

through her scalp. Flailing helplessly against the current, she realized something had her by the hair. She shrieked and kicked, swallowing more than her share of the river as the water gave her up to a greater force. Seconds later, she hit solid ground with a rude thump, deflating her lungs upon impact. Gasping and choking, she crawled to her knees, struggling for breath. When she could finally breathe, everything came out in a screech.

"Ye bleedin' sod!" She swiped hair and water from her face and eyes. "Were ye about trying to drown me?"

Eyes Like Mole jerked and stared directly at Caitie. Not because he could suddenly see, but because the voice was female. His interest grew. So it was a white woman that he'd rescued! But her manner of speech was strange. She was from a tribe he did not know. He thought of his vision quest. Maybe she was the answer to his prayers. Maybe his ancestors had guided him to this woman from a faraway tribe. He thrust out his chest.

"You did not swim."

Rage wilted into terror as Caitie looked up into the implacable copper face of the mounted Indian. With water streaming from her hair into her eyes, she dropped to her knees and made the sign of the cross. "Holy Mary, mother of God, help me now in me hour of need."

Eyes Like Mole frowned. The woman was strange in ways other than her mode of dress. Now that he'd saved her from the river, she was on her knees, talking to herself at a rapid pace, and in a tongue he couldn't understand.

He did not know that as Caitie lapsed from English into Gaelic, she was swiftly calculating the distance between herself and the horse's hooves, certain that if she tried to run, she could be squashed like a mouse underfoot. Believing her plight to be hopeless, she fell forward upon the ground in a weak, helpless heap.

Shrieking aloud, she pounded the earth in anger and fear. "Sweet Jesus and Mary, dear mother of God, how dare Ye be lettin' me live through hell on the streets of Dublin only to be bringin' me here to this godforsaken land to die at the hands of a heathen."

Eyes Like Mole looked down at the shadow upon the ground, trying to squint past the blur to the woman beneath. It was no use. She was nothing but a vague shape with a loud mouth.

"You not die," Eyes Like Mole scolded.

"I, Eyes Like Mole, saved you. Get up, woman! You do not cry!"

Caitie choked on her last sob and lifted her head from the ground as reality sank in. *He's speaking the English tongue! Maybe there'll be hope for me yet.*

"How are ye knowin' the English?" she asked.

"Scout for Army at fort. Know plenty about white man."

Caitie glared. He might know plenty about white men, but he didn't know beans about white women or he wouldn't have treated her so roughly.

"So ye were draggin' me by the hair of the head and out of me bath. To what purpose?"

His answer was slow in coming. Taking a chance, Caitie got to her feet and took several steps backward for a better view. From where she stood, he looked to be only a few inches taller than she was. His body was as brown as the earth beneath her feet, and his long black hair was bound up in two hanks over his ears and wrapped with colorful cloth all the way down. His face was broad. His mouth was wide. And he stared down that hook of a nose at her like a bird of prey. But little did Caitie know that those small, dark eyes saw nothing of her person other than a shape.

While Caitie had been surveying him, Eyes Like Mole had been doing some thinking of his own. She'd asked him a question. It was time to answer.

He pointed at her with his chin. "I take you. You come with me."

She took two more steps back and muttered. "Like hell! And why should I be comin' with the likes of a heathen?"

"I take you for wife."

His announcement was as plain as the small brown horse he was riding. But Caitie took it no better than the unwanted rescue.

"Ye'll be taking yer'self to hell and back first," she screeched.

"You come," Eyes Like Mole repeated and swung his horse around, heading toward what he hoped was camp while motioning for her to follow.

As was her bent, Caitie O'Shea reacted, rather than thought. She came forward all right, but not to follow. Eyes Like Mole only saw her move. He did not see her purpose.

She raised her hand and slapped the horse's rump with a sharp and vicious blow. It shot forward like a scalded cat, leaving chunks of sod and blades of grass soiling the air behind him.

Eyes Like Mole wasn't prepared for the jolt, or the runaway horse. Instinctively, his knees gripped the horse's belly as he fought for control. A skilled horseman, he soon had his mount in line, but relocating the woman was a serious problem. He rode up to the crest of the nearest hill and turned to look at the view far below. Seconds later, he grunted. A smile slid into place as he kicked his horse and rode back down the hill.

Caitie ran and never looked back. Her heart thundered in her ears and her lungs burned as she struggled for breath between each chop of her legs. And because she didn't look back, she never heard the horse, or saw the Indian, until it was too late.

Eyes Like Mole stared passively at the shape upon the ground. His horse grazed nearby.

The scent of horseflesh.

The sweet smell of grass being harvested by his horse's teeth.

A shrill cry from a hawk overhead, and the slow,' even breathing of his woman at his feet.

All were familiar sounds and scents he could identify. At that moment, he was satisfied. And then Caitie came to.

"Wha' happened?"

She rolled her tongue around a mouthful of dirt and grass that was imbedded between her teeth, then crawled to her knees and spit. Everything came back in a rush as the Indian's small feet encased in moccasins, as well as his leggings and a breechcloth, moved into her line of vision. She didn't like to think what lay beneath.

"You fall."

"Like hell. Ye pushed."

He shrugged. Arguing with a woman was not something an Arapaho warrior should have to do. Eyes Like Mole started toward his horse.

"We go." He felt for the dragging reins of his horse and once he'd located them, vaulted onto its back in one smooth leap.

"I'll not be goin' anywhere," Caitie argued, and then choked and gasped at the tug of the rope around her neck. She couldn't believe it! While she was lying unconscious, he had hog-tied her like a pig being led to slaughter.

"We go," Eyes Like Mole repeated, and nudged his horse forward, giving the woman no time to escape.

As an honorable Arapaho warrior, he might make a mistake now and then. A man was allowed a few in his lifetime. But he knew better than to let this woman get too close again. Keeping her on the far end of a long rope would serve his purpose nicely. The farther away she was from him and his horse, the better he could see her. And once they were on the move, she'd be too busy trying to keep up to save herself from being dragged.

Pheasant flushed from their nests as the odd duo passed. Eyes Like Mole turned often to check behind him, making certain that his woman was still at the end of his rope.

Caitie O'Shea was there, and almost at the end of a rope of her own. Blind with exhaustion and weak from hunger, she felt her legs giving way.

"Stop!" she begged, and tugged on the rope with both hands. "I cannot be runnin' another step."

Eyes Like Mole reined in his horse and frowned. His ancestors had sent him a woman as he'd asked, but she seemed to be weak in the ways that counted.

"You come?"

Caitie dropped to her knees, heart pounding, head aching.

"I'd be delighted," she muttered, and tried not to cry.

They entered the Arapaho village to the tune of barking dogs and shrieking children. All work stopped as the people ran out to gaze at the unbelievable sight. Eyes Like Mole was riding in with a white man in tow. It took the second, and then the third look before the people in the village realized it was a woman, and not a man tied at the end of Eyes Like Mole's rope.

Chief Little Deer was torn between admiration and shock. Eyes Like Mole had never been able to accomplish much past being a good, long-distance scout. To see him come riding into camp with a prisoner was quite a feat. On the other hand, it was a white woman that he'd captured. At this time, the Arapaho had a peaceful relationship with the white man and wanted to keep it that way. This was about to present a great problem.

Chief Little Deer ran forward. "Eyes Like Mole! What have you done?"

Eyes Like Mole dismounted, trailing the rope in the dust as he swaggered toward the sound of his chief's voice.

"I have had a vision. The spirits of my ancestors sent a woman to me. She is to be my wife."

Caitie groaned and sat down in the dust,

eyeing the tepees, the barking dogs, as well as the suspicious glares of the Arapaho women with total disgust. "And I'm thinkin' this couldn't be gettin' worse."

"She speaks with a strange tongue," Chief Little Deer said, noting, as Eyes Like Mole had, the odd catch to the white woman's voice. "And if the spirits sent her to you, why is she tied?"

"She does not come willingly."

Chief Little Deer frowned and felt compelled to add.

"It is difficult to keep a woman who does not want to stay."

Eyes Like Mole thought a bit before he answered. He'd given that point some thought on his own.

"I believe it is because she did not hear the spirit's voices as I did."

Chief Little Deer felt obliged to warn him while taking careful note of the fact that Caitie O'Shea did not look weak and distraught. In fact, when their gazes had collided moments earlier, he'd had the distinct impression that he'd just faced an insurmountable foe.

And then Caitie got her second wind. "Ye'll be untying me now," she said, and yanked the rope from Eyes Like Mole's unsuspecting fingers.

He spun, staring glassy-eyed in the direction of her voice, but all he could see were the vague outlines of the people surrounding him. He couldn't distinguish Caitie from any of the others.

The sudden shock, and then fear that swept across his face startled her. What the hell could he possibly be afraid of? She couldn't outrun several dozen people, even if she tried.

"I'll be wantin' food . . . and water . . . and a place to sit down."

So great was his relief, Eyes Like Mole seemed to wilt on the spot. Even her demands were music to his ears.

He motioned toward what he hoped were the lodges.

"My woman gets such things for herself."

Caitie sensed something more than her capture had taken the tribe's attention. It was then she noticed they were not watching her. They were watching him, as if they expected to see him fail. She looked closer. Eyes Like Mole seemed to be waiting for the same thing.

She grabbed him by the arm and started dragging him away from their prying eyes.

"Listen you bleedin' sod. I can be smellin' fear as good as the next. I'm not knowin' who's worse afraid, the likes of you, or the likes of me."

A small child darted forward and clasped Eyes Like Mole's hand. As Caitie watched, the child tugged at him, changing their direction toward a tepee near the edge of the camp. It seemed abandoned.

No fire burned outside its doors. No spirit designs had been painted upon the skins around his lodge. Eyes Like Mole's small brown horse had instinctively wandered to the area and now stood with head down, reins hanging, waiting to be cared for.

"What's happening? Why is everyone about treatin' you like a child?"

He stopped outside his lodge, drooping like the small brown horse who waited, searching for the English words to explain himself.

"I am weak." It was humiliating to admit the truth to a woman, but if she was to be his wife, it must be said.

Caitie's stomach tilted. His dejection was so obvious she felt compelled to find the source of his pain.

"You walk, talk, and ride like any other man. Where is your weakness? And why have ye need of stealing a woman when I'm seein' dozens of your own kind. They can't all be wed."

Eyes Like Mole turned toward the sound of her voice and tried a fierce glare. It did not feel comfortable explaining himself to a mere woman. But it was hard to glare at someone you could not see.

"You give me your hand."

His order was so unexpected that she complied. He held it up before him, splaying her fingers apart like the feathers in a bird's tail.

"I cannot see this."

"See what?" Caitie asked.

"This hand, or you." He pointed around him. "I know what is there. I see it from afar. But when I ride close, it disappears, like the dust before a windstorm."

Caitie slipped her hand free and then stepped close, waving her hand before his face in a wide sweep. He barely flinched.

"Oh. Oh me, oh my."

There was little else she could say.

"Food is inside. Water is nearby. You find. Later we talk."

With stoic face, he turned toward the sound of his grazing mount, moving carefully with outstretched arms until he reached the shadowy bulk before him. He walked away, leading his horse. But he wasn't the only one who could not see. Surprised by the hand fate had dealt the little man, Caitie found herself looking at his world through a blur of tears.

The sun was only hours old as Joe Redhawk squatted low to the ground, watching the Bolin Brothers camp, constantly searching the thickets beneath the trees for a sign of the girl.

He saw nothing but the brothers, heard nothing but their quarrels, and felt a growing sickness in the pit of his stomach that had nothing to do with missing breakfast.

She'd been so pretty. Feisty and young as she was, she should have been fighting off beaus, not the likes of Milt and Art. Yet no one knew better than Joe Redhawk that life had a way of being unfair.

Had been pretty? he thought. *Why do I keep thinking that way? She can't be dead. I don't want her to be dead. Hell, I don't even know her name.*

Anger made him careless. When "Breed" got careless, people often died. He walked into the camp with both guns drawn.

"Where is she you sorry sons-a-bitches? And don't be tellin' me she's dead, or you're next."

Milt spilled hot coffee on his hands. Art fell backward off the stump in the act of trying to draw his gun and busted his head on a rock.

For Milt, this was the last straw in a series of disasters. He wished to hell and back that he'd never even seen Mudhen Crossing or that stable girl.

"It's all your fault!" Milt yelled, glaring at Art who'd addled himself when he fell.

Art, on the other hand, had more things to worry about besides the gunslinger who'd surprised them in their camp. "My head! I think it's broke."

"I asked you a question," Joe drawled, and just to prove he was serious, cocked the hammers on both guns.

Glassy-eyed with pain, Art heard the hammers click and looked up. Unaware that the blow to his head had nearly tripled his vision, it looked to him as if a whole posse had them surrounded, but was hard pressed to see which man it was who was aiming down on him.

"How many are there?" Art asked, and staggered to his feet. "I'll get the two on the right. You take the rest."

Joe crouched. "I said, drop your guns! Do it now!"

Milt cursed and spit, then followed the Breed's orders and dropped his piece in the dirt. At Milt's insistence, Art followed suit, then followed his gun by passing out, face forward into the dirt.

Milt rolled his eyes and glared at the big half-breed. "Just shoot me now and put me out of my misery. You'd be doin' me a damned favor, and that's a fact. Look at him! I never saw such a poor excuse for an outlaw in my entire life."

Joe shot in the dirt between Milt's feet, and then smiled. He had Milt Bolin's attention.

"Next time I won't miss."

Art groaned as he clutched his head and rolled over onto his back. "Is it her? Is she back? If she is, so help me God, I'll take her back to Mudhen Crossing myself," he said, and then puked all over himself.

The urge to kill slid out of Joe's body as quickly as it had appeared. If they feared she was back, then that meant she must still be alive!

"What've you done with her?"

Breed's angry voice rang in their ears. For the first time in his life, Milt wished he could trade places with Art. "She got away. I don't know where she is."

"The hell you say," Joe growled, and shot again.

"Jesus Gawd!" Milt screamed. "I'm done for!" He fell to the ground in pain, his foot clutched tight within his hands.

"That was just your toe. I'm aimin' higher next time."

Milt dropped his foot and clutched his bloody hands to his crotch. He got the message.

"We thought she'd passed out. When we untied her, she kicked me in the balls and ran. I couldn't 'a straddled a horse to save my hide, and Art there, well, see for yerself. He ain't never done nothin' right yet. She's gone. I cain't rightly say I care where to, either. If you're going after her, take her gol-danged pack with her. I don't want no reminders of that bitch anywhere around me."

He reached behind him and slung the bag he'd been leaning on toward Joe.

It hit the dirt at Joe's feet. He picked it up, hefting it easily in one hand. All her worldly possessions. At the thought, his stomach listed slightly, like a sinking boat.

Joe stared at the pair before him and thought of just drilling them now. It would stamp paid to a lot of misery and he was pretty sure he'd feel a whole lot better. He could only imagine how frightened the girl must have been. Yet he couldn't help but feel some admiration for her spunk. No matter what she was dealt, she kept making the better play. He waved the gun in Milt's face one last time.

"I'm going now. But if I don't find her tracks leading out of this canyon alone, I'll come back and shoot you both where you lay, then look for her body by myself."

Milt paled. "You're a goddamned Injun. You people are supposed to be good at trackin'. Look hard. I ain't gonna die for somethin' I didn't do."

Joe's voice was just above a whisper. "Maybe not. But you're likely to die from something I do, if you don't shut the hell up."

Milt sucked in the sides of his cheeks, and bit his tongue. Breed got his point across better'n any damned man that he knew. Art tried to get up and groaned. Out of frustration, Milt kicked him in the belly, simply because he could.

Joe was a few hundred yards from his horse when he saw the first set of tracks. Relief overwhelmed him. A slight grin split the seriousness of his expression as he knelt, tracing what she'd left behind with the tips of his fingers. Such a small foot. Such a small woman. But what a big heart. He had a sudden wish he'd been different. Living out the rest of his life with someone like her would be fine. And then he straightened and cursed himself all the way to his horse.

"Women like her don't have anything to do with men like me."

"Talkin' to yourself?"

Joe looked up. Sheriff Bud Williams was leaning against a rock while his horse grazed beside Joe's.

"I see you haven't lost your skill at trackin'," Joe muttered.

"Oh, I could find you just fine. It's the Bolin brothers I can't seem to locate. Maybe you could help me out." He gave Joe a long, studied look and then frowned. "I heard some shots a while back. I hope you're not gonna tell me that they drawed down on you, or anything stupid like that."

Joe grinned and shook his head. "Naw. They're back there in the canyon. Pevehouse's horse is there, too, but the girl is gone. She got away from them. When I find her, I'll bring her back so she can watch them hang."

"Who'd you shoot?" Bud knew his friend too long to imagine that it had been birds he'd been shooting at.

"More like *what* I shot, not who. Milt's only got four toes on his right foot now, but that don't matter. It'll just make his boots fit better. And Art puked on himself.

Other than that, they were fine when I left. However, if you want to bring both of them back alive, you'd best hurry. Old Milt was right pissed at Art. Wouldn't surprise me if they did each other in."

Bud started to grin as Joe mounted his horse. "You keep havin' all the fun, and I wind up doing cleanup duty."

"Yeah, but you're the one who's gettin' paid. Remember?"

Minutes later, the canyon was silent, save for the sounds of the sheriff's horse as he rode into the Bolins' camp to take them back to jail.

They went quietly.

It had not been a good day.

An Armed and Less Than Shiny Knight

Joe Redhawk started out to find the runaway stable girl with the sun in his face. Now, it rode at his back like a weak, but persistent partner. When night came, he'd be forced to stop and wait for next light before continuing his search. All he could do was hope he found her before it rained. If he lost her trail, chances were that he would lose her, too. The Territory was vast, and the residents within were either widely scattered, or constantly on the move.

"She's just so damned little."

The sound of his own voice startled his horse and himself, as well. Joe shifted in the saddle as his horse shied past a pile of rocks. When they were clear, Joe gave the horse its head, trusting its instincts when he could not see the cause of its alarm. Chances were that a snake lay among the stones, coiled and ready to strike.

His eyes narrowed as he gauged the mood of the sky and the surrounding hills. Many unseen dangers lie in wait for the unsuspecting, and the girl was as unsuspecting as they came. How she thought she would be able to hide her identity was beyond him. He got mad all over again, remembering what she'd endured at the Bolin Brothers' hands.

He kicked his horse in the flanks, moving it from a canter to a lope as the image of her face danced before his eyes.

Damn those Bolins. If the sheriff don't hang them, I just might.

And so they went, man and horse across the prairie in search of a girl with no name. A half-hour later, his horse snorted again, but this time Joe saw the reason why.

Water!

A riverbed with a good, steady flow beckoned in the shallow valley below. Moments later he dismounted and knelt to fill his canteen a few feet upstream from where his horse was drinking.

That's when he saw the tracks at the edge of the bank. The same tracks he'd followed out of the Bolins' camp and halfway across the prairie. Boot prints like those of a child, or a small woman. His eyes narrowed and a slow smile changed the contours of his face.

"So, girl, you found yourself some water after all."

Relief settled. She was still surviving on her own with little help from anyone. A sense of pride at her accomplishments kept growing within him. This was the kind of woman a man could trust out here.

He began to retrace her steps, beginning from the point of entry into the water, to her point of exit, but when the unshod tracks of an Indian pony suddenly mingled next to those of the girl, Joe Redhawk broke out in a cold sweat.

The first few years of his life had been spent with his mother's people, the Cheyenne. He knew only too well the fate of captive white women within the tribes.

He glanced at the tracks one last time and then straightened. Resolve settled the nervousness that he'd first felt.

"This is Arapaho country. At least I know where to start looking. I just don't know if I'm gonna like what I find."

His horse's ears twitched at the angry rumble of Joe's voice. He grabbed the trailing reins of the bridle, and in one smooth motion, swung up into the saddle and rode away.

Mile after mile, Joe let himself be led by

the faint trails in the prairie grasses and the scent of wood smoke on the night breeze. He found the Arapaho camp just as the new moon rose in the dark night sky. Careful to stay downwind and not alert the camp dogs, he considered his options.

Riding in now *was* a possibility. He was well known in the Territory. By his birth alone, the Arapaho would acknowledge his right to be in their midst. But his black, bone-straight hair was no longer worn in the fashion of the Cheyenne. Now, it barely fell below collar length. He'd abandoned deerskin leggings and a breechcloth for white man's pants. He wore boots rather than moccasins, and shaded his face with a wide-brimmed felt hat. And he rode a saddled horse, not an Indian pony with a hand-woven blanket. In the dark, the differences could prove fatal. Being the cautious man that he was, he opted to wait for daylight before riding in.

Hours later when daylight came, he rode in expecting to find her a hostage. He didn't expect to see her in charge.

One day at a time. One night at a time. That was the way Caitie O'Shea had endured her life thus far. Being held captive by Eyes Like Mole had barely changed her situation. The only difference now was that somewhere between being dunked in the river and nightfall, she'd begun to feel sorry for the weak-eyed little man.

"You eat now!"

Caitie rolled her eyes. She'd already eaten when he wasn't looking and nearly upchucked it all. Now he expected her to swallow more of the foul-looking concoction he kept bubbling in a pot while he hovered only inches away, trying to peer past the shadows between them.

Aware that he operated on sound as well as sight, she stirred the wooden paddle several times around the pot, making it seem as if she was mixing before dipping.

Eyes Like Mole grunted, satisfied that she was cooperating with his orders, and settled next to the door of his lodge. If she tried to make a run for it, he would hear her.

"You will give me fine sons," Eyes Like Mole announced, just as Caitie was considering the possibility of slipping past him.

His audacity was unexpected. Caitie crawled to her knees, the wooden paddle from the noxious stew held tight in her fist like a club. "I'll be givin' ye a fat lip if ye try a damned thing."

Eyes Like Mole sighed and wondered why the spirits of his ancestors had sent him such a stubborn woman.

"The spirits told me you would come," Eyes Like Mole argued.

"I didn't *come*. It was after bein' dragged." Her voice had risen to just below a shout. When he stood and started toward her, she started to shriek. "And I'm not about layin' with some weak-eyed heathen just to be provin' a point."

Before he could react, she stormed past him, stomping out of the tepee with blood in her eye, looking wildly around for something larger than the flat stick to use as a weapon.

Joe Redhawk was on the slope of the hill, several hundred yards away and about to ride into camp, when he saw a woman running out of a lodge. The long fringed tunic she wore looked just like any other Indian woman's style of dress, but it was the short red hair and unbounded fury that gave her away.

He reined in his horse, watching as she grabbed a stick of firewood then turned toward a small, bowlegged man who staggered out of the tepee toward her. From where Joe sat, things didn't look good. He nudged his horse into a gallop.

Caitie turned to face her captor with fury in her stance and fear in her heart. It might be her last action on earth, but she was ready to go out fighting. And then as before, it was the unexpected sound of jeers and laughter that stopped her cold.

She pivoted. They had an audience. And from their gleeful expressions, they expected Eyes Like Mole to fail. Her anger died.

Panic, mixed with that of defeat, layered the wild blank look in Eyes Like Mole's expression. Caitie groaned.

A memory of her own childhood came rushing back. Of a time when she'd been humiliated on the streets of Dublin by a gang of young bullies who'd whipped her soundly then laughed when she'd cried. She dropped her head and walked back to Eyes Like Mole, dragging the stick she'd pulled out of the stack.

"Here." She handed it to him in as subdued a manner as she could muster. "I'll not be arguin' with ye again."

It was hard to say who was more shocked, the onlookers, or Eyes Like Mole. He took the stick, aware that she offered more than herself to be beaten. She'd given up her own freedom for his pride.

His heart swelled. He couldn't see it, but he knew that his own people were looking at him with respect, and he had the woman to thank. For that reason alone he could not do as she'd asked. But he could give them both an out by showing that he could be generous, as well as forceful. He waved the club above his head and puffed out his chest.

"It is good. You have learned lesson."

Caitie sighed. "I'm thinkin' I'll be needin' me head examined," then she buried her face in her hands. It was while she wasn't looking that Joe Redhawk rode into camp.

"Girl, I'm thinkin' trouble follows your trail."

Caitie jerked with shock, then stumbled backward. She'd heard that voice at her back before! In Mudhen Crossing. Just as the Bolin Brothers were about to do her in. She pivoted and at that moment, wished she hadn't given Eyes Like Mole her stick.

"You!"

He looked mad as hell and twice as scary. Although he sat his horse with apparent ease, there was a sense of violence within him she couldn't ignore.

And then he spoke, and his rough drawl

grated across her conscience. "I've tracked you across more miles than I care to count, girl. You sure can cover the territory."

Her chin jutted. "And not a whit of me own accord!"

In spite of the low murmur of the crowd around them, Joe laughed. By damn, but he wanted this woman for himself. He just wasn't sure she'd be thinking the same. However, all of the feelings he had for her must be dealt with later. He turned to survey the crowd.

Chief Little Deer knew the man who'd ridden into their camp. Breed was known throughout the Territory. But it remained to be seen what purpose he could possibly have for coming here.

Eyes Like Mole sensed the familiarity between the stranger and his woman and knew that he should do something to regain his status as master. He stepped forward and shouted.

"Woman! You come!"

When he heard nothing, the frown on his face deepened.

Caitie flinched at the tone of his voice, looking to Joe Redhawk for an answer. Joe gave her a nod, yet when he started to talk, it was not what she'd expected.

"I am Red Hawk of the Cheyenne. I

have come for my woman. She became lost on the prairie and I have been tracking her. Who do I have to thank for her care?"

Eyes Like Mole lurched forward, blindly reaching out for a woman he could not see. "No! She is my woman. You lost her. If you meant to keep her, you should have taken better care of what is yours."

Caitie bit her lip. Just when she thought it couldn't get any worse, it did.

Joe gauged the passion in Eyes Like Mole's voice. Although the man stood straight and proud, something about him didn't seem right. Someone was tugging at the leg of his pants. He looked down.

"Ye can't go fightin' the likes of him," Caitie begged. "He's not seein' his blessed hands in front of his face. T'would be nothing short of murder."

She stepped back as he dismounted, watching as he unbuckled his gun belt and hung it across the saddle horn in a gesture of good faith, then gave her an odd, almost affectionate look.

"You do find the oddest assortment of villains."

She tried to glare, but was too weary and heartsick to do more than blink.

"Just don't be hurtin' him," she muttered.

As far as Joe Redhawk was concerned, her last request settled her fate. If she could feel compassion for her captor, then he might actually stand a chance with her, too.

"I promise," he said, and untied her bag, willing to sort through the ownership business later. "Here." He tossed it to her through the air. "Milt and Art send their regards."

"Me things!"

Her face lit up like a candle as she dropped to her knees and began digging through the bag to make sure that all she owned was still intact.

Eyes Like Mole stepped forward and in doing so, almost fell on top of her. She jumped up to steady him. Somewhere within the gathering of the tribe, a woman giggled.

"Get lost the lot of you," Caitie shouted, waving her arm at the crowd.

Joe frowned. The warriors looked none too happy. If he didn't do something soon, the situation was going to go sour. His posture shifted as he pointed toward Caitie.

"I came for my woman. I will barter for her."

"You have nothing I want," Eyes Like Mole said.

"Oh, but I do. You want my woman." Joe turned and stared at the small, shorn woman as his mouth quirked at the corner. "And, so do I."

Caitie was in shock. The gunfighter had laid claim to her right in front of an entire band of heathens. She wondered how much of it was truth, and how much of it was simply a ploy to get her out of her latest predicament. While she was pondering the last question, Breed lapsed into Indian dialect and she became lost as to what was now going on. Several of the women standing in the crowd started to glare at her and shout what she suspected were insults.

"Blessed Jesus," she muttered, aware that her future and her safety had suddenly been tossed up for grabs.

There was always the possibility that they'd be forced to make a run for it and if that happened, she wasn't about to be leaving her precious possessions in the hands of heathens. Her movements were frantic as she began shuffling her belongings back into her bag.

The bag was small, and spilling the contents had rearranged the spare space until she was having trouble making it all fit back. But when her fingers slid across a small leather case, her pulse gave a kick.

Maybe, just maybe.

She yanked it from the bag, then jumped to her feet.

"Joe! Wait!"

He frowned. What was she up to now? He'd been about to make his offer and she had messed up his speech.

"Girl?"

Warning was thick in his voice as Caitie bolted toward him with the small leather case in her fist.

"Look! They were belongin' to me father. He was afflicted with poor eyesight, as well. Maybe?"

Joe's eyes narrowed. "I'd say give it a try. It beats fighting a blind man all to hell."

As Caitie turned toward the little Indian, her conscience pricked. If a body wasn't too picky about the details, he had sort of saved her life. There was no telling whether she would have survived a night on the prairie alone. If this gesture would set her free, it was the least that she could do.

"You! Eyes Like Mole."

He turned toward the sound of her voice as Joe Redhawk began to translate Caitie's words into the language of his people.

"It's time for me to be goin'," Caitie

said. "But before I do, I'll be rewardin' ye for your kindness and bravery. Ye saved me from drownin', as well as gave me shelter and food."

The Arapaho began to mutter among themselves. They had not known of Eyes Like Mole's bravery in these things. They thought he'd simply stumbled over a lost woman and dragged her home behind his horse like a stolen calf.

Eyes Like Mole started to argue, but Caitie stopped him with a touch of her hand. "And because of yer kindness, I'm bringin' great magic to ye."

She opened the case and pulled out her father's eyeglasses. The wire rims were old and worn, but the glass was still intact. When she unfolded the earpieces and extended her hands toward his face, he stepped back in fright.

Whatever Joe said seemed to calm the little man. Caitie proceeded again. And this time, he stood, bowing slightly as she slipped the glasses up his nose and settled the earpieces behind his ears.

"You can be openin' yer eyes now," Caitie announced.

"Aaiiee!"

Eyes Like Mole's cry was somewhere between a war whoop and a shout of pure joy. He began to run. Darting from people to places, touching and feeling, seeing that which had eluded him all his life. His small brown eyes seemed huge beneath the prism of the lens, but for the first time, he was seeing the world in clear colors and shapes.

"Ye must be careful!" Caitie warned. "Or the magic will break!"

Joe translated again, and this time Eyes Like Mole nodded. Of course they could break. Magic could not last forever unless great care was taken.

To the amazement of those gathered, Eyes Like Mole strode directly toward Chief Little Deer.

"I was wrong," he announced grandly, speaking in English so that his woman could understand. "The spirits of my ancestors did send this woman to me. But not to take as wife. She brought great magic with her instead. She brought me eyes so that I would see."

He looked at Caitie, then frowned. "While she has given me a great magic, I do not think she would give me many fine sons. She is too small and has no hair."

Joe laughed at the disgust on Caitie's face. "Mount up while you've got your chance, girl, and quit fussing about the fact that he no longer wants you."

Caitie did as she was told. Minutes later, they rode out of the Arapaho camp in a more dignified manner than that in which she'd come.

A coyote howled from the ridge beyond their fire. The sky was dark but clear. It was one of those nights that you could see forever. But Caitie O'Shea was not looking past the man who sat beside her. She was too intent upon making sure that certain rules stayed fast.

"I'll be wantin' to know, Joe Redhawk, why did ye keep comin' after me?"

Joe looked into the flames between them while he struggled for an answer she would be willing to hear. Would she accept the truth of what was in his heart, or should he simply lie and let her go when they returned to Mudhen Crossing? The latter thought didn't bear consideration. This small person had become fixed in his heart.

He looked up. "You never told me your name."

Caitie rolled her eyes and tucked her buckskin tunic a little tighter around her knees. "Yer not about askin' me to believe ye've came all this way, fightin' outlaws and Indians just to be askin' me name."

Joe hid a grin. "I might."

Caitie frowned. "I'll be wantin' the truth."

"You might not be wantin' to hear it," Joe said, mimicking her mode of speech to perfection.

Her nose tilted upward just the tiniest bit. "The truth is best, even if it's sometimes painful."

"Then hear this," Joe said. "At first I came after you because I felt I owed it to you. But I kept looking because I didn't want to lose you, girl."

"My name is Caitlin O'Shea. My family called me Caitie."

"I didn't want to lose you, Caitie O'Shea."

Her heart thumped twice in rapid succession. This sounded awfully like a declaration of love.

"And why would that be?"

He looked away. If she said no, it would kill him.

She wouldn't be swayed. "I'm waitin', I am."

He stood and Caitie resisted the urge to run. He was so terribly big and intimidating.

"I had in mind that you and I . . . that

256

maybe we could —"

She jumped to her feet. With nothing between them but a small campfire, she doubled her fists.

"Ye'll be comin' no further, Joe Redhawk. I'm not about sleepin' with a man unless we're wed."

Joe grinned. The perfect opening.

"Then, Caitie O'Shea, I wonder if you'd consider coming with me to Lizard Flats."

"Why? What'll there be in Lizard Flats that's not in Mudhen Crossing?"

"A preacher. A real one from back East. I thought if you were a mind to, maybe we could get hitched."

Caitie gasped. This man was offering her his hand in marriage. It was an enticing, yet frightening thought. "Horses are hitched. It's people who are married," she muttered.

Joe scooped her into his arms. "Oh hell, girl. Anyway you say it, it still comes out the same. Will you be my wife?"

Caitie grinned. "I'll be givin' you many fine sons," she offered, mimicking the demand of her weak-eyed captor.

Joe Redhawk laughed.

The next day, they struck out for Lizard Flats.

Eulis was standing at the end of the bar near the back wall, watching for the odd customer who left without finishing a drink. It was his job to clear the tables. He considered it his right to finish off the liquor before Will wiped out the glasses, and the way business was booming tonight, he had started hoarding the dregs in a jar in the back which he could drink later after he'd swept up the floor. No sense making Will angry by passing out before he'd done his job. Will might cut him off from his three free drinks, and then what would he do on the nights when business was slow?

A tall, scrawny man was sitting at the far table with his back to the wall. Eulis watched as the man suddenly laid down the hand of cards he was holding. He rolled the unlit cigar in his mouth from one corner to the other, then leaned forward and raked the coins on the table toward him.

As far as Eulis knew, the man had been at that table for almost thirty-six hours. Except for the times when he'd gotten up to relieve himself, he hadn't budged. And he hadn't seen him lose. Either the man was the best card player to come to Lizard Flats, or he was a damned good cheat.

Eulis thought about telling him what had happened to the last gambler who'd come into town, then decided to mind his own business.

Suddenly, one of the men at the table jumped up with a shout and threw down the cards in his hand.

"You cheatin' bastard! You couldn't have a full house. Not unless this deck has five kings."

Before anyone could think what might come next, the man standing had a gun in his hand and put a bullet between the gambler's eyes.

Eulis flinched.

"God all mighty," he muttered, and made a run for the back room as the place erupted.

Upstairs, Letty was in the act of pocketing her dollar from the last man she'd pleasured when she heard the shot. The man, a liquor salesman from up north, grabbed his sample case and his hat and bolted out of the room.

It wasn't the first time there had been gunshots in the White Dove, but it was the first time she'd heard them since Jim had died. The sound made her sick to her stomach, but she was curious as to what was going on. She slipped out of her room and peered over the railing just as Will the Bartender pulled a shotgun from underneath the bar. She got a brief glimpse of a man lying in a pool of blood and a dozen others in a rip-snorting fight, and ran back inside her room and locked the door. But the moment she'd done it, another round of gunshots went off. At that point, she panicked. She was mad at the world, but not ready to die and the floors in this place were as thin as the walls. She could get shot here as quickly as if she were downstairs. She grabbed a shawl and made a run for the back stairs, exiting onto the street just as she heard running footsteps behind her. Still nervous, she darted into the nearby alley, then held her breath as the men ran past. Like her, they'd just wanted out of the way of flying lead. Another round of gunshots sounded. Letty resisted the urge to duck, she knew she was far away enough now to be out of danger.

Figuring that work was over for the night and knowing it was too soon to go back inside, she stood for a moment, uncertain of where to go next. She ventured out of the White Dove only rarely, and never at night. But the air was cool and the way she figured it, the farther she got from the saloon, the safer she would be. Pulling her shawl a little closer around her shoulders, she started to walk.

At first, it was only to put some distance between herself and the gunshots, then it became a journey of a different kind.

It only took three blocks before she ran out of sidewalk. Although she was now walking on dry ground, she kept moving. She passed the barbershop, then the livery stable and finally came to the house where Sophie Hollis lived.

From outside, the house looked like something from a storybook, all clean and pretty with lamplight in the downstairs windows. As she stood, she saw a silhouette pass between the curtains and the light and knew that Sophie must have heard the gunshots, too. When she saw the curtains part and then saw Sophie peering out, she moved back into the shadows. But as she watched, she saw something she hadn't expected to see. There was fear on the pretty widow's face.

Letty frowned. She had never considered that someone who had everything would still be afraid. There was a brief moment when she felt a kinship for another woman alone, but the feeling disappeared. The only thing she and Sophie Hollis would ever share was that little weasel of a man she was going to marry.

There was a soft fluttering of wings above her head, then a whippoorwill called, so close that she imagined if she took just one step backward, she would hear its tiny, beating heart.

"Who's there?"

Letty jerked. While she'd been daydreaming, Sophie Hollis had walked out on her porch, and wonder of wonders, she was carrying a gun. Afraid she'd be shot in the back if she walked away without letting herself be known, Letty knew that she had to speak up.

"It's me, Leticia Murphy. I'm just out for a stroll."

It took Sophie a moment to realize who she was speaking to and then stepped back in shock, as if speaking to a woman such as Letty would soil her own reputation.

"Get out!" Sophie cried, and waved the gun in the air. "Get away from my house this instant or I'll shoot."

"Perfect," Letty drawled. "Then you'll be no better than the fools down at the White Dove."

Sophie gasped and then hurried back into the house, slamming and locking the door behind her.

Disgusted with herself for even having a

moment of softness for this woman, Letty started back to the White Dove. Sophie Hollis had her place in this world. Letty Murphy had hers and wherever she went, her life would be the same.

She thought of the preacher as she retraced her steps. He would probably be as out of place in this town as the Widow Hollis. The only difference was that when the wedding was over, he would be gone. Sophie would still be here, married to the town banker, and Letty would still be smiling and flirting and pretending that each man who rode her was the best lay she'd ever had.

It wasn't much to look forward to. So when the whippoorwill called again, Letty didn't break stride as she yelled.

"Stupid bird! Whatever you're looking for sure as hell isn't here."

I Baptize Thee . . .

Gravestones littered the hillside above Isaac Jessup's farm. It was a poor testament to the Jessup name that Minna Jessup gave birth and then gave up more babies than Isaac could name. It was for that reason that their last, and only surviving child, had never been named.

Before, they'd lovingly named each baby that had come from their union. But nine years ago when their next to the last child had died, Isaac had put his foot down, refusing to put a name on another baby he was certain he'd have to give up to the Lord. When the next baby was born, he stayed true to his word.

So delighted was Minna that her child was surviving, that she was indifferent to her husband's decision. Even if she had deigned to disagree, in the times in which they were living, a husband's word was as strong as God's law. To their joy, their child not only continued to survive, he thrived. Soon Minna was too busy chasing him about to prompt Isaac into rescinding his vow. The years passed and as they did, Baby Boy Jessup began to outgrow his name. But it wasn't until a schoolteacher came to Crawler's Mill that Isaac's omission created a new set of problems for their little family.

It was the first day of school and Minna Jessup's joy knew no bounds. Her child was going to get the education that neither she nor Isaac had ever had. Her son would amount to something better than the dirt farmers they were, or she'd know the reason why. Even Isaac was perfectly willing to sacrifice his son's help on the farm so that he could get an education instead.

Everyone was happy with the situation except Baby Boy. At the tender age of seven and one half years, he stood a head taller than most of the children his age, and yet regardless of his size, it was his name he couldn't live down.

Poor Baby Boy. In the first week alone, he came home with a busted lip, a black eye, and had irreparably torn the only pair of good pants he owned. When Monday of the second week of school rolled around, Baby Boy bowed up like a pissed-off skunk and ran away from home. It was only after

Isaac found him on their farm and hiding in the cave above the spring, that matters finally came to a head.

Minna was in hysterics as she ran about the prairie, calling out Baby Boy's name. And every time she stopped to listen, hoping for an echo of his little voice answering her call, she got nothing for her trouble but the wind whistling down her back. Fear settled deep in her bones as she searched the vast prairie, refusing to glance upon the hillside where the small brown crosses stood, believing if she did it would jinx their luck of finding Baby Boy alive.

Just as she feared all would be lost, she heard shouting and turned toward the crosses on the hill. Isaac was running between them as he shot down the hill, waving his arms and shouting something that she still couldn't hear. But the longer she stood, the more convinced she became that Isaac had found Baby Boy. She gathered up her skirts and started toward him, praying with every step that she took.

Baby stood knee deep in the creek with grass roots stuck in his hair from hiding in the cave and cockleburs caught in the frayed edges of his britches. His little hands were fisted; his face was tear-streaked and filled with dismay at having been found.

His mother was on the creek bank crying, begging him to come out and into her arms. As badly as he wanted to hide underneath her apron, he'd taken a stand from which he couldn't back down. His father stood nearby with a switch in his hand that would have felled an ox. In spite of his mother's comforting presence, the size of that stick gave him great pause for thought.

He shuddered on a sob and swiped at the snot running down his nose with the back of his hand. They just didn't understand. Here he was nearly a man and didn't have a man's name. He was sick of school and sick of fighting. He'd decided last night that learning to read wasn't worth the trouble it was going to take.

"I ain't a goin' back to that there school and you can't make me," he cried, then covered his backside with both hands, certain that his ultimatum would warrant a whipping of severe extent.

Isaac was in a quandary. On one hand, Minna was weeping with joy over the fact that they'd found Baby Boy alive and well. On the other, Isaac considered a direct refusal to obey a father's orders should merit some sort of punishment. However, it was the condition of his son's face and Minna's joy that slowed his intent.

He waved the switch above his head. "See here, Baby, you just cain't go and —"

"That's just it, Pa. I ain't a baby no more. I'm plumb close to growed. I hunted winter meat with you last snow, and you said I could go on my own this year and see if I could fetch down the first deer. I plow, I cut wood, and I know how to do near everythin' you do."

The truth of his son's words hit Isaac hard. He slumped against a willow overhanging the creek bank while Minna stood beside him, making promises to Baby Boy that Isaac knew he could never deliver. Finally, he'd had enough. His voice echoed from one side of the creek to the other as he waded into the water after his boy.

"Son! You get out of that water and get on back to the house, and you do it now! I won't have no young'en of mine smart-mouthin', you hear me?"

Isaac waved the switch for effect, but both he and Minna knew he wouldn't use it. Not now.

Baby Boy quailed at the tone in his father's voice. His small shoulders slumped.

"I'll come," he muttered. "But I ain't goin' back to that school." With a defeated air, he began climbing up the creek bank and out of the water.

Minna Jessup was barely five feet tall to her husband's six-foot height, but when their child was in her arms, she lit into Isaac with all of her might.

"You've got to do somethin' and I mean now, Isaac Jessup! He's my only livin' child, and I cain't be havin' him runnin' off like this again out of fear. You're the one who wouldn't put a name to him when I gave him birth, so you're the one who's gonna have to find a way to make this right."

"Well, hell, Minna," Isaac grumbled. "I want him happy as much as you do. You ain't the only one who lost all them babies. I had to dig the holes for each and every one. It takes a lot out of a man when he has to dig graves for seven of his own."

Just thinking of all her precious babies set Minna to crying even harder.

Isaac groaned and then pulled his son out of Minna's arms. "Run on to the house now," he said gently. "And wash your face good, too."

"Yes sir," Baby Boy mumbled, and took off running across the prairie.

Minna fell into Isaac's arms with a sob. "I know you suffered, too, Isaac. And I ain't puttin' any blame on you. What happened was God's will. I've accepted that. But what about Baby Boy? What are we gonna do?"

Isaac held her close, marveling at how so tiny a woman could bring him so fast to his knees.

"I'll figure out somethin' Minna, honey. Don't you fret none, you hear? I'll make it right and that's a promise."

She sniffed twice and then wiped her face with the hem of her apron, much in the same way she'd survived her losses.

"Well now, that's that, I suppose. Let's get on back to the house. Most likely Baby will be starvin'. He missed his breakfast and his dinner, too."

Minna hurried on ahead, anxious to get to her single, precious chick, leaving Isaac alone to come at his own speed. And left alone, Isaac had to admit that his sin of omission had done much toward the suffering that Baby Boy was now enduring.

"Lordy be," he muttered, as he followed his family home across the prairie. "Who would'a thought there'd be so much fuss over a name?"

Long after supper was over, Isaac pondered the dilemma his family was in, but it was near morning when the answer came, right out of a dream, and as if God himself had spoken.

Isaac sat straight up in bed and reached for his gun, still not certain the voice that he'd heard had been in his head and not inside the cabin with him and his family.

Minna rolled over in bed and clutched the covers beneath her chin. "What's wrong, Isaac? Is there a varmit prowlin' outside?"

Isaac's heart was still pounding as reality sank in. He set the rifle beside his bed and then laid back down. Slipping an arm beneath Minna, he cuddled her close.

"No, Minna honey, there's no varmit. I reckon I was just dreamin'."

She snuggled her face against his chest, relishing the safety of his presence, and soon fell back to sleep. But Isaac couldn't have shut his eyes to save his soul. He was too busy planning the best way to confront the enemy and bring him to heel.

And so the week passed while Baby Boy followed his father about their farm and pretended his life wasn't hanging in the balance. Each day that a sun came and went without being forced back to school was, for him, a day of joy. But with each new sunrise came an unsettling fear that his mother would put the coveted education over his personal feelings and force him back into an impossible situation.

"Pa, where are you goin'?"

Isaac paused in the act of harnessing the mules to wipe sweat from his brow.

"Into town to get some things for your momma. Want to come?"

Baby Boy ducked his head. The offer of a wagon ride and the possibility of a sweet treat at the general store was hard to pass up. But if he went, it would be near to impossible to bypass the blacksmith's son. He was the one who'd started the teasing Baby had endured, although Baby Boy privately thought that Arnold Detter's son didn't have a name that was all that much to brag about, either. Going through life with the name of Pearl had to be hell for a fellow to live down. If Baby had been a little older, he might have understood Pearl Detter's need to ridicule someone besides himself, but he wasn't. Wisdom doesn't normally come to a man until some time after he's bedded his first woman and survived a fight for his life. Baby Boy had yet to do either. He was just hoping to get past his eighth birthday with all of his permanent teeth intact, and he feared if his momma made him go back to that school, it wasn't going to happen.

Isaac suspected the reason why Baby didn't want to go with him. But he also knew that to run from a fear was the single worst thing a man could do, no matter what his age. Once in the habit of ducking a problem, the habit seemed to stick throughout life. It made a weakling out of a good man every time.

"I'll let you drive," Isaac offered.

Baby Boy vaulted into the seat. He'd suffer a bloody nose any day for the opportunity to drive his pa's fine team of mules.

"I'm ready when you are, Pa," he said, his palms fairly itching to take the reins in hand.

Isaac hid a grin. "Just let me get yore momma's list and we'll be off."

Minna had overheard their conversation and met Isaac at the door with the list and a warning he knew meant business.

"You bring him back in one piece, Isaac Jessup, or so help me God, I'll take a stick to you, myself."

Isaac grinned, then lifted Minna off of her feet and danced her around the kitchen.

"You're awful pretty when you're mad."

Then he stole a kiss she didn't much bother to dodge.

"And you are a scoundrel, Isaac Jessup. Now get! I've got things to do."

"We'll be back before chore time," he promised.

She stuffed the list in his shirt pocket. "Tell Baby I'm making apple pies, but I don't want to milk that darned cow by myself. She kicks worse than a mule."

Isaac grinned. He heard more than complaint behind her words. She was telling him she loved him and needed him as best she knew how.

"You won't have to, honey," he said. "I'll be back in plenty of time to do chores."

"Pa! Let's go!"

Isaac grinned. "Sounds like our son's impatient to get his lights punched."

Minna frowned. "All I know is, Baby better not be the only one who comes back with a bloody nose."

"Dang, honey, Arnold Detter is twice my size."

"And Pearl is near twice Baby's size."

The smile slid off of Isaac's face. "I get the message."

Minna stood in the doorway and waved until she could no longer see so much as a dust trail. After that, she went inside, cried until she gave herself a headache, then walked up the hillside toward seven small tombstones and sat down among the wild flowers that blanketed her babies in a way she could not.

Crawler's Mill was no different from any other Territory town except that it had no mill to explain the significance of the name. Main Street was the only street. It was head high in dust when it was dry and knee high in mud when it rained.

The general store was the only establishment that welcomed women as customers. The other businesses, few though they were, catered solely to men, which was the way of the West at this time.

Dump's Saloon was a dump, but it was Dump Smith's pride and joy. Where else could a man with his meager abilities and education make a living such as this? In a land where shade and drink were at a premium, he boasted the only place this side of Lizard Flats where both were available, and only one for sale.

Each year he promised himself that he was going to retire and go back East where civilized amenities abounded. He had a hankering for houses with fine floors and indoor baths. Where everyone he met didn't smell like sweat, horses and manure, or a combination of all three. And this year, like all the rest, he found another reason to stay on. The reasons never amounted to much, but in spite of his grandiose plans, it didn't take much to satisfy Dump Smith.

Detter's Blacksmith and Livery did a good business as well. Arnold Detter could shoe a horse in the blink of an eye and was training his young son to follow in his footsteps. It gave the residents of Crawler's Mill and the surrounding area a sense of stability to know that there were two generations of blacksmiths at their disposal.

Arnold's son, Pearl, was still young, but for a boy of ten, quite strong and as brawny as some men. Unfortunately for Pearl, his opinion of himself was larger than he was. More than once, he'd gone to bed with a fat lip and skinned knuckles, compliments of the fights he'd had with bigger boys who'd laughed at his name.

When the new teacher started a school, Pearl had been delighted to learn there was one youth in the Territory who had a name worse than his own. Pearl Detter decided that making Baby Boy Jessup's life a living hell might alleviate some of his own.

The plan worked clear through the first

week of school. After that, Baby Boy Jessup didn't come back and Pearl was again on the defense, daily pounding the jeers from other boys' lips.

That was why when Pearl heard the squeak of a wagon wheel in need of grease and turned to look, he began grinning from ear to ear. It was the Jessup wagon that was coming toward their livery.

While Pearl was gloating at his good fortune, Baby Boy flinched in fear as his father turned toward the stables.

"Pa! What are we going to the livery for?"

Isaac heard the terror in his son's voice, but could find no words to explain that his son must face his nemesis. With every day that passed, Pearl Detter became bigger in Baby's mind than he actually was.

"Wheel squeaks."

Baby knew that. It had been squeaking all the way to town. Had he realized the significance of it, he might have bolted from the seat and run back home. It was too late now. Pearl Detter was coming out of the livery with a smile on his face the size of a watermelon slice.

"Mr. Jessup. Baby Boy. What can I do for you?" Pearl relished the silly sound of the boy's name on his tongue.

Isaac heard the taunt in Pearl Detter's voice and, for the first time, began to understand the hell his son had been enduring at his expense.

"My wheel's a squeakin', Ruby. I wondered if you had any wheel grease."

Baby gawked. Pa knew the Detter boy's name was Pearl. He fidgeted on the seat, certain now that when Pearl got the chance, he'd whomp him twice for his pa's insult.

Pearl frowned. "My name is Pearl, Mr. Jessup. Not Ruby."

Isaac pretended not to notice the indignation in the big boy's voice.

"Oh, sorry." He crawled down from the wagon to kneel near his wheel, pretending to inspect it as he gave Baby Boy the list Minna had put in his pocket. "Son, you run on over to the general store and start gatherin' up your momma's necessities while Pearly and I fix the wheel."

Pearl Detter turned red in the face and wished he were a man grown. He'd bust Isaac Jessup in the nose for sure.

"It's Pearl, not Pearly," he muttered.

Isaac shrugged. "Sorry. I ain't much good with names."

When he was certain Baby Boy was too far away to hear, he gave the smithy's son a steely glance. "I ain't too good with names," he repeated, " 'cause I don't think they matter all that much. My daddy always said it was what's inside a fellow that makes him a man. It don't matter how big he is, or how good he is with his fists, if he's a coward, it'll show. Somehow, someway."

Pearl flushed. He recognized the rebuke. He would have liked to be angry, but was too shamed before this big, gentle man to make the effort. Pearl Detter knew the misery of being made fun of and he'd spent every day Baby was in school making sure his life had been hell.

Pearl ducked his head. "I s'pect you'd be right about that, Mr. Jessup. I'll be gettin' that wheel grease if you don't mind waitin'."

He ran back into the livery just as his father was coming out.

"Jessup." Arnold offered his hand. "What can I do for you?"

Isaac shook the man's hand. "I'm fine, Arnold, just fine. Your son is takin' real good care of me and mine. He's a boy to be proud of, I reckon."

Arnold beamed. When Pearl came back with the bucket of grease, Arnold gave him a sharp thump on the shoulders and knelt to help remove the wheel.

"You're sure right about Pearl, Mr. Jessup. I am proud of him."

Pearl's belly flopped. He felt like he'd swallowed a worm and now it was squirming on him from the inside out. When they'd finished with the wheel, Pearl dusted off his hands.

"Pa, can I go and say hello to Mr. Jessup's boy? He sits behind me at school."

Arnold nodded. "I reckon, but you hurry on back. There's still work to be done."

When Pearl darted off toward the store, Isaac suffered a spurt of worry, then let it settle. Whatever happened now was up to the boys. He'd interfered all a man should in a case like this.

Baby Boy was leaning on the counter, watching the jar of peppermint sticks next to his left ear as if they might suddenly jump into his mouth. And because he was staring so hard at the jar, he missed seeing Pearl Detter come into the store.

"How you doin', Baby?" Pearl asked, and then took a couple of steps back just to prove he meant no harm.

Baby Boy pivoted, and looked toward the door. Pearl was too close, and it was too far away to make a run for it.

"Your pa is talkin' to my pa," Pearl offered, and then stared at the candy jar for something to do.

Baby Boy thought about running anyway, then doubled his fists and stood his ground. Whatever happened, it couldn't be too bad with the storekeeper nearby.

Pearl dug in his pocket. "I came to get myself a sweetie."

Baby glared and pretended he didn't care that Pearl Detter had two whole pennies to call his own.

The storekeeper was in the back room weighing Minna Jessup's flour into a sack. "Mr. Calley, I'll be gettin' myself two of these here candies," Pearl shouted.

While Baby looked on, Pearl plunked down a penny and dug two of the biggest sticks of candy out of the jar. To Baby's surprise, Pearl shoved the biggest stick in his face.

"Want one?" Pearl asked.

Baby didn't know whether to say thank you, or wait for Pearl to ram it up his nose.

Pearl persisted. "So, do you want it or not?"

Baby wasn't giving in this easy. Not after what Pearl had put him through.

"Why are you bein' so nice?"

Pearl shrugged and stuck his candy in his mouth for lack of anything else to say.

Reluctantly, Baby took the peace offering.

Isaac Jessup walked into the store just as Baby stuck the candy into his mouth.

"Hey now, Baby. I didn't say you could have one of those."

"It's my treat, sir," Pearl said, and ducked his head. "I reckon I owed him."

Isaac's expression softened. "So you reckon you owed him a candy?"

Pearl nodded. "Yes sir."

Baby Boy couldn't quit staring. Something was going on, but for the life of him, he couldn't bring himself to care enough to figure it out. All he knew was his worst enemy had just bought him a peppermint stick and his pa was grinning like a possum in a persimmon patch.

"See you at school," Pearl shouted, and ran out the door.

Isaac sighed. At least when he went home Minna wouldn't take that stick to him that she'd promised.

"That'll be a dollar and twenty-three cents," John Calley said, as he plopped the last of the items from Minna Jessup's list onto the counter.

Isaac dug into his pocket and pulled out the hard-to-come-by coins.

"Pa, look!" Baby was pointing toward a colorful poster on the wall behind the counter. "What's a mine-is-ter of the fath?"

Mr. Calley grinned. "Minister of the faith, son. It says, minister of the faith. That means there's a bonafide preacher from back East coming to Lizard Flats. I hear tell they're planning a wedding and a revival and who knows what else."

Isaac's thoughts took a sudden turn. "Hey John, when does it say that preacher is comin'?"

The storekeeper squinted at the date then counted on his fingers, estimating to-day's date against the printed date of the preacher's arrival.

"In a week and two days. Yes sir, an honest-to-goodness preacher from back East is coming to Lizard Flats."

Isaac grabbed at the two largest packages. "Baby, you get the rest and hurry on out to the wagon. We'd best be gettin' on home."

"Yes sir, Pa." Baby Boy poked the candy to the side of his mouth like a fat cigar and did as he was told.

By the time Isaac and Baby Boy were home, his idea had taken firm root. When Minna came running out to meet them, Isaac jumped down from the wagon and caught her in his arms.

"Why Isaac Jessup, what on earth?"

And when he kissed her behind both ears before claiming the spot dead-center on her lips, she gasped.

Baby Boy grinned. He'd seen his momma and his pa kissing before, but he'd never seen them do it in broad daylight. He giggled behind his hand and tied the reins of the team to the hitching post near the porch.

Minna was still blushing when Isaac set her on her feet. "I swear, what will Baby say?"

Isaac tweaked her nose just to see her blush. "It doesn't matter, 'cause we're goin' on a trip."

Minna couldn't have been more shocked if Isaac had asked her to strip naked and run to the creek with a bucket in each hand just to see if she could do it. "A trip? Where 'bouts are we goin'?"

"We're goin' to Lizard Flats."

Minna was trying not to get excited by the prospect of seeing new territory after eighteen years of seeing nothing more than their farm and Crawler's Mill. "But why? What's in Lizard Flats?"

"A preacher from back East is comin' to Lizard Flats, and we're gonna be there when he arrives."

"Whatever for?" Minna asked.

"We're gonna have our son christened! I

ain't never gonna give another child of mine a name without the blessin' of a man of God to keep him safe."

Minna burst into tears. Isaac smiled. He knew the difference between happy tears and sad tears, and these tears were full of joy.

Baby Boy couldn't believe what he was hearing.

"You're gonna give me a real name, Pa? I ain't gonna be called Baby Boy no more?"

"That's right, son."

"What is it?" Baby asked, his voice full of excitement. "What are you gonna name me?"

The look Isaac gave his son was one he would have given an equal.

"I reckon you're about big enough to pick one for yourself, don't you?"

Minna cried even harder.

Baby Boy couldn't believe his ears. "Are you sayin' that I can pick out my own name?"

"I reckon so."

Baby started running.

"Hey, boy, where are you goin'? We ain't unloaded the groceries."

"I'm a goin' to pack my things, Pa. I want to be ready when that preacher comes."

CHARITY BEGINS AT HOME

During the day, Letty was like a bear with a sore tooth. She griped and complained about everything to Will and Eulis, and at night, gave the men hell who came to her for a dance. She teased them and taunted them and laughed when the fights over her favors broke out.

Will knew that a reprimand was in order, but the truth was he feared she would bolt. Ever since that gambler had been killed, she'd been impossible. He'd tried to tell her she couldn't keep causing all that trouble or she'd put him out of business. She laughed in his face and then ordered Eulis to bring her a bath. Even Eulis was keeping his distance from the heartbroken woman who seemed hell bent on making everyone as miserable as she was.

He didn't know that she'd lost the last bit of hope that she'd kept close within her. She no longer spent evenings out on her balcony listening for the small whippoor-will. All he knew was that she refused to

286

sing. Pete pounded the keys of the piano as he'd always done, but without the accompaniment of Letty's voice. Even the customers sensed all was not right at the White Dove, but the whiskey still flowed and the music still played, and if their luck was with them, they could still get a dance with the soiled dove still flying at the White Dove Saloon.

And, although Letty Murphy and Charity Doone had never heard of each other, they were grieving for a similar loss.

Ever since Charity Doone's night with Randall Ward Howe, she'd been in a bad way. More than three days had passed since she had fainted in Wade James' arms and she had yet to speak a word about what had happened to her. Her eyes were all but swollen shut from crying. She wouldn't come out of her room, and she was refusing to eat.

Mehitable was beside herself with worry. She had coaxed and begged, promising Charity everything from a trip back East to a ship's ticket to Europe. Once the very mention of such delights would have sent Charity running to pack. But not now. Now it was too late. In Charity's eyes, her future was ruined before it was over. Since she was no longer pure, being a nun was out of the question. And no decent man would have her now that she was no longer a virgin.

Mehitable wasn't the only one in a state of panic. The delay in going after Randall Howe was making Wade James nervous. With each passing hour, he feared the preacher was getting farther and farther away from justice. But Wade had seen the state Charity was in. She would never have been able to travel, and leaving her alone seemed impossible, as well. He wanted to just pack up and go after the man alone, wreaking his own kind of vengeance. But the fear that when he came back, Charity Doone would have done herself in, kept him here. Like Mehitable, he loved Charity enough to wait.

Charity had been trying all day to die.

It wasn't as easy as she had believed. On the surface, it seemed simple. A simple cessation of breath and a few seconds later, blessed peace. But no matter how much she tried, she couldn't hold her breath long enough to even pass out. So she'd tried bargaining with God instead.

She stretched out on the bed, crossed her arms across her bosom like a laid out corpse, then closed her eyes. Maybe if she prayed the right prayer, God would just take her. In fact it would be better if it happened that way. She'd accomplished nothing by holding her breath except giving herself a terrible headache. So she laid on her bed, trying to relax and waiting for God to do the deed for her. All she did was fall asleep.

She woke up later, still in her room, still on the ranch, and still a deflowered virgin ashamed to show her face. It would seem that even God had let her down. The disappointment was too much to bear.

Suddenly, all her anger at Randall Howe spilled forth. She leaped from her bed and began running in circles, sobbing and tearing at her hair. Across the room, a cheval mirror reflected her insanity. She stopped in mid-step, staring at the image without recognition. When it finally dawned on her that she was seeing herself, she snapped.

Grabbing the nearest object, which happened to be a Dresden figurine of a shepherd and a lamb, she flung it at the mirror, shattering it and herself into pieces. Satisfaction was swift, but brief. She needed more! Much more! Wild of eye and hair, she let out a shriek and ran out of the room, her nightgown billowing about her feet.

Mehitable heard the first scream as she was standing on the front porch. Guilt hit her like a fist to the gut. She knew her sister's mental state was unstable. She shouldn't have left her alone. The sound of breaking glass and another shrill scream sent her reaching for her gun.

Was Charity in danger? Had she already done herself harm?

Palming her pistol, she dashed into the house, only to find Charity in the drawing room with a vase in her hands, standing in a puddle of water and roses. From the look in Charity's eyes, the only thing in danger was their mother's crystal vase.

Mehitable groaned. Quickly holstering her gun, she reached for her sister. Charity lifted the vase in a threatening gesture and took a quick step back, careful to stay out of Hetty's reach.

Mehitable's eyes narrowed until they appeared to be closed. Any other time, Charity would have been petrified to know she had angered Hetty this much. But not today. Because Charity had not been able to destroy herself, it would seem she was trying for their belongings instead.

Mehitable took a deep breath, calming

her voice and relaxing her posture as she might have done with an unbroken horse.

"Sister. Hand me the vase."

Charity laughed.

The sound sent chills down Mehitable's spine. She lunged for the vase, but it was too late. Mehitable ducked as the vase hit the wall then exploded in a shower of crystal shards.

At that point, Charity started to curse without pausing to breathe and in more detail than Mehitable would have believed. She cursed herself and cursed God, then cursed the ground all men walked on. Then she broke into sobs — harsh, choking sobs that leeched all the anger from Mehitable's bones and left her frightened and shaking. She reached for Charity again, desperate to restrain her in some manner before she did herself harm.

"Sister, Sister," Mehitable crooned. "It's all right. It's all right."

But Charity kept on screaming, fighting every boundary before her, including her own sister's arms.

Mehitable tried reasoning; she tried sympathy, then tried shouting back. Finally, at her own emotional limit, she drew back her hand and landed a sharp, healthy slap on the side of Charity's face.

The silence that came after was startling. Suddenly there was nothing between them but shock and a widening, red flush on the side of Charity's cheek. They stared, sister to sister, and then started to cry. Quietly. Openly.

This time when Mehitable opened her arms, Charity fell into her embrace without hesitation.

"It will be all right," Mehitable said.

"It will never be all right," Charity sobbed.

Mehitable took Charity by the shoulders and shook her gently until she was forced to look up. "By God, I said it will!"

"But how?" Charity asked.

"Because we're goin' after the bastard, and we're gonna make him pay."

Charity's eyes widened. "We can't."

"The hell we can't," Hetty argued. "We Doones take care of our own."

"But Hetty, think of the dangers of two women traveling alone. Besides that, we don't know where he's gone."

"Oh, I'll find him," Mehitable promised. "And we ain't goin' alone. Wade James is comin' along."

"Wade James?" Charity's face paled. "Our Wade James? That hard-eyed young cowboy you hired last year?"

Mehitable nodded.

"But why him?"

"Because he wants to, and because you dragged him into this mess when you passed out in his arms."

Charity groaned. "I didn't!"

"You did. He heard everything, including the part about you wanting to die. The past few days it's been all I could do to keep him here. He was set to go after the preacher right then."

Intrigued by having a champion, Charity bit her lip and looked away. "I must have looked a fright when I fainted." And then she slumped. "But what could it matter? He must think I'm nothing more than a whore."

Mehitable sighed with relief. This was a good sign. If Charity was worried about her appearance, she was beginning to heal. And while there was a lot she could have said as to what Wade James thought about Charity, she decided to leave the telling of it up to him.

"I don't know what he thought. All I know is he was ready to kill. We leave first thing tomorrow," she said shortly. "Pack to ride, girl. We'll be movin' fast."

They'd gone first by train, following the same route that Randall Howe had taken.

By a stroke of bad luck, they missed the stop where he'd disembarked and lost two extra days retracing their steps before picking up his trail again. It wasn't until they found a stagecoach driver who remembered a preacher getting on board that their luck took a turn. After that, it had been a matter of following the stage lines south.

Wade James and the Doone sisters camped in a hollow near a deep, narrow creek, seeking shelter from the ceaseless blast of wind through which they'd been riding. It had been blowing for days. Their eyes were red and irritated, their skin chapped from the air-driven dust, and they were edgy, both with the situation and with each other. Although the wind wasn't as strong down where they'd camped, it seemed to be shifting and stirring, like batter in a bowl.

Wade had tethered the horses in trees, giving them some shelter as well, and now the animals stood with their heads down and their tails to the wind — like their masters, enduring.

The land looked the same as the last three nights' camp, but Wade James wasn't a man to take things for granted. As soon as he'd seen to his chores, he began scouting the area on foot, making sure there would be no surprises after sundown.

Mehitable was across the creek near their small campfire, skinning a squirrel Wade had shot for their supper. Although she was standing upwind and kept her back to the fire, the occasional streak of smoke still drifted into her eyes. She looked up as Charity came into the clearing, carrying an armload of wood.

She frowned, which made her natural squint even more pronounced. Charity was walking like a woman on her way to be hanged. Mehitable looked at the spindly bits of wood her sister had gathered and shook her head. Bill Doone should not have sent his youngest daughter to finishing school. He should have taught her to rope instead.

Charity dropped the wood near the fire.

"That ain't gonna be enough wood," Mehitable muttered.

Charity looked stricken. Silently, she turned and went back for more.

Mehitable sighed. She shouldn't have been so short with Charity. Charity had been sheltered in a way Mehitable had not ever since the day she'd been born. And then Hetty amended her own thoughts. If

Charity was old enough to get herself into trouble with a man, she was old enough to help set up camp.

A few minutes later, she gave the last bit of skin on the squirrel a quick yank. It came away from the meat like the peeling off a hot, new potato. Mehitable shrugged. The squirrel was small. But it would make a good stew. She reached for her knife and began hacking it up, dropping the chunks, one by one, into the pot of boiling water.

Wade glanced toward their camp. It was a good thing they weren't in Indian country. Thanks to this everlasting wind, the smoke from their fire would be noticeable for miles. He could even smell it from here. Then he frowned. That didn't make sense. He was standing upwind.

Before he had time to consider the thought, something snapped behind him. He spun toward the trees. Instinctively, his hand went to his holster. Just the feel of the pistol against his palm was reassuring, but when he looked back at the camp, Charity was nowhere in sight.

Before he could worry about the fact, a deer suddenly burst out of a thicket, coming toward him at a full run. The animal's eyes were dark and wild, its body flecked with sweat. Before Wade could move, it leaped the creek and disappeared into the trees near where their horses were tied.

Wade stared in disbelief. A few moments later a pair of raccoons came scurrying out of the underbrush and waded into the creek as if he wasn't even there.

"What the hell?"

Then he took a defensive step back as the woods were suddenly alive with animals.

All running. And in the same direction.

The hair crawled on the back of his neck. Before he lifted his head, he knew. It wasn't their campfire he'd been smelling after all.

"No, oh no," he groaned, and started running, yelling Mehitable's name.

She looked up as Wade came running through the creek.

"Where's Charity?" he screamed.

"I sent her back to get more wood."

"Christ!" he muttered. "Which way did she go?"

"There," Mehitable pointed. "What's wrong?"

Wade pointed toward the other side of the creek. It was crawling with animals of every kind and size. And now the air was darkening with flocks of birds, all in a desperate race to outrun the wind and the fire on its back.

"Prairie fire. Saddle the horses."

Mehitable's stomach clenched with fear. She'd seen only one before, and that time six families in a wagon train had burned to death before her eyes. She shuddered with fear. In this wind, only God could save them from a similar death.

Wade started toward the trees at a lope.

"Where are you going?" Mehitable screamed.

He paused long enough to look back. "After Charity. And if the fire gets too close, don't wait."

Mehitable drew her gun. It was a stupid thing to do, but what he said scared her so bad that she did it out of instinct.

"You better make it back or so help me God I'll kill you myself," she snarled.

Wade grinned and then started to run.

Charity was lost. She knew it as well as she knew her own name. What was worse, she knew she was still within shouting distance from the camp because she could smell the fire. All she would have to do was yell and Hetty or Wade would come running. But the shame of failing again, and at the simplest of tasks, kept her silent. Instead, she began to mark her own trail, aiming sticks in the direction she was walking and stacking rocks by the sides of trees. Every now and then she would break a limb, leaving it dangling down at an angle. Not because it told her where she was at, but just to make sure she wasn't walking in circles.

Time passed and frustration set in. This didn't make sense. Camp couldn't be far. The smoke was so thick she could taste it. She cursed beneath her breath. It was all the fault of these infernal winds. They mixed everything up. Then she frowned. That made no sense. As hard as the wind was blowing, it should be impossible to smell smoke, or anything else, unless she was standing in it.

She looked into the trees, then up at the sky. The hair rose on the backs of her arms.

"No. Oh no."

There was too much smoke. Unless Hetty was cooking a moose, there was no way their campfire would cause all of this. Terror struck. She started to scream.

Wade was shouting her name as he ran. When he came upon the first marker she'd left, his heart skipped a beat. My God, she'd gotten herself lost and was trying to find her way back. The smoke was thick now, burning his nose and bringing tears to his eyes. Without hesitation, he followed her trail.

"Char-i-tee! Char-i-tee! Where are you?"

Less than ten yards ahead of him, a cougar leaped out of nowhere, as startled to see Wade as he was to see it. It froze and crouched flat, its yellow eyes glittering, its mouth twisted into a snarl.

"Get!" Wade yelled, and went for his gun.

The cat hissed. But at the moment, fire was a greater foe than man. It leaped off the path and disappeared. Wade holstered his gun and kept on running into the smoke, still shouting Charity's name.

When Charity first heard his call, she turned toward the sound like a baby turns to its mother's breast. A sense of peace filled her heart. She should have known. It was Wade.

"Here!" she screamed. "I'm here!"

Seconds later, he emerged through the smoke at a lope and caught her in mid-leap, and for a split second, allowed himself the luxury of holding Charity Doone in his arms. He'd found her. They were together. He took a deep breath and then reality surfaced as the acrid smoke slid down his lungs. Unless a miracle occurred, they would die together, too. He grabbed her by the shoulders, fixing her with a swift, hard look.

"Are you hurt?"

"No."

"Then follow me, girl, and whatever you do, don't let go of my hand."

They started to run back in the direction Wade had come, blindly following instinct rather than trails, as the smoke was too thick now to see. Small limbs from low-hanging branches slapped them in the face. Stinging. Cutting. Laying open the flesh. And still they ran.

Just when Charity feared all was lost, Mehitable came running through the trees, leading their horses.

"Mount up," she screamed.

Wade all but threw Charity into the saddle, then mounted his horse on the run.

"Ride!" he yelled. "Everyone ride . . . and don't look back!"

A few minutes later they came out of the hollow, racing up the slope of the land and out onto the rolling prairie. It was then that they took time to rein up and look behind them. All they could do was stare in growing horror at the pillar of black smoke rising into the sky, and then below, to the layer of fire beneath.

"Are we safe?" Charity asked.

Wade couldn't help himself. He reached out and cupped the side of her face where the scratches still bled. Her blood was warm beneath his fingers.

"Not yet, girl," he said softly. "But we will be."

Mehitable looked back at where they'd been.

"I reckon that squirrel's gonna be a mite too done to eat," she muttered.

They looked at each other and then, because they were still alive to do the deed, laughed until tears made clean tracks down their cheeks. Filled with the joy of being able to breathe, Wade yanked his hat from his head and waved it high in the air.

"Yeehaa!" he shouted.

Charity's heart swelled at the sight of him there; undefeated, indomitable, and fell the rest of the way in love. But there was no time to dwell on the fact that Wade James was not a man who would take another man's leavings.

"Let's ride!" he yelled.

Neither the horses nor the Doone sisters needed a second urging. The horses leaped forward, taking them all out of danger.

The elation that came with outrunning the fire soon dissipated. The next few days became a series of frustrating failures. At each way station they came to, their inquiries netted the same results. Yes, a preacher had been on board, but he'd taken the next stage south. By their best guess, they were about five days behind him, but closing in. Trail weary but determined, they kept on moving.

And then everything came to a halt.

The stage line ended in a place called Thomasville and when Randall Howe was nowhere to be found, they had to face the fact that his trail had come to an end.

Wade James was fit to be tied, cursing himself up one side and down the other for not following his inclinations and striking out on his own. If he had, the bastard would already be rotting in the ground.

Mehitable was disappointed beyond words. She kept staring at the distant horizon with her customary squint, as if trying to conjure up an image of where the man could have gone.

Charity was strangely quiet. Her days on the road had been healing for her in more ways than one. Channeling her anger into a purpose had been healthy. But anger wasn't the only emotion that she'd begun to channel. After the way the preacher had tossed her aside, she'd planned to hate all men. But the days and nights she had spent in the company of Wade James had changed that forever.

His quiet ways and cold handsome face intrigued her. His kindness charmed her. And ever since the prairie fire, there were times when she caught him watching her. It was those moments, more than anything else, that made her wish she could turn back time. If only she'd noticed him before. Before she'd committed her unpardonable sin.

So here they were, stuck in Thomasville with no idea of where to go next. Without benefit of a hotel, they made camp at the creek outside of town. The night was hot, made hotter by their campfire and the rabbits Wade had shot earlier sizzling over a makeshift spit. The air was still. Nearby, horses stomped nervously, as if they sensed the trio's dilemma.

"I think we should just give it up," Charity said. "We've been gone too long. There's the ranch to run and things to do." She couldn't look either Wade or Mehitable in the face as she continued.

"After all, it's not as if he killed me. I'm still breathing."

Wade stood up with a jerk. "Well I'm not breathin' so easy. And I won't be until I get him in my sights."

Mehitable sighed. She was torn between wanting to avenge her sister and worrying about her beloved ranch. Granted she had good hired help, but things still happened.

She looked at Charity then, seeing the changes that the days on the trail had brought. Gone was the fussy young girl with the flyaway dreams. In her place was a hard-eyed young woman who rarely smiled. She remembered Charity's smiles. Virginity wasn't the only thing Randall Howe had stolen from Charity. He'd taken her joy, as well. It was that alone that made Mehitable say what she did.

"Let's give it one more day," she said. "There's a freight wagon due in tomorrow. We'll talk to the driver. If he ain't seen the man, then I vote with Charity to go back."

Wade stared into the fire until his eyes began to burn. His hands fisted as he looked up, straight into Charity's face. His voice was quiet — too quiet.

"I'll see you ladies back to the ranch and then I'll be movin' on."

Charity's face crumpled. It was just as

she had feared. Whatever Wade had done for them, he'd done out of a sense of duty, not because he cared for her in any special way. She jumped up from the fire and disappeared into the darkness.

"What the hell?" he muttered, and turned to Mehitable for understanding.

She shook her head. This was why she'd never bothered with marrying. It was the getting to it that was so damned much trouble.

"Ain't you goin' after her?" Wade asked.

Mehitable snorted. "It ain't me that she's runnin' from. It's you. I reckon she thinks you're quittin' because you're disgusted by her."

He turned pale in the firelight. It was then that Mehitable knew his true feelings.

Wade's guts were in knots. That he'd hurt her, however innocently, was more than he could bear

"Miss Hetty, you know that ain't so. Go get her. You have to tell her she's wrong."

But Mehitable didn't budge. "Nope. *You're* the one who needs to do the talkin'. She already knows how I feel about her. It's you she's mixed up about."

Wade didn't know what to say. His feelings for Charity were mixed up with an urge to kill the man who'd wronged her.

And then there was the fact that she was the boss's sister. He gave Hetty a cautious look.

She frowned. "Don't look at me. I ain't the one in a swoon."

He swallowed nervously. "Uh . . . yes, ma'am. Then I reckon I'd better go bring her back. It ain't safe for her out there in the dark."

Mehitable stifled a grin. "I reckon you'd better at that."

Moments later, he was gone. Hetty tossed another stick onto the fire, hoping that the smoke would be enough to keep off the mosquitoes and then leaned back in her bedroll and closed her eyes. No sense waiting for the pair to come back. The way that cowboy stuttered and stammered, it might take him all night to get said what was in his heart.

The water spilling down the creek made soft rippling noises against the half-submerged rocks. Overhead, a three-quarter moon painted the ground with a luminous glow. An owl hooted from a nearby tree and out on the prairie, a coyote yipped, followed by an answering chorus from the rest of the pack. Charity Doone stood at the banks of the creek, too hurt to cry.

During the trauma of the last few days, she had learned something about herself. She wasn't shallow. Things did matter to her. And while she hated herself for being so blind and weak, and Randall Howe for taking advantage of her naiveté, something good had come out of this that she would never have believed.

She'd found out what she was made of. She'd endured the rigors of the daily hard rides, and survived a prairie fire. But the best of it was, she had learned exactly how much Hetty loved her.

For years she'd believed herself to be nothing more than a burden in her sister's life. But now she knew that was false. In a way, Randall Howe had almost done her a favor. She and Hetty might have gone through life, skirting the issues of being sisters without knowing each other's true heart.

And then there was Wade James, her reluctant champion. A strong man. A good man. A man who'd rescued her twice in her hours of need. Over the past few days she'd even let herself pretend that if things had been different — if she hadn't shamed herself before God and man — then he might have cared for her.

She looked down at the water. Moonlight reflected there, like liquid threads of pure silver, but she didn't see the beauty, only the shadows of the night in between.

She pressed the flat of her hands to her belly and moaned. It was the truth of it all that hurt the worst. He felt duty-bound to get them home, and then he was leaving. She didn't know why — she should have been expecting it — but the news had shocked her. Once having learned the truth about her fall from grace, no self-respecting man would want to be around her.

A twig snapped in the trees behind her. She spun around, expecting to see Hetty. The man who came out of the shadows made her heart skip a beat. And because she was so hurt, she lashed out at him.

"What are you doing here?"

Wade flinched. The anger in her voice was unexpected. "You hadn't oughta be out here in the dark alone."

"There's nothing left in this world that can hurt me more than I've already hurt myself."

"Don't say that," Wade begged, and stopped her when she would have run past him. "Wait. You don't understand."

She laughed then, but it was not a happy sound. "Oh, I think I understand everything just fine. I have disgraced myself and my family."

Wade's hands slid up the length of her arms of their own accord. He could feel the softness of her flesh beneath her blouse. And then he thought of that preacher, putting his hands on Charity in much the same way and he froze. What if he was frightening her? What if his touch disgusted her? He turned her loose abruptly.

"I'm sorry, Charity, girl. I shouldn't have touched you like that."

To Charity, it was a slap in the face. She'd been right all along. He loathed what she stood for. That's why he had let her go. That's why he was leaving the ranch. She looked up at him then. At the way the moonlight lit the contours of his face, making him seem older, harder, even angry. Her voice was trembling.

"I disgust you."

The despair in her voice broke his heart. "No, Charity, no!"

"Don't pretend with me Wade James. I can't bear it. I've had my fill of men who say one thing and mean another." Then she bit her lip to keep from crying. "Besides, I understand your feelings. Yes, I was wronged by Randall Howe, but it was partly my fault."

"No, Charity, you misunderstood my —"

"Please, Wade, let me finish."

He bowed his head. Even though the pain in her voice was like knives in his heart, he did as she asked.

She sighed then, as if the weight of the world was square on her shoulders. Her gaze bore into him, wanting him to believe and needing him to understand. Not so he might love her. Just so he wouldn't hate her.

"It was my dream, you see. I'd had the same dream seventeen times. I thought it was God telling me what to do with my life. I told Reverend Howe about it. He was going to help me become a nun."

Wade's head jerked up like a gutshot steer. A nun? This was the first he'd heard of such folly. His eyes narrowed angrily as he looked at her there in the moonlight. A nun. Not only no, but, hell no. A woman like Charity Doone was meant for a man's empty bed and warm embrace. And he had both. If she would only care.

Charity continued, unaware of what was running through Wade's mind.

"I told him everything." Her mouth tilted in a bitter smile. "I let myself believe something false. I deserved what he did."

Wade's face was hot. His daddy used to say that Wade let his anger show more than any boy he'd ever known. Thankful for the gentleness of moonlight and the darkness of night, he cleared his throat. She'd had her say. Now it was his turn.

"No ma'am, you did not deserve to be mistreated. He was a man of the cloth, a man you were raised to trust. It was him that stepped over the line." Then he touched her hand, then her arm. "Charity, girl, it doesn't matter what he did to you. You're what matters."

Charity was stunned. She mattered? But did she matter to him?

"Those are kind words," she whispered. "But find me a man who can ignore what I've done and I'll show you a saint."

Wade laid his hand at the side of her face. "I reckon you're lookin' at one now, but I ain't no damn saint. I'm just a man who's in love with a fine, gentle woman."

A Drunk by Any Other Name

For a drunk whose normal speed was crawl, Eulis Potter came awake all too suddenly and wondered why. Immobile, he contemplated the bright light of day through the slits in his eyelids and the fact that there was nothing between his head and the hard packed earth but his hat.

He'd passed out in the alley, which meant he hadn't made it to his room, after all. He knew where he was because he recognized the roof line of Goslin's General Store. But something was different. Something he couldn't quite name. He wrinkled his nose. An odor of sweetness wafted up his nostrils, which was puzzling because good smells and Eulis did not coincide.

Molasses, he thought. That's what he smelled. When he was a tyke, no more than four or five, his mother had made him molasses cookies. He closed his eyes against the glare of the sun and thought of the face of Kiowa Bill on the wanted poster in his room at the White Dove Saloon.

Funny how smells could bring back memories.

His arms felt like fence posts. His legs felt like lead. That last batch of rotgut Will the Bartender had bought wasn't fit to sell. And yet Eulis had drunk his fair share, and from the way he was feeling, everyone else's. He licked his lips and then frowned. Damned if he wasn't tasting that molasses as well. This was quite a memory.

Someone giggled at the end of the alley. He didn't bother to look. Someone was always laughing at him, or calling him names. But he'd long since quit caring what other people thought. He couldn't be bothered with their business when he was so involved in his own.

Something crawled on his leg. He needed to move. Once he'd passed out and woke up with a snake up his pants. But that had been in the fall of the year and the snake had been looking for a place to get warm. God knows it was hot enough for snakes in Lizard Flats without them having to crawl up a poor man's pants.

Someone giggled again. Then again.

"G'way," he mumbled. "Leave me be."

The giggles increased. And so did the crawling sensation. In fact, now that he thought about, the crawling wasn't just up his leg. It was all over. On his ankles. On his arms. On his face. In his beard. He opened one eye just enough to peek out. Hell's fire. Even crawling up his nose.

He lifted his hands, frowning at the tiny brown rash all over. And then his eyes opened wide. Oh God. That rotgut had been bad — real bad. He was worse off than he thought. He was hallucinating, and even worse, the brown rash was starting to move.

The giggles exploded into wild bursts of laughter.

The scent of molasses was strong in his nose. The taste sweet on his lips. He licked them again, amazed at how strong his memory had become. Then he turned his head and spit. Something was wrong. Molasses didn't have seeds.

The crawling sensation was making him crazy. He sat up with a groan and slapped at his pants near his knee. The crawling was worse now. Swaying where he sat, he bent his knee and pulled up his pants, just to make sure it was absent of snakes. To his dismay, the dancing brown rash was down there as well.

"Oh Lordy," he muttered. "I been poisoned, that's what. I been poisoned and I'm a' goin' to die."

A tiny pain shot behind his ear, then in the bush of beard below his chin. He crawled to his feet and started toward the street. Maybe Matt Goslin had something in his store that would help cure his rash.

He stumbled. Something crashed against the wall. He looked down, frowning at a jug lying in the dirt. It was too small for whiskey and too large for liniment. He picked it up, lifting it to his nose, just in case he'd been wrong about the whiskey part.

To his surprise the molasses smell was even stronger. He poked his finger into the narrow neck. It came away covered in thick, brown syrup . . . and ants. He could see them now. Crawling out of the lip of the jug and down the sides like little soldiers on the march.

It took a few moments, and another pain down his neck, for reality to sink in. He looked at the trio of tow-headed boys peeking around the corner of the building and knew it wasn't a rash he was suffering. Coupled with their hysterical giggles and the contents of the molasses jug that they'd poured onto his person, he'd knew he'd been had.

"You little devils," he shrieked. They'd used him for bait. He came out of the alley, shedding clothes as he ran.

His coat fell at the feet of the black-smith's wife as he staggered across her path. She screamed and danced sideways as the coat hit her shoes.

Still on the move, his hat and shirt were the next to go as they landed in the middle of the street. A rancher's daughter took one look at Eulis's white hairy belly, still crawling with ants and started to laugh.

By the time he got to the watering trough in front of the livery, he was clawing at his hair and his beard. Desperate to stop the stings, he went in face first, landing with a belly flop and sending a spray of water high into the air. Moments later, he came up gasping and looked down. Hundreds of ant carcasses were floating on the water. He sat down in the trough, groaning in pain and disbelief as Pete Samuels, the owner of the livery, came out on the run.

"Eulis, dang your hide. That ain't no place to take a bath."

"Ain't bathin'," Eulis muttered, while combing his fingers through the sticky gunk in his hair and face.

"Then what the hell are you doin'?" he shouted.

Eulis pointed. "Ants."

Pete gawked. Sure enough, the surface of the water was littered with them. It didn't take long for the three laughing boys and the stench of a sweetened down Eulis to make things clear. He shook his head. Those little dickens had sure caused a stir, pouring molasses on a passed-out drunk.

"Well, get the damned things off and then fill up my trough with clean water, you hear?"

Eulis nodded. "Be glad to," he offered. "Just as soon as I pick the rest of these ants out of my beard. Durn things sting hard, don't you know?"

Pete went back into his livery, muttering to himself.

Eulis continued to pick off the ants, splashing himself now and then with the murky green water, heartily glad he hadn't been forced to shed his pants. His last pair of long johns had fallen apart last winter. He'd been doing without ever since.

Alfonso Worthy was on his way to Sophie's house for supper. But it wasn't the thought of her food that was hurrying his steps, it was the telegram he had in his pocket. The preacher was coming with the next wagon of freight. He could hardly wait. Not until he heard Sophie Hollis say the words, I do, was he going to rest easy.

And because he was so engrossed in his own bit of news, he missed seeing the clothes lying in the street. But he did see a small crowd gathering around the livery. He pulled out his pocket watch and checked the time. He was a little bit early and his curiosity won out. He stepped off the sidewalk and into the street just as a trio of young boys came barreling past him.

"Hooligans," he muttered, settling his hat a bit firmer on his head.

The frown was still on his face as he pushed his way through the crowd. It did his blood pressure no good when he got to the front and saw Eulis sitting in the watering trough. His ire rose. With a proper gentleman preacher coming from back East, he'd done everything within his power to increase the social amenities in Lizard Flats. He'd even hired a man to whitewash the bank, only now it stuck out like a sore thumb in a town where every other building was a plain, weathered gray, but Alfonso didn't care. It was a sign of prosperity. For a banker, a necessity indeed.

But now this? How would this town fare in the preacher's eyes if the town drunk was allowed to take public baths?

"What's the meaning of this?" he shouted.

Eulis looked up. His head was throbbing and his vision had doubled. To make matters worse, the little roosters suddenly dancing in front of him looked a lot like Worthy, the banker.

"Have you all gone insane?" Alfonso continued, staring about in great confusion. "Why is this man being allowed to bathe in public? It's a disgrace, I tell you! In fact, he's a disgrace!"

"I ain't bathin'," Eulis muttered. Then he felt something crawling at the back of his neck and thrust his fingers through the wet, sticky mass of his hair, digging and picking until he felt the small ant. He mashed it before it could bite, ending its futile bid for freedom.

Alfonso was livid. Everyone watching seemed to think this was terribly funny. They were snickering and pointing at the man like a sideshow freak. It was all he could do not to scream. He thought of Sophie. Now that she was his intended, he felt obligated to protect her in every way that he knew. He gritted his teeth and leaned closer until he and Eulis were almost eye to eye.

Water clung to Eulis's hair and beard, mixing with the remnants of molasses to give him a rather interesting appearance. If it wasn't for the stink of his body and the condition of what was left of his clothes, he might have looked sugarcoated.

"If not a bath, then pray tell what do you call this?"

"I been anted," Eulis muttered. "I'm just pickin' 'em off."

Alfonso frowned. Anted? He'd never heard of such a thing. Then he looked down at the water. Hundreds of dead ants were floating upon the surface. He gawked.

"Good Lord! How did such a thing happen?"

Eulis frowned. For a banker, old Worthy was pretty dim.

"Wal, you take a jug of somethin' sweet and —"

"Oh for pity's sake," Alfonso snapped. "Get yourself out of there!" He straightened and glared at the crowd. "And you people are no better for gawking at a fool. Someone get him out of Pete's trough and off the street. What would the preacher think if he was to come into town right now?"

They began to mutter among themselves. They hadn't thought of it quite like that.

"Right, Mr. Worthy," someone said.

Alfonso stomped away, satisfied that he'd dealt with a sticky issue in a satisfactory manner.

The guilty crowd dispersed, leaving Eulis to get himself out of the trough. His steps were dragging as he recovered the rest of his clothes from where they lay. Holding them between his thumb and forefinger, he dragged them through the dust to the trough, then doused them up and down a few times to remove all the critters before putting them back on, dripping wet.

With his head throbbing and his mouth gone dry, he went about the business of draining the ant-ridden water, then re-filling the trough with clean water just as he'd promised to do. Every step that he took squished. Every move he made dripped. And there was still a bit of mo-lasses in his hair and beard that he hadn't gotten out. But the ants were all gone and he was some cooler than he'd been in quite a while. All in all, it wasn't such a bad way for him to start his day.

Dust boiled beneath Eulis's feet as he trudged up the hill at the south edge of town. Makeshift crosses lined the horizon, markers for the dozens of people who'd gone before him. He shifted the shovel he was carrying from his right shoulder to his left and pulled his hat down a little farther over his forehead. The sun was hot, the wind brisk. When he breathed, he got dust up his nose for the trouble. He thought about that watering trough down at the livery. The dunking hadn't been all that bad. In fact, he could do with another one right about now.

Then he sighed. Baths weren't on his social calendar. In fact, hadn't been for some months. He didn't know why he was thinking so hard on them now. Maybe it had to do with the sticky bits he still felt in his hair. And maybe it was because he'd rather do anything than dig another grave.

But word had gotten around that the preacher was due any day and Eulis was stuck with the job of gravedigger, just like that molasses was stuck in his hair. Added to that, the trapper who'd dragged his dead partner into town was now in need of a hole in which to plant him.

As he topped the hill, he paused at the first set of markers.

Frank Smith.
Dolly Smith.

Husband and wife, as he remembered. He frowned at the place where Dolly Smith lay. He'd passed out in that hole right after it was dug and dang near drowned before he came to. It wasn't often that thunderstorms came to Lizard Flats. But when they did, they caused a good deal of trouble. Eulis was real careful now about getting drunk when it stormed. If he was going to die, he wanted to drown in his sorrows, not the rain.

He moved to the next marker, squinting to read the inscription, although he knew it by heart.

Yankee Dan.

He frowned. It was a shame they hadn't known his whole name. He moved on past the fresh mound of dirt and the scrawny gambler that they'd buried yesterday. No one had known his name. They'd put a cross at his grave and someone had dropped a deck of cards into the grave before he'd covered him up. It was the best they could do.

He didn't dwell on the fact that the man now lay in an unmarked grave. The way he figured, he'd brought his demise upon himself. For now, Eulis had a job to do and he needed new ground.

He paused at the marker bearing Jim

LaSalle's name and noticed a small bunch of withered wild flowers had been laid near the cross. He knew where they'd come from. Poor Letty. She was taking his dying real hard. As he passed, he gave the unsettled mound of dirt a quick tap with his shovel.

A few minutes later, he'd located an empty spot and began scooping out the dirt and piling it off to the side. Eulis was worthless when it came to most things, but he did dig a good hole.

Neat.

Deep.

Like the farmer his father had been, he was preparing the soil for planting. And like the fields they'd once planted, this ground, too, would be barren. Nothing to raise here but the occasional ghost.

He dug and he dug while the whiskey-stained sweat soaked his body and clothes. The sun was near setting by the time he had finished. He stabbed the shovel into the ground and started back down the hill toward Lizard Flats. Will would likely have some stew done by now. Eulis's belly growled. He stuck his finger in his pocket. It came away sticky. He licked it a bit, just to test. The sweetness that came was faint, but it was enough to remember, one more time, those cookies his momma used to make.

Will was sweeping the floor. Letty Murphy had gone upstairs with a man who only had one eye. But Eulis figured it didn't matter how many eyes a man had, as long as his pecker stayed hard. As for Eulis, his pecker was too whiskey-soaked to do him much good any more. He didn't really mind all that much. The glow he got from a good bottle of booze lasted a hell of a lot longer than a dollar a poke on a whore.

"Hey, Eulis," Will the Bartender yelled. "If you think you're gonna still get your drinks, you're gonna have to help me clean up."

Eulis groaned. It wasn't that he objected to the work. But his legs were of one mind, his convictions of another.

"I'd be glad to," he said. "Only I ain't so sure I can stand."

Will the Bartender slid his broom across the floor. It came to a halt a couple of inches from Eulis's face.

"You'll figure somethin' out," Will said.

So Eulis did.

Upstairs, the one-eyed man suddenly let out a whoop.

Eulis paused in mid-sweep.

Will the Bartender nodded his head and reached for another glass to dry, thankful that while Letty now refused to sing, she was still willing to give the men a poke.

"That Letty . . . she sure knows her business."

Eulis thought about it some. "Yeah, I reckon she does," he agreed and stirred up a little more dust.

A short while later the one-eyed man came downstairs. He was grinning from ear to ear and there was a swagger to his step that hadn't been there before.

"Drinks all around," the man said.

Will the Bartender glared. "Ain't no one here but me and Eulis," he muttered.

But Eulis was already bellied up to the bar and waiting for his drink to be poured. His hands were shaking as he reached for the glass. He toasted the one-eyed man and then downed it neat. It burned all the way and brought tears to his eyes. At that point, he remembered he'd been meaning to talk to old Will about the quality of his drink.

"Have another!" the one-eyed man said.

Eulis shoved his glass forward. And he would talk to old Will for sure. As soon as he finished this drink.

"Right kind of you, mister," Eulis said.

The one-eyed man nodded magnanimously, finished off his own drink, then sauntered out of the saloon. Eulis's gaze was locked on the bottle in the bartender's hands.

"Gonna cork 'er up?" he asked.

Will frowned and poured Eulis one last drink. "This is all for tonight, you hear me?"

Eulis nodded and drained the shot glass in one gulp.

"I better not come back here tomorrow and find out you been into my stuff," Will warned.

"Oh, I wouldn't do that," Eulis said. "I ain't no thief."

Before Will could respond, footsteps sounded on the stairs behind them. Both men looked up. It was Letty, coming back to join the ranks. She'd overheard the last bit of Eulis's remark and was wearing a smirk on her face. She was pissed because the one-eyed man had insisted on having his poke with his boots still on. Letty accepted her lot in life, but she had her rules. To her, there was something crude about a man who got his pleasures without taking off his shoes. And because she was pissed, she took her anger out on

Eulis, instead of herself.

"That's right, Eulis Potter. You're no thief. But you're damn sure the biggest drunk I ever seen."

Owl-eyed by the liquor fogging his brain, Eulis managed to frown.

"I ain't never denied my lot in life, Miss Letty. It might behoove you to do the same."

Both Will the Bartender and Letty stared at Eulis as if he'd just grown horns. Will whooped.

"Behoove? Where did you come up with a big word like that?"

Eulis swayed, then gripped the broom handle harder to steady himself. The room was beginning to tilt. Letty's face was starting to melt in the middle, like it did about this time every night.

"There's things about me you don't know," he muttered. "Now if you will 'scuse me. I think I am goin' to sleep."

The broom clattered to the floor. Eulis staggered toward the back room, leaving the pair alone.

"You hurt his feelings," Will said.

Letty shrugged. "He ain't got any feelings, and if he does, I warrant they're as numb as his lips."

And then, because she felt guilty for

taking her frustrations out on an innocent man, she poured herself a drink and downed it like medicine.

She looked around; the saloon was as empty as Letty's heart. "I'm goin' to bed," she said. "I heard tell that preacher man is due in tomorrow. I want to be lookin' my best when he comes."

Will snorted. "That preacher ain't goin' to be messin' with the likes of you." Then he added, "No offense, Letty. Just facts."

She shrugged. "None taken. But you still never know."

She sauntered back up the stairs, her skirt tail swishing and her bosom bouncing with every step that she took.

Will tossed his towel aside and hung his apron on a nail. At the door, he stopped and turned, giving the room one last look. Eulis still hadn't swept and there was a table in the back that had yet to be wiped down. But tomorrow was another day. And like Eulis, he was ready for sleep.

He closed the doors behind him and walked across the street to the livery. A few minutes later, the steady clop, clop sound of a shod horse could be heard as he rode toward his house at the north end of town.

Upstairs, Letty stood at the window, watching as the lights came on in the scattering of houses. Down on the flats at the south edge of town, a single candle burned. She frowned.

That would be Matt Goslin's place. He was as stingy with himself as he was with everyone else, choosing to eat by the light of one candle, rather than a lamplight like everyone else. She folded her arms across her breasts and leaned against the sill. The only thing Matt didn't short himself on was his manly pleasures. Truly Fine had serviced him on a regular basis until she'd left town. After that, Letty had been stuck with him. It was enough to make her consider upping her rates. Except for Eulis, Matt Goslin needed a bath worse than any other man in Lizard Flats.

Her gaze slid from Matt's candlelit window to the small one-room shanty at the other end of town. For its size, it was lit up like a church. Letty grinned, thinking of the Dumas family and their three little boys. They were devils for sure, but they did make her laugh. Their latest stunt was still the talk of the town. Anting Eulis while he was passed out drunk had been a good one. It was something she might have done when she was a kid.

At the thought, her smile froze and then died. When she was a kid, if she'd had a jug of molasses, it wouldn't have been wasted on a passed-out drunk. There'd been too many nights in her life when she had gone to bed too hungry to waste food on a prank.

Angry with herself for letting go of such feelings, she thrust her hands into her hair and started taking out the pins, yanking and pulling until they were gone and her hair was a jumble around her face. She didn't want to think about her childhood. She couldn't bear to remember how her mother had looked all laid out in that box, or how the Indians had peeled her father's scalp from his head. She reached for the brush and started pulling it through her hair. As she did, she closed her eyes, remembering when she was small, how her daddy used to love to do this for her. When the Indians took Daddy's hair, they had taken the rest of her childhood, as well.

Then she sighed and started removing her dress. It didn't matter. None of it mattered. Not anymore. She'd gotten where she was by her wits, her willingness to let men think they were perfect, and would not offer an apology for either. Then she thought of Jim and the pain twisted in her chest. At least she was alive, which was more than she could say for some.

She tossed her dress on the back of a chair and then slipped on her wrapper. Here, in the dark, alone in her room, her body was hers once more. Here she could sleep and dream, and savor the silence without pretending to bask in some man's afterglow.

A dog barked suddenly, viciously. She glanced out the window then finally relaxed. Probably nothing more than a warning to some coyote who'd come too close to town.

Her gaze shifted to the dark silhouette of Sophie Hollis's house. The lights coming from there were not stark in the night, but rather muted behind the gathers of fine lace. Letty stared for a while, trying to imagine what life must be like for a woman upon whom society did not frown. Then she shrugged and turned away. There was no need dwelling on something she would never have.

She poured some water in a glass and took a long drink, then walked across the room to the bath awaiting her there. The water wasn't as hot as it had been when Will had filled it up, but it didn't matter. She and Will had a deal. Every day, regular as clockwork, she got her bath and Will's customers got whatever they wanted from the whore in the red satin dress.

Her wrapper fell to the floor at her feet as she stepped into the tub, the water enveloping her as she sat. She would never be able to cleanse the filth from her soul, but she could have a clean body.

She thought of the preacher's imminent arrival and picked up her soap and began to scrub. One thing would be certain. For the duration of his visit, her business would probably be nil. Which, when she thought about it, suited her just fine. It would be good to have her body to herself for a while.

Howe Low Can He Go?

Randall Howe was getting used to eating dust and jackrabbit. In fact, he considered it part of his penance for seducing a virgin and then running from the scene of his crime. The wagonmaster had assured him that they were only a day out of Lizard Flats now. His journey was coming to an end. After this, the destinations he chose would be his own. He thought of the wedding he was to perform and the sermon he was supposed to give in the makeshift church afterward. The thought made him ill. He wasn't fit to bless the union of matrimony, and he certainly wasn't fit to speak the word of God.

At this point in his life, Randall Howe was a sorry sight indeed. He hadn't slept the night through in days and couldn't remember the last time he'd shaved. He kept seeing Charity Doone's sweet face and knowing that he had ruined her life. But, he reminded himself, he had made many promises to God in return for forgiveness. Surely God had heard.

335

Then he sighed. God might forgive him, but Randall feared he would never forgive himself. There was a terrible weakness within him that he didn't know how to fight. Prayer didn't help. Promises didn't work. Even fear for his own life had not been enough to stop him from tasting the sweetness of womanly wiles. And, no matter how far he traveled from Mehitable's ranch, it would never be far enough for him to forget what he'd done.

His misery increased with each miserable jolt of the wagon wheels into the deep, hard ruts. And with each jolt, he repeated the solemn promise he'd made to God a few days earlier. No matter what, he would never partake of worldly things and wanton flesh again.

"We'll make camp here for the night," the wagonmaster announced.

Randall stirred, taking note of the creek and the stand of trees on the bank. This was good. He would bathe, maybe even shave. In the morning, he would put on fresh clothes. He would arrive in Lizard Flats as close to the man he'd been when he left Boston, or know the reason why. He owed it to himself, and to the people who awaited him there.

When morning came, Randall awoke with a new sense of purpose. Just the scraping of the dirt from his body and the whiskers from his face had given him a new sense of purpose. It had been a symbolic cleansing of his soul.

He'd learned his lesson. Yes, he had. No women. Not ever. Again.

It was coming on evening when they pulled into Lizard Flats. The wagon came in from the far end of town, stopping at the largest building in sight, which happened to be the White Dove Saloon. When Randall Howe saw Leticia Murphy standing on the porch beneath the sloping roof, his heart skipped a beat. The red satin dress was like a beacon of hope in a long, dark night and the cascading curls she'd pinned up off her neck begged to be taken down. At that point, every promise he'd made to himself — and to God — began to sink with the swiftly disappearing sun.

God give me strength.

When the feathers decorating the neckline of her dress suddenly fluttered with the evening breeze, he added an amendment to his previous prayer.

And then strike me blind.

But when his prayers were not immediately answered, he knew himself well enough to recognize the symptoms. Unless a miracle occurred, he was about to do sin.

The streets were deserted save for a dog and a couple of kids running for home before dark. The wagonmaster climbed down from his rig and began to unload Randall's bags, but Randall hardly noticed. Framed by swinging doors and the lamplight from the hanging chandeliers in the room behind her, Letty Murphy was a sight to behold.

The lines in her face were softened by the shadows of dusk, and so Howe did not readily see them. Her overblown body looked soft and welcome to a man who'd ridden a wagon seat until it felt as if his hip bones had come through his rump. And then she smiled and he started convincing himself that this one wouldn't matter. Because she sold herself on a daily basis and that nothing he did to her could be misconstrued as a lie. It wasn't as if she would expect anything from him other than her pay. It wasn't as if she counted. She was only a whore. He never even noticed when the wagonmaster drove away.

Letty had seen the clerical collar. It was the preacher everyone had been waiting on. She was beside herself with glee. Will the Bartender would never believe it, but she, Leticia Murphy, was going to be the one he would first greet. She pulled her feather boa across her cleavage in an attempt to cover her breasts and took a step forward.

"Welcome to Lizard Flats," she said.

It was all Randall could do to nod.

Then Letty got nervous. Embarrassed by the flush that spread up his neck and cheeks, she looked away. It shamed her to think he must be shocked by her appearance. But curiosity won out and she started the conversation over again.

"You are him, ain't ya? I mean . . . you are the preacher everyone's been waitin' for?"

Randall doffed his bowler, bowing just low enough to get a better than average view of her barely concealed bosom.

"Yes, madam, I am. Reverend Randall Ward Howe at your service. Maybe you would be so kind as to show me to the hotel?"

His voice made Letty shiver. It reminded her of the culture in Jim LaSalle's speech. Then, angry that he'd made her think of Jim, she blurted out, "The hotel has been full for days, but there's a couple of rooms over the saloon that Will the Bartender sometimes rents out. Only he went to get himself a haircut for the funeral, so I can't let you have no key until he gets back."

Howe frowned. "What funeral?"

She eyed the preacher up and down, taking absent note of the fine cut of his clothes and thinking of how this man was going to put his blessing on Sophie and Alfonso's wedding.

"I guess the one you'll be performing tomorrow after the wedding, and as I hear it, none too soon. The old codger they brought in to bury is stinkin' up the place somethin' fierce."

Howe dabbed at the sweat dripping from the roll of fat beneath his chin. "Good Lord! Don't you people have an undertaker?"

This time Letty laughed aloud and pointed behind her to a man who was passed out on the floor and slumped against the bar.

"Yes, another drunk like Eulis over there. When Eulis is sober, which is hardly ever, he digs the holes and plants the bodies. When he's drunk, he sometimes forgets to cover 'em up. The undertaker is even worse."

Howe tried not to show the horror he felt. Maybe he'd been wrong last night. Maybe God had truly forsaken him by abandoning him to this wasteland. And if that were so, then it shouldn't matter if he sinned just one more time — for old times sake — before he continued down the missionary trail that fate had set him on.

Howe gave her one of his show-me-pity smiles. "I'm travel-weary to my bones. And since your boss isn't here, would you be so kind as to consider letting me . . . ah . . . rest in your rooms until his return?"

Letty had heard too many invitations in her lifetime to ignore the one she'd just been handed. She started to snort, and then inhaled instead. Maybe she was mistaken. It would be a disaster if she offended the man the whole Territory had been waiting for. Then his gaze slid downward and she saw that he was peering through the feathers to the valley between her breasts.

Letty knew leers when she saw them. *So preacher man. You've got an itchy dick just like every other man who comes through these doors.*

"Would you care to follow me?" she asked.

Howe picked up his bags, watching her ample hips swaying beneath her dress as she led the way upstairs. His loins were beginning to surge as he watched the ripple and roll of her body beneath the tawdry silk.

I'm not going to mind this ride at all.

When the door closed behind them, Letty turned, and the glitter in her eyes was as hard as Randall's dick. "It'll cost you a dollar."

Howe's hands shook as he dug in his pocket. He would have given her a five-dollar gold piece and considered himself getting the best of the bargain.

Letty took the money and tucked it away when he wasn't looking. It didn't pay to trust any man. Even a man of the cloth.

Reverend Randall Ward Howe would never imagine, not in his wildest dreams, that it would cost him a dollar to die. But that is exactly what he did. Right in the middle of a hump. And right on top of Leticia Murphy.

Letty felt the air and the life go out of him all at once. In her line of work, men often shot their wad before they even got it in. And no matter how loud they bragged to their buddies about their prowess, she'd watched their lust go limp on a regular basis. But she'd never, not once, had one die on her, or in her, before.

With a panicked grunt, she pushed him

up, then off her. His purpling face and deflating belly were more than she could handle. She grabbed her pillow, clamped it over her face, and commenced to screaming until goose feathers came out between the threads in the ticking and into her mouth.

But time passed and Randall Howe continued to hog his share of Letty's bed. When she could think without coming undone, she knew she had to make a plan. And since she was naked, the first thing to do was get dressed. Ever so often, as she yanked on her clothes, she would give his body another push, just to make sure she hadn't made a mistake. To her continuing dismay, she hadn't.

"They will hang me for sure! People have been coming for days to hear the preacher from back East, and I've gone and killed him in a bed of sin." With that, she began to shake.

But as with everything bad, there comes a time when weariness can overtake grief and fear. It happened to Letty just about the time she began to get mad. She leaned over the bed, peering into the preacher's sightless eyes.

"It's all your fault, you stupid lout," she muttered, then reminded herself, "I can't just let him lay here. I've got to do something!"

No one argued with her decision.

She yanked his hands across his belly, then folded his arms across his chest and covered him with a spread. Now he looked like the corpse he was, lying cold and still beneath the makeshift shroud. And with that thought, came another, followed on the heels of the wildest scheme she'd ever concocted. But if it worked, everyone would still be happy, and she just might escape the hangman's noose. She bolted for the door.

The silence down in the bar was odd, almost eerie. She couldn't remember a day when there hadn't been at least a half-dozen men milling about, unwilling to go home.

Will the Bartender was still gone. She thought of Truly Fine, who'd left here over a year ago, and while she wished now that she'd been on that stage with Truly, the solitude in which she found herself was all the better to play out her hand.

To her relief, Eulis was right where she'd seen him last, passed out on the floor beneath the bar. Letty nudged him several times with the toe of her shoe. He didn't budge.

"Eulis!"

He didn't move. He didn't blink.

Letty bent down and grabbed his long, bushy beard, yanking it back and forth until his head lolled on his neck like a yo-yo.

"Dang it, Eulis, wake up!"

He groaned and rolled, squinting through swollen lids as the overhead lights all but blinded his vision.

"Letty? Izzatchu?"

"Yes, it's me," she hissed. "Get up."

"Wha' the hell are you doin'?" he muttered, and swiped at Letty's hands. "Dammit, 'at hurts."

She glanced nervously toward the door. If anyone came in now, her plan would be ruined before she had a chance to set it in motion. Thankfully, there was no one in sight.

"Get up!" she whispered. "I need your help."

"Can't. I'm in my cups," Eulis said, and rolled over on his side.

Letty grabbed him by the ear, yanking hard enough to bring tears to Eulis's eyes. "I will skin you alive and stake you on an ant hill if you don't get up."

As drunk as he was, it was the word *ant* that got his attention. Every now and then he still found a dead one in his tangle of beard.

He groaned and staggered to his feet. "What the hell do ya' want?"

"Come with me," Letty said, and all but dragged him up the stairs.

"Now see here," Eulis mumbled, trying to regain his freedom before the whore pulled him into her room. "I ain't able to help you out like this none. I've been drunk too long to get it up, and that's a fact."

"I don't need that kind of help, you ass. I need you to help me hide something."

She pushed him through the door, then slammed it shut behind them.

Even for a drunk, the body on the bed was impossible to miss. Eulis staggered backward. He'd seen plenty of dead men in his days, but none laid out on a whore's bed, covered with a thin cotton spread, and not a stitch of clothes to his name. It was a sobering sight that sent the last fumes of alcohol flying from his whiskey-soaked brain.

"What the hell did you do to him?"

She thought about crying, then swallowed the urge, although her voice was shaking. "I didn't do nothin' to him that I don't do to any other man. How was I to know he was goin' to croak on me?"

Eulis felt bad. He hadn't meant to upset her none.

"There, there." He patted her shoulder. "I'm sure it couldn't a been helped. I always say, 'when it's a man's time to go, it's his time to go.'" He grinned through a drunken fog. "Besides, I can't think of a better way to die than gettin' a little of the good stuff on the way out."

Letty hit him up aside the head. "Don't make jokes. This is serious."

Eulis grimaced and rubbed at the side of his face where she'd smacked him. "Not for him it's not. He's past worryin' about anything."

Letty bit her lip as she confessed her sin, although saying the words made her belly quake. "That there's the preacher everyone's been waiting for."

Eulis gawked. He looked from the mound of flesh beneath the spread, to Letty, and back again.

"You killed the preacher?"

At this point, she began to shake and moan, wondering if it hurt much to hang.

"Oh hell, now, let's don't start that all over again," Eulis muttered. "We'll figure somethin' out." The sounds coming out of her mouth were giving him a serious headache.

Letty sniffed, then blew her nose on the

skirt of her dress. "We've got to hide the body."

Eulis stared at the mound of man beneath the spread. "That might take some doin'. He's right portly."

She rolled her eyes and then punched Eulis on the arm. "You aren't telling me anything I don't already know. I lay odds you have never been humped by something the size of a buffalo."

Eulis considered the fact and had to agree. And then he thought. "We could bury him."

Letty's face brightened. It was the first sensible thing Eulis had ever said in her presence.

"Where?"

"I done dug a hole for that trapper they're waitin' to plant. Maybe I could dig it a little deeper and put the preacher-man in first. If I cover him with a few inches of dirt, no one will be the wiser when they drop the trapper in on top. Hell, the old trapper smells so bad now that I doubt anyone will even come to watch the buryin', save maybe his partner who brought him into town."

Letty's eyes widened as she considered the notion. With one last sniff, she clasped her hands beneath her bosom in a prayerful gesture.

"Oh Eulis! If you help me do that, you can poke me free forever."

Even though his pecker was useless, he brightened at the thought.

"All right then," he said. "Help me wrap him up good. We'll drag him out the back door and into Will's wagon. I'll have him at the cemetery before you can say amen."

Reverend Howe would have been highly incensed at the casual way in which his earthly body was handled. He was rolled, thumped, and bumped down a single flight of stairs then dragged up a plank and into the wagon with little ceremony.

The only snort of disapproval came from the horse pulling the wagon. And it was not at the manner in which the body was being handled. It was because he was still hitched to a wagon, rather than a feed bag.

But Letty was borderline hysterical, and Eulis was on a mission. The horse's meal would have to wait. Together, they made it out of town and up the hill to the cemetery then did what they had to do. Later, still hidden by the shelter of darkness, they re-entered town a weary, but calmer, pair than when they'd left.

"I need a drink," Eulis muttered, as he unhitched the horse and bedded it down in a stall.

Letty's eyes narrowed. She had other plans for Eulis. Plans that she'd been concocting while he'd been digging a deeper hole.

"What you need is a bath."

Eulis shrugged and brushed at the dirt on his hands and clothes. It mattered little to him. There was so much of it, that one more layer of grime hardly mattered at all. Besides, if he could stand himself, why should anyone else care?

"Naw, I'm fine." Eulis combed his dirty fingers through his long hair and beard to prove that it was so. "I had me a dunkin' a day or so ago in Pete Samuels' waterin' trough."

"A dunking is not enough. Not if you're going to preach tomorrow," Letty said, and started pulling him toward the door.

"Not if I'm gonna what?"

Letty was too busy guiding him toward the back stairs that led up to her room to answer. Her bathtub was full and waiting for her to crawl in, but tonight it was going to see better use.

More than once, Eulis tried to run, but Letty had him by the beard, and it hurt too much when she pulled.

"Dagnabit you witch! Turn me loose or else," he warned.

"Or else what, Eulis Potter? Who are you gonna tell? And what will you say? That you helped a whore hide a dead body? That makes you an accomplice. They can hang you as high as they hang me. You'd best remember that."

Eulis groaned. He had just remembered why he'd become a drunk. It had been a woman who'd driven him to the bottle, and she'd been too much like the one who now had him by the balls, and by the beard, to argue with.

The door slammed, and they were suddenly alone. The tub beckoned although the steam had long since quit rising from the water.

"Take off your clothes," Letty ordered.

Eulis groaned. He was some sober, but not enough, he feared, to do her any good.

"Not for that, you ass," Letty muttered, and started ripping at his jacket and shirt. The rotting garments fell away in her hands. "Get in the tub. By the time I get through with you, you won't recognize yourself."

Eulis was feeling too sick to argue. He needed a drink, but from the look on Letty's face, he wouldn't get the time of day unless he did as he was told. He crawled into the water with the reluctance of a drowning man. The tepid water covered, then shriveled, his prick and his balls.

"I'll get some more warm water," Letty said, and bolted out of the room. She was back within minutes, having snitched the big pot of water off the stove that Will kept ready for making coffee. When she tilted it into the tub and poured, Eulis started to shriek.

"Christ all mighty!" he yelled.

"Preachers don't curse," Letty muttered.

"I'm going to be sick."

"You do, and you'll be bathing in it," she warned.

He swallowed the bile and took the soap that she offered.

Two hours later, he stood before her mirror, a shorn and saddened man. His own mother would not have recognized him. He was, as near as Letty had been able to create, a passable re-creation of Reverend Randall Ward Howe, right down to the part in the middle of his hair, and the clean-shaven face and double chin.

Letty handed him the preacher's clothes and robe. "Try them on," she said.

Even though he knew it would add to his believability he eyed the preacher's heavy robe with distaste. The idea of sweltering in that garb did not appeal to him.

"That'll be too hot. And he was fatter than me," Eulis argued.

"Well, forget the robe. And your beer belly will hold the rest of 'em up. You can belt in what sags."

Letty was still holding the scissors she'd used to cut off his hair and beard, so Eulis figured an argument of any sort would be a lost cause. Reluctantly, he began to dress, and when he finished, stood back to view himself.

All told, he didn't look as bad as he'd feared. He even pranced and preened a bit at Letty's instructions, trying to mimic the walk of the man whose final act on earth had consisted of committing a sin. By the time dawn arrived, Eulis had been coerced into a plan of collusion that could fall apart at any given moment. Neither of the culprits had any notion of whether Banker Worthy or Widow Hollis had known the irreverent reverend on sight. If they did, it was all over. But, Letty and Eulis were counting on the fact that they had only known him by name. So, if Eulis didn't go and get himself drunk before the ceremony, they'd be home free.

Letty pushed a sweaty lock of hair away from her face. "It's nearly daybreak. I'm gonna clean myself up, then we're both going down and pretend nothing is wrong."

Eulis grinned. His mouth was dry. And he would have killed two snakes for nothing stronger than a smell of cheap whiskey, but he was starting to enjoy himself. He looked real good in these fine clothes. And Letty didn't know it, but he'd been raised on the Good Book. He knew plenty of passages to get him by the worst of it.

What he didn't know was if he could keep a straight face. In the years that he'd spent in Lizard Flats, he'd been kicked aside, ignored, or spit at on a daily basis. This was too good to fathom. He kept thinking of Sophie hitting him with her umbrella and the trouncing Alfonso Worthy had given him while he'd been sitting in Pete Samuels' trough. Now Eulis was going to perform their marriage ceremony and it wouldn't be worth a hill of beans. It was the best sort of vengeance a man could ask for. Bloodless, but binding, nevertheless.

By breakfast, he was in full swing, bestowing compliments on women who, yesterday, wouldn't have let him sweep the dirt from beneath their feet, and blessing babies as if he'd brought them into the world himself.

Letty watched from a safe distance away, horrified by the monster that she'd created, yet unable to turn him off for fear of ruining herself in the process. There was nothing left for her to do but ride out the day with as little panic as possible.

No sooner had she sworn to react with calm, than Alfonso Worthy entered the dining room adjacent to the saloon with his fiancée, Sophie Hollis, in tow.

"Reverend Howe, I presume?"

Eulis grinned. Yesterday Alfonso Worthy had stepped over him like a dog turd. Today he was fawning at his feet. Justice had never been so sweet.

"That's me. I mean . . . yes, I am he . . . uh, him." Eulis stuttered. He had to remember to talk fancy. "And this must be your charming bride-to-be."

Eulis rose to the occasion by standing, then bowing over Sophie Hollis's hand before bestowing a gentle kiss upon the knuckles of her right hand with princely grace.

Sophie giggled and blushed as Alfonso announced his news. "We came to inform you that the wedding will be held in exactly one hour . . . if that meets with your approval."

Eulis pulled a small book from the

pocket of the preacher's coat, and pretended to consult it for several moments, as if checking a schedule that was actually nonexistent. Howe hadn't been in town long enough to do anything but die.

Finally, he raised his head and nodded in a pleasant, and what he hoped was a benign manner. "That will be fine. And where, pray tell, is the ceremony to be held?"

Letty rolled her eyes in disgust at the flowery words Eulis was spouting. If he wasn't careful, he'd outrun his own wind and blow himself down.

"We're holding the ceremony at dear Sophie's house, of course," Alfonso said, and smiled as Sophie blushed.

She'd been all over him like a cat scratching fleas for the better part of a week. Alfonso would get the ceremony out of the way, and then get Sophie in bed or know the reason why. Going from the front parlor to the upstairs bedroom seemed the simplest and best way to accomplish both.

"I'll be there promptly in one hour. No sooner. No later. A man of God always keeps his word," Eulis said.

Alfonso nodded, content that he'd done his part in satisfying propriety. Once he satisfied Sophie Hollis in bed, he would have it made.

Sophie pranced and giggled. "Do hurry, dear Reverend. I just don't like to be kept waiting a minute longer than necessary to call this wonderful man my husband."

Eulis nodded, burped, then took another sip of his spiked tea. The weakened whiskey settled his queasy stomach just enough to get him by. It was one thing to become a preacher overnight. It was another thing altogether to get religion and go on the wagon at the same time. Some men might be able to do it. Eulis Potter knew his limitations better than most. He'd do what he must, but he'd do it with a glow, or not at all.

The moment the affianced couple was gone, Letty rushed to his table and snatched the cup from beneath his mouth and sniffed it.

"I should have known," she hissed. "You're drinking whiskeyed-down tea. You get drunk on me, Eulis Potter, and I'll hang you myself."

"Reverend Howe, to you, my dear. And hadn't you better get changed? We don't want to be late for the ceremony."

"What's wrong with my dress?" Letty grumbled, smoothing down the red silk with sweaty palms.

"It reveals too much of your, ah, womanly charms." He waggled his eyebrows and leered at her breasts for effect. "Don't you agree?"

He had her over several barrels and they both knew it. Unable to argue, Letty raced to her room to dress. In her panic, she tore both the underarms of her only decent dress and had to cast it aside. She ran to the window, as if looking for answers, then started to grin. There was a blue-sprigged muslin in the window of Matt Goslin's store that had been hanging on a store dummy for the better part of three years. It was sun-faded in the front, and stained in the back from the time the roof had leaked and wetted down everything in the front of the store. But it was high-necked, and long-sleeved, and by God, it would hide everything, including her damned neck, if she buttoned it just right.

LET THE GAMES BEGIN

It looked as if the entire population of Lizard Flats was in Sophie Hollis's yard, ogling for the best view of the ceremony about to take place upon her front porch.

Matt Goslin, storekeeper and rejected suitor, glared from a place near the porch steps. If Alfonso Worthy was going to snatch up his sweetie, he was going to get as close as he could.

Letty Murphy had picked her place early. She was less than five feet from the spot where Eulis, the drunk-turned-preacher, had taken his place. She figured if he got out of hand, she should be as close as possible to try and prevent a disaster from occurring.

And while she waited, she tugged at the neck of her new dress, not for the first time, wishing she'd worn one of her own and said to hell with propriety. It was no wonder that the upright women of Lizard Flats often had pinched expressions about their mouths. These high-necked, long-sleeved dresses were uncomfortable as all get out.

Letty fidgeted beneath the stares of the guests milling about the yard. She supposed it was because they'd never seen her dressed in such a fashion, when in fact, they were curious as to why her dress was faded to a near white in front and still bright blue in the back. No one recognized the dress as having come from Matt Goslin's store. What they did notice was that the dress was about a size and a half too small, and that Letty's ample charms were pressing with prominent persistence at the boundaries of the buttons running down the front of the dress.

Just then the bride and groom came out of the house and paused beneath the roof of the porch and everyone's attention turned. A small gasp of admiration rose from the assembled females. Sophie Hollis was wearing a pink dress with a complexion to match. Truly a blushing bride.

Alfonso was strutting as he took his place before the preacher.

Eulis cleared his throat and Letty held her breath. It was time to begin.

"Do you, Sophie, take —"

"I do." She giggled and cast a flirtatious eye toward her little banker.

"Not yet, my dear," Alfonso cautioned with a whisper. "He's not through saying his piece."

Just the word "piece" made Sophie quiver inside. She sighed and squeezed her legs together as a reminder to stay calm, smiling over her nervous need.

"Reverend, pray continue," Alfonso said loftily.

Eulis nodded, and did as he was asked.

Eulis's voice rolled up and out of his throat in deep booming consonants, echoing from beneath the porch roof where the ceremony had commenced. But the mighty tone was not because he'd suddenly felt the call to preach. It was because he'd talked more in the past eight hours than he had in the last eight years and his throat was getting hoarse. He continued where he'd left off.

". . . this man to be your awful wedded —"

"Lawful," Letty hissed. "The word is lawful . . . lawful."

Eulis glared and paused for effect. "Lawful wedded husband. To . . . a . . . hold all the time and to a . . . have forever. Even when you're sick?"

Eulis paused at the end of this statement and nodded toward the blushing bride.

Now it was time for Sophie's answer, but the preacher had left something out that Alfonso felt needed mentioning. He smiled at Sophie and patted her arm and then leaned forward.

"What about obey?" Alfonso asked. "You didn't say anything about obeying."

Eulis sighed and wished them both to hell and back. What possible difference could the omission of one teeny little word possibly have? Then he looked at the pout on Sophie Hollis' face and knew that the banker probably had a point.

"Of course, of course. I'm sorry. The trip was just so tiring, that I fear I'm not myself." He cleared his throat and began again.

"Sophie Hollis. Do you promise to obey this man in every way until death do you part?"

She'd been a little miffed at Alfonso's interruption until the preacher had mentioned the word 'death'. The memory of her dear Nardin's untimely demise made her forget her ire. Of course she should obey. It was, after all, the mode of the day.

"I do. I do."

Her gasp was tinged with just a hint of a sob. Alfonso squeezed her hand in a comforting manner and sent her into spasms of delight. She could hardly wait. For everything.

"And do you, Alfonso Worthy, take this woman to be your wife? Will you take care of her and all that's hers forever until one of you dies?"

"With pleasure," Alfonso said, thinking of Sophie's womanly body, and then amended by adding, "I do, too."

Eulis felt euphoric. He was getting to the good part and hadn't messed up yet.

"Then by all that's holy, I say you're man and wife. And no man here should put it under."

"Asunder," Letty groaned. "The word is asunder."

But Eulis's second faux pas didn't matter. As far as everyone assumed, the two were now legally wed. The gleam of relief in Alfonso's eyes matched the lust in Sophie's. Each had gotten what they most desired.

A rousing cheer went up.

"Food and drinks inside," Alfonso announced, and stepped back as the crowd surged forward.

Sophie shivered in her shoes and pressed her new husband's arm against her breast as she held fast to him to keep from being swept off the porch. When he caught an arm around her waist to steady her, she knew that she'd done the right thing. One day she would even confess to him that she'd figured out who her secret admirer had been, but for now, she was just happy to call him husband.

When Eulis would have willingly joined in the celebration, Letty grabbed him by the arm and hauled him off the porch before he imbibed too much to finish the rest of what he must do.

"Come with me," she hissed.

Eulis yanked his arm free and looked back at the house. "But what about the party?"

Letty pointed toward an old man who was sitting astride a horse just outside Sophie's fence.

"You don't have time for partying. You're the preacher, remember? That old trapper has been waiting for days for you to get here and bury his partner."

She wiggled her eyebrows and glared. It was enough of a reminder to Eulis about the need to cover up their own dirty deed that he quickly bolted off the porch. A vision of the real preacher bouncing down into that deepened hole came back with full force. The few inches of dirt he'd tossed over the man would not suffice long unless the real corpse was laid neatly on top and planted beneath six feet of Territory dirt as planned.

"Lead me to him," Eulis said.

Letty did as she was told.

Henry Wainwright held his breath as best he could. He and Parson were about to take their last trip together. And when it was over, Henry would be going on alone. The need for haste outweighed whatever lingering sorrow Henry had mustered. Old Elmer smelled to high heaven, and that was a fact.

By the time they got to the outskirts of town and entered the cemetery, Henry was plumb lightheaded from lack of oxygen, and the preacher and the whore in the two-tone dress looked green.

"Maybe you'd best tip him on in and begin covering him up," she suggested, unwilling to think of Jim and desperate to have the last of her sin buried as quick and as deep as possible. "The preacher here can talk while you shovel."

Henry nodded. It sounded like a plan to him. Will the Bartender had promised to come to the burying, but it was obvious that he'd forgone Parson's burying for the celebration taking place down at Sophie

Hollis Worthy's home. No one else had bothered to follow them out of town. Possibly because Elmer and Henry had been strangers to Lizard Flats. And possibly because Elmer Sutter stunk.

Henry untied the travois from the horse and pushed it to the edge of the hole that Eulis had dug yesterday. A quick film of tears covered his eyes as the buffalo robe and all that it held slid down into the grave.

Dust boiled up into Henry's eyes as the body raked the sides of the hole, making them water even more. It was just as well that he couldn't see. He might have wondered why old Elmer hadn't settled as flat as he should have in his earthly resting place. The portly paunch of Reverend Randall Ward Howe was a hard hump upon which to rest. But it was of little importance in the scheme of the living still left on earth. Henry bent down, picked up the shovel, and started to scoop as the preacher began to speak.

"All in all, a man's time on earth is short," Eulis began. Henry paused in the midst of his third shovel full of dirt and nodded in satisfaction. The words were big and deep, just like he'd expected to hear from a 'real' man of the cloth. Old Elmer would be proud to know that he'd kept his word.

Anxious that the funeral not become a public scene, Eulis felt the need to hurry. Someone might actually wonder why it was that the bereaved was doing his own burying when it was the place of the grave-digger, namely himself, who usually did the honors.

"Therefore it is only fitting that a man's burying should also be the same. Ashes to ashes and uh . . . dirt to dirt."

"Dust," Letty hissed, and wiped at her eyes with the sleeve of her dress. "It's dust to dust."

Eulis nodded. "So it is, little lady. So it is. It's mighty dusty out here, at that." And he proceeded to repeat the Twenty-third Psalm. It was the only thing out of the Bible that he knew by heart.

Letty sobbed. Henry gave the woman a kindly look. It was a nice touch to the solemnity of the situation. It was right nice of her to shed a few tears for a man she'd known only briefly in her bed.

Little did he know that she was shedding tears for her own misdeeds. The body lying beneath Parson Sutter would be forever hidden from the eyes of man, but it wasn't them she was worried about. It was God.

He saw everything and knew everything. And He knew that Leticia Murphy had been hating Him for some time now, and after the incident with the preacher, had committed a grievous sin. It was for herself that she cried the most.

Within the hour, it was over. Eulis and Letty stood silent witnesses to the last thump of the shovel upon the hand-carved cross that Henry Wainwright had planted at the head of the grave. Or maybe it was at the foot. After the bear and the time that had passed, it had been hard to decide which was heads and which was tails of what was left of old Elmer.

"There now. It's done," Henry said, and jammed the shovel into the ground for the next grave that would be dug.

He took off his hat, revealing a rim of yellow-white hair and a shiny spot of skin at the crown of his head that was encrusted with an accumulation of grime and scars. "Elmer Sutter . . . you've been a good and true partner. I might even find myself missin' your damned preachin'." He sniffed and swiped at the tears and snot running down his lip. "Rest easy old pard. I reckon I'll be seein' you soon enough as it is."

This time, Letty cried for the man who'd

died, and not the one she'd killed. Even Eulis was hard-pressed to keep a straight face. When he died, he doubted a single man or woman would shed tears over his body. It was a soul-searching thought and one on which to end the occasion.

"Well now," Eulis said, thumping the old trapper on the back. "It seems you've been a true friend to this man. Giving him a proper burial was a fine thing to do."

"Oh hell," Henry said, as he turned to catch his horse's reins. "I didn't bring him all this way just for a funeral. I brought him so that a real preacher could say the right words over his body. It's what he always wanted. Now he can rest easy in heaven."

With that, Henry Wainwright mounted and rode off. West out of Lizard Flats. Back toward the Rockies and his untended traps. He just hoped to hell that when he got there, the danged Indians hadn't made off with them all.

Eulis couldn't look at Letty, and Letty couldn't find the words to say to make it right. Because of their deception, a man's dying wish had not been fulfilled. And then Eulis had a thought.

"Well hell," he said, and pulled at the vest over his belly. "Maybe a real preacher didn't say words over his body, but by God, he's gonna spend eternity in the arms of one."

Letty brightened. She hadn't looked at it all that way.

"You're right," she said. "Come on. We've got to get back."

"What for?" Eulis asked. "I done performed the wedding and buried the corpse. What else could possibly be left?"

Letty grabbed him by the arm and aimed him toward town. It only stood to reason there would be more who needed the services of a man of God. It didn't occur to them that some might wonder why the town whore had taken it upon herself to be the escort for the preacher they'd waited so long to meet, and they were too busy trying to save their own hides to care.

Isaac Jessup sat on the bench in front of Matt Goslin's general store, waiting patiently for the preacher to come back from the funeral on the hill outside of town. He knew that the worthy reverend would be a busy man. He also knew that the preacher had already married some and buried another, but Isaac had his own urgent need for the man of the cloth.

He needed God to give a blessing on his

one and only son. If he and Minna lost Baby Boy, she wouldn't survive another burying'. Truth was, he would lose her, too. And if he lost Minna, he might as well put a gun to his own head and do himself in while he was at it. Going on without her didn't bear consideration.

While he watched for the preacher, Minna and Baby were inside the general store, marveling at the newfangled goods that marked Lizard Flats as a place of unbelievable refinement.

Even Isaac had been stunned to see real peaches in tin cans, and had been disbelieving of the marvel until Matt Goslin had opened a can right before their eyes and offered them all a bite.

Isaac leaned his head against the outer wall of the store and licked his lips. He could still taste the peach juice.

A horse neighed. He looked up. A man and a woman were walking down the sidewalk. Isaac took a deep breath and stood up. Although he'd never seen Reverend Randall Ward Howe in his life, he recognized the man by his clothing.

Just as Letty and Eulis thought they had things under control, a man stepped into their path.

"You'd be the preacher?"

It was more question than statement, but Eulis knew what the response demanded.

"Why, yes I am," he said. "What can I do for you, my son?"

Isaac shifted his stance. He'd found the right man after all. The fellow even talked like a preacher.

"I reckon I'll be needin' you to baptize my boy," he said shortly.

Eulis relaxed. Surely he could handle the naming of one small infant without causing a disaster.

"And where would the sweet child be?" Eulis asked kindly, hoping he sounded as fatherly as his position demanded.

Isaac turned toward the store. "Baby Boy! Minna! Come on out here! I found the preacher!"

Eulis gawked. He'd never heard a man shout that way at an infant in his life. His confusion increased when a strapping youth and a pretty woman came running from the store.

"Who are they?" Eulis asked, wondering where the baby was.

"That there's my wife, Minna, and our son, Baby Boy."

"But where is the child you want baptized?"

Letty elbowed him so hard he stumbled.

"That's him, you dolt." She pointed at the tow-headed youngster at his father's feet. "It's got to be him. He called him Baby, remember?"

Eulis was sorely in need of a drink and an explanation. He didn't get the drink, but he did get an explanation as Minna Jessup began to speak.

"We buried seven babies before this one here came along," she said softly, and then combed her fingers through Baby Boy's hair to smooth it down. "Isaac couldn't bring hisself to name this one for fear of jinxin' him, too. But Baby's growed some, and he's a mind to take a name, so we brought him along for you to give the blessing."

Eulis swallowed a knot of panic. *They want me to bless a child for good luck? Dear Lord, I haven't had a run of good luck in so long, I wouldn't know it if it ran up my ass and shouted whoopee!*

Letty began to sweat. This was getting too complicated for words.

"Son, have you decided what you're gonna call yourself?" Minna asked.

Baby Boy straightened up and stepped away from his mother's touch. He needed to act like a man when he took a man's name.

"I'm gonna call myself Isaac," he said. "After my pa."

Isaac felt the ground swaying at his feet, and then his spirit rose inside him so high that at that moment, if he'd suddenly taken flight, he wouldn't have been surprised.

"Why, Baby, I think that's a wonderful idea." Minna threaded her fingers through her husband's hand and squeezed gently for comfort.

"Come on, Preacher, let's do it," Isaac said suddenly. "Where do we go and what do we do?"

"We'll be needin' water to sprinkle on his head," Minna said. She remembered seeing her younger sisters and brothers christened back home in Massachusetts.

"How 'bout some peach juice?" Baby Boy asked. "It was right tasty, and there's plenty left in the can inside."

Before anyone could stop him, he'd bolted for the store to retrieve the can from Matt Goslin, and not a grown-up among them could bring themselves to stop his intent. It was, after all, his christening. He should be able to have it done the way he wanted.

Eulis leaned against the hitching post to still his rolling belly. "This is a fine mess," he whispered.

"Straighten up," Letty hissed, and goosed him in the ribs to make her point just as Minna turned to them and smiled.

Eulis wiped the sweat from his brow and nodded.

"Right hot for this time of year, don't you think?"

Minna smiled as Baby Boy came back with his juice.

Eulis accepted the can with all the dignity he could manage, and right there in the middle of the street in Lizard Flats, Baby Boy Jessup changed his name with a spoonful of peach juice and the blessing of a man who, until yesterday, had only used the word of God in profanity.

"I christen thee, Isaac . . . uh, what's your last name, sir?" Eulis looked to Isaac for an answer.

"Jessup."

Eulis nodded and repeated. "I christen thee Isaac Jessup. And, uh, let no man put asunder."

Letty groaned then muttered beneath her breath. "That's for weddings you dolt."

But the Jessups didn't seem to mind. And when Eulis sprinkled another dollop of peach juice on the child's head for good measure, there wasn't a dry eye among the family from Crawler's Mill.

For lack of something else to say, Eulis suddenly lifted the can of peach juice in a toast.

"To young Isaac Jessup," he said, then took a sip from the edge, careful not to cut his lip on the jagged opening.

As if it were every day that a preacher baptized with a can of peach juice, the can was passed from hand to hand with dignity as if it had been a magnum of champagne.

Each witness to Baby Boy's emergence from the chrysalis of childhood into manhood sipped from the tin. When it came to Isaac, the father, he had to swallow tears before he could swallow the juice.

Eulis beamed. It was over and he hadn't messed up yet. "Congratulations, young man. It's been a pleasure to meet you."

Baby Boy threw back his shoulders and tilted his chin. "My name is Isaac."

Minna cupped the back of her son's head. "Come along home, young Isaac. You and your pa have a lot of work to catch up on, and you've got a week's worth of schoolin' that you missed."

"Yes, ma'am," young Isaac said proudly.

"Yes, ma'am," his father echoed, and then winked at his wife.

About the time that the Jessup family was leaving Lizard Flats, Miles Crutchaw was pulling his team and wagon to a halt in front of the White Dove Saloon.

"Whoa!" he cried. The mules slowed and then stopped.

He wrapped the reins around the hand-brake and then smiled down at the woman sleeping in his lap. Truly was not a woman accustomed to the trail and had suffered greatly through the trip from Sweetgrass Junction to Lizard Flats. She'd been bounced and bruised until Miles had taken pity and cradled her on his lap.

As he watched her, Truly sighed and then started to stretch. As she did, she came close to falling out of her dress. The once-yellow satin was now nearer in color to dusty butter, her henna-red curls had come down long ago and hung around her face in wild abandon. The rouge that she wore on her cheeks and her mouth had long since disappeared. She'd never been so mussed, nor had Miles thought she'd been prettier.

"We're here, Truly. Just like I promised. While you're getting a bath and some new clothes, I'm gonna find us that preacher. Before we leave here today, you'll be Mrs. Miles Crutchaw or I'll know the reason why."

Truly wiggled with joy. She'd never believed that a whore like her could be redeemed by the love of a good man, but she was about to change her mind. Right now, she'd lie down and die for Miles Crutchaw.

A man and a woman turned the corner and headed down the street toward Miles' wagon. When he saw the white clerical collar around Eulis's neck, he grinned.

"Hey Preacher!" Miles called.

Eulis groaned beneath his breath. He wanted a drink and something to eat. But he could tell by the look on Letty's face that it wasn't about to happen. Not here. Not yet.

"Yes sir, I'm Reverend Howe."

"I reckon I'll be needing your services," Miles said. "This here is Truly Fine, my fiancée."

He pronounced the word, fi-ancy. Truly could have cared less. He loved her. He could call her mud for all she cared and it would make her no difference.

"We want to be married today. Got ourselves a long way to go and want to do this proper."

Letty's eyes widened. She tried not to stare, but it was impossible to stop. The big man in the wagon was dressed to the hilt. Fine clothes. Good leather on his shoes. A smile that was as bright as all outdoors. And he was sitting there claiming to be in love with Truly? Her friend, but still a whore in a yellow satin dress?

Truly's chin went up. She saw the look of disbelief on the woman's face, but at first didn't recognize her old friend, Letty. The faded dress from Matt Goslin's store window had gone a long way toward changing Letty's appearance. Without the red satin and black fringe, her brown curls looked almost proper.

"I'll be needing a bath first," Truly said.

"And clothes," Miles added. "Whatever she wants, she can have. Nothin's too good for my Truly."

Letty's eyes teared with envy and remorse. She thought of her Jim, who lay rotting in his grave, and of the preacher that she'd killed, then she sighed. It was too late for her to realize her dreams. Jim LaSalle was dead and so was the preacher, and she was in cahoots with the town drunk in the name of God and all He stood for. She looked away, believing that Truly didn't want her man to know that they'd been friends. But once Truly was down off the wagon, Letty whispered in her ear.

"Truly, it's me, Letty. Matt Goslin's down at a wedding. I'll help you find some clothes and show you where you can bathe."

"Letty? Is it really you?" Truly cried, and then promptly threw her arms around Letty's neck and started to cry.

Concerned, Miles started toward her when Truly turned and hugged him next.

"Miles, this is my dear friend, Leticia Murphy. She and I worked together at the White Dove."

Relieved, Miles grinned and held out his hand. "Pleased to meet you, Miss Murphy. I trust that you'll stand up for my Truly as her maid of honor?"

Letty gasped as if she'd been stomach punched as her heart filled with shame. She didn't deserve such an honor. Could this day get any worse?

"Let's hurry," Truly said. "I've put this off far too long."

Letty led her away, still pondering Truly's good luck, while Truly tried to ignore the fact that Letty's dress was faded in front and not in the back, then shrugged off the thought as no concern of hers. The only one who mattered in her life was Miles. She'd see to it that he spent the rest of his life with a smile on his face.

The store offered little in the way of choice, but a brown homespun with a narrow white collar and a fitted bodice suddenly became the most beautiful of dresses on Truly Fine.

Still damp from her borrowed bath, she pulled and tugged at the fabric, anxious to get back to Miles and bolted out of the back room of the general store with the last two buttons still undone. Letty followed in a daze, hoping that Eulis hadn't disappeared on her. When Miles saw her, the smile slid off his face. He inhaled slowly, amazed by her transformation. The worldly look was gone with the satin. The fussy red curls were pulled back from her face, giving her the appearance of a girl, rather than the woman she'd been for years.

"Oh my, Truly, you look just fine — truly fine."

She grinned.

"I'm ready, Miles."

He swooped her from the sidewalk and into his arms, twirling her around beneath the afternoon sun and laughing at the dust that coated his boots and pant legs.

"Not half as ready as I am, girl. Not nearly by half."

For the first time in her entire life, Truly Fine blushed.

"Preacher man. Do your thing," Miles

ordered, and set his blushing bride down beside him before she could change her mind.

"Here? You want me to marry you right here in the street?"

Miles shrugged at the preacher's question. "Why not? One place is as good as another. Beside, it ain't the place, it's the woman that matters."

At that vow of love, Letty couldn't hold back. Tears flowed down her cheeks. She was sick — sick to death at the hand fate had dealt her.

"Stop sniveling, Letty, and hand me my book," Eulis grumbled. Every time he looked at her, Letty seemed to be bawling. She should have the headache he had, then she'd have something to bawl about.

Letty did as she was told.

"Ashes to ashes, dust to —"

Letty kicked him in the shins. "That was for the buryin'," she muttered. "This is a wedding, you dolt."

It had ceased to matter to Letty or Eulis that anyone should think their banter strange. They were too busy trying to endure that which they had wrought.

"I knew that," Eulis argued, and turned several pages in his book. He smiled benignly at Miles. "I had turned to the wrong page," he said. "Please excuse me."

Truly smiled and leaned against Miles' massive arm. She didn't care what page they were on as long as it got her married.

Eulis began. "Dearly beloved . . ." And a few minutes later, he stood on the sidewalk, watching with a bemused expression as the big man scooped his new wife into his arms and carried her to the wagon across the street without letting her feet touch the ground. Then to Eulis's surprise, Miles Crutchaw came back.

"Here," Miles said, and handed Eulis a small pouch.

"What's this?" Eulis asked.

Miles grinned. "I reckon you could call it payment for services rendered."

Eulis's eyes brightened. He hadn't thought about getting paid for any of this. Only getting it over without being hanged.

"Well now, this is very thoughtful of you," Eulis said. But when he peeked inside, the smile on his face froze. He gasped, then poked a finger into the sack, just to make sure he wasn't seeing things.

"Is this —"

Miles nodded. "Struck it rich a while back. Thought I ought to share some with the man who made my dream come true."

"And that would be me?" Eulis asked.

"Thanks to you, Truly is my wife."

Eulis beamed. "It was my pleasure, I'm sure."

Miles grinned. "I reckon we'll be movin' on," he said. "It's a ways to Dodge City."

"Is that where you live?" Eulis asked.

"No. I'm thinkin' of takin' Truly to San Francisco. I hear tell they've got a lot of refinement out there. Truly deserves to live like a lady. The West is hard on women, you know."

Eulis kept fingering the pouch full of nuggets. Making small talk wasn't easy for a man who hadn't said much more than, 'give me a drink,' for the last ten years of his life. But the man had paid him in gold, and he felt obligated to visit until the man called it quits.

"So, Dodge City is just a whistle stop on your way to bigger and better things is it?"

Miles shook his head. "Naw. But I heard tell that they're hangin' Kiowa Bill up there sometime next week. He once killed a friend of mine. Thought I might stay around long enough to see that."

Miles Crutchaw's voice faded away as Eulis's head started to pound. Kiowa Bill was in Dodge City. He was going to hang.

Eulis's fingers were twitching as he retied the string around the pouch and dropped it in his pocket while Miles Crutchaw and his wife drove away. He could hear Letty sniffling as she sidled up, but for the life of him, he couldn't find the words to speak. He kept seeing his mother's blood on the ground and hearing his little brother's screams.

Letty thought briefly of the pouch of gold and then dabbed at her eyes as the newlyweds pulled out of town.

"Wonder where they're going?" she asked.

Eulis shrugged. An idea was forming in the back of his mind. It was radical, but he'd gotten away with the impersonation so far. Who was to say it couldn't continue. "Dodge City. They're goin' to Dodge City," he mumbled. "And I need a drink."

Letty grabbed his arm. "Only a small one," she urged. "There's still tonight."

Eulis stopped. "What the hell's tonight?"

"The revival under the brush arbor everyone's been building. And don't curse. Preachers don't curse," Letty warned.

"I can't preach no full-blown sermon, and most preachers don't poke whores neither," Eulis grumbled. His frustration set off a new spate of tears to running down Letty's cheeks. "Well hell, I mean heck. I didn't mean to go and make you cry.

Come on. Let's go get ourselves somethin' to eat while you tell me what else it is I got to do before I can get myself some rest."

Consoled by the fact that Eulis seemed ready to do as she bid, Letty took him by the arm and headed toward the White Dove Saloon. She could fry up some side meat and put it between biscuits. Will always kept cold biscuits just in case.

"It's just a sermon," Letty said. "One little sermon. After that, the preacher will be on his way to the next stop on his missionary trip. You can handle one little old bitty sermon, now, can't you Reverend?"

Eulis sighed. He wished his body could rise to the occasion that her look demanded, but so far, the only thing hard on his body was the preacher's change jingling in the pockets of his pants.

"I reckon I can," he said. "What's one more sermon in the face of what we've already done?"

Tears dried on Letty's face, replaced by an expression of relief.

"That's the spirit!"

"Don't say that word," Eulis muttered. "The only spirit I want is in a corked bottle."

Letty grabbed him by the arm and led him across the street. "All in good time,

Reverend Howe. All in good time."

Eulis didn't even notice that she'd called him by his ill-gotten name, because he was beginning to believe his own deception.

A small child darted across the street after a runaway kitten just as a big black horse entered town. The couple upon its back rode tall and quiet with little wasted motion, moving with the horse's gait as if they were one.

It took Matt Goslin exactly thirty seconds to remember where he'd last seen that man. And when he did, he bolted inside his store and checked to see if the gun he kept behind the counter was loaded. It was. But little good it would be against the Breed if he chose to wreak the havoc for which he was known.

Joe Redhawk felt the stares before he saw the people. It did no good to care. For years it had been the same. If the sight of his brown skin and black hair didn't strike fear in a white woman's eyes, the gun on his hip did. It made no difference that he'd abandoned his Indian way of dress, and for the most part, his Indian ways. To them, he would always be a half-breed.

But that was before he'd met the woman

who rode behind him. Before Caitie O'Shea. Now, unless something or someone stopped them, he was about to do something he'd never imagined. Not even in his wildest dreams. The half-breed was taking a wife.

Within moments of the sighting, word of the gunfighter's appearance in Lizard Flats spread. Alfonso Worthy rolled from his marriage bed in fear that the bank was in danger of being robbed. The news left Sophie Hollis Worthy in a fainting fit, certain that her latest bed partner would suffer a fate similar to that of her first, and she would be forced to bury another man before she'd barely tried him out.

The smithy fired up the forge for no other reason than to have something to do, although a coal fire would do little to stop a man of Breed's reputation.

Will the Bartender polished a few more glasses and popped the top on two new bottles. If things went according to usual, everyone in town would belly up to the bar for a shot of false courage.

Letty sat at a chair by the window in her room, watching Eulis sleeping the sleep of the dead. At the thought, she shuddered. She'd had her fill of dead men for one day.

But when she glanced out the window

and saw the man riding in on that big black horse, she figured it was possible, just possible, that they'd be needing a new grave dug. And if Eulis came up missing in the middle of the need, someone might notice that the preacher wasn't all he should be. Her anxiety increased as she watched him ride past.

The rider's face was shadowed by a wide-brimmed hat that was as black as the hair hanging down around his collar. But she saw the way he wore his guns, and the way he sat loose in the saddle and knew she was right to worry. A gunslinger had come to Lizard Flats. Of all the faceless men who'd come and gone in her life, he was one she had not forgotten. He'd been kind, even gentle when he'd taken her to bed, and if she remembered correctly, had left her a five dollar gold piece instead of the dollar for which she'd asked.

As he passed, Letty noticed someone rode at his back. Someone small and shorn like a boy, but dressed in the fringed tunic of an Indian squaw. Someone whose bare legs shone as fair and white as the skin on Letty's own breasts.

"What on earth?" Letty muttered.

"Jus' pass me the bottle."

She frowned at the lump of a man on her

bed, walked over to where he was sleeping, and thumped him in the middle of the belly with a balled-up fist.

"Wake the hell up," she hissed. "Trouble just rode into town."

Eulis grabbed his belly as he rolled out of the bed. "Why did you hit me?"

"Look out the window," she said.

Eulis kept rubbing his stomach. "I still don't see why you had to go and hit me. I wasn't hurtin' you none and I don't see what you're so all-fired —"

He leaned all the way out the window, then choked on his complaint. He'd seen the man before, in person as well as on wanted posters. He shuddered and ducked back into the room.

"I need a drink."

Letty handed him a dipper of water.

"Not that kind of drink," Eulis grumbled, and poured it back into the pitcher on the dresser.

"It's that or nothin'," Letty warned. "Put on your coat. Maybe you can stop whatever's about to happen."

Eulis gawked. "Why on earth would I be doin' somethin' like that?"

"Because you're the preacher, that's why," she said, and handed him his suit coat. "And because if that gunslinger kills someone, they're gonna be needing a grave. And if there's no one to dig it, they might get to wonderin' just where you have gone."

Eulis went pale. With each passing moment, they kept getting deeper and deeper into the lie. And like Letty, he was so lost between fact and fiction that it hardly mattered anymore. He left the room, buttoning his coat and slicking down his hair. He needed to look good when he confronted the gunslinger. Maybe a killing could be averted. It was, after all, what a real man of God should do.

And So It Continues

Eulis was running when he got to the sidewalk. But the closer he got to the man on the horse, the slower his steps became. His first suspicion had been right. It was the Breed! Then Letty pushed him forward, and it was too late to change his mind about retreat.

The gunfighter's eyes held no expression, except when he looked at the tiny woman riding behind him. When he did, something within him seemed to change. It was that single spark of humanity that gave Eulis the courage he needed. He looked up at the gunslinger, meeting his dark, brooding stare. While he was trying to find the right words to say, the Breed spoke first.

"Are you the preacher?" Joe Redhawk asked.

"Yes, I'm Reverend Howe. How may I be of service?"

Joe dismounted and then turned, lifting Caitie high into the air and then standing her down beside him.

Caitie lifted her chin. "We've come to marry."

Eulis was momentarily speechless. It was Matt Goslin who spoke up.

"You ain't tryin' to tell us that you, a white woman, are gonna marry no half-breed?"

Joe went still. Caitie felt his anger, but it was nothing to the rage that overwhelmed her.

"I'll not be tellin' ye anything, ye randy old goat."

Shocked by the viciousness of her manner, Matt frowned.

"Now see here —"

"Be gone," Caitie raged, waving him away with one sweep of her hand. "If I was after lookin' at apes, I would have been stayin' in Mudhen Crossing and watchin' Milt and Art Bolin hang."

Letty gasped. She'd heard of them. They were troublemakers of the worst sort. Too stupid to hurt anyone except themselves, they still managed to raise hell wherever they'd gone.

"The Bolin Brothers are going to hang?" Letty asked.

"And happy to be doin' so," Caitie said. "It was meself, or the noose. They chose the rope, I'm told."

Joe grinned. The residents of Lizard Flats were getting a giant dose of Caitie's blarney. They had no way of knowing that the Bolins were safe in a Territorial prison. For the time being, well out of Caitie O'Shea's way.

But Caitie wasn't through. She glared at the fancy dressed preacher and the woman beside him, daring them to add to Matt Goslin's remarks.

"Now, as for the marryin'. Are ye about performin' the ceremony, or are ye of a mind to stand with your jaw to your knees, tryin' to swallow yerself whole?"

Eulis shut his mouth. It was the least he could do in the face of such fury.

"I'd be pleased to marry you, Miss . . . Miss. . . ."

"Caitlin O'Shea, late of Dublin, Ireland, now residin' wherever this man chooses to take me."

"I hope you ain't livin' here," Matt muttered. "People ain't gonna feel right with a gunslinger in town. And they won't take kindly to no white woman marryin' up with an Injun, even if he is half white."

It was the insult to Caitie that Joe couldn't ignore. His hand was on the hilt of his gun and Matt Goslin was wishing he'd kept his big mouth shut when Caitie stepped between them and poked her finger sharply in the middle of Matt's belly.

"Joe Redhawk and meself will not be lingerin' long in this hole of a town, so don't concern yerself where we'll be layin' our heads."

Faced with the fury of such a tiny female, Matt decided that a retreat was in his best interest.

"I'll just be goin' now," he said.

No one seemed to care, and he'd never been happier for being snubbed. He quickly disappeared into his store.

"Where do you want me to hold the ceremony?" Eulis asked.

Joe had no answer. Where had not been an issue. Asking Caitie to marry him had taken all the guts that he had. The actual ceremony was an afterthought. In his heart, she was already his.

But Caitie had other issues to raise. "I'm seein' that ye're not a priest."

Eulis sighed. He wasn't even a preacher, but at this point, that fact was redundant. He shook his head.

She frowned. "I'm supposin' it hardly matters. I haven't been to confession since I was seven years of age." Then she glanced at Joe, gauging his patience before turning to Eulis again. "I don't suppose ye'd be havin' a church here, either?"

Since everyone else had been running their mouths, Letty decided it was time she tossed her opinions around.

"We have an arbor. It's new. Brand new."

Caitie frowned. "An arbor? I'm not knowin' the name."

"It's sort of an outdoor church. We built it special, for the preacher's arrival," Letty said. "He's giving a revival sermon in it tonight, but you could have the use of it first if you wanted."

"Is it far?" Caitie asked.

"At the edge of town. Up on the hill opposite the cemetery."

Joe lifted Caitie back into the saddle. For him, the decision had already been made.

"Just a little further, girl. Are you with me?"

Caitie nodded. "Aye, Joe. All the way."

He sighed. The sound of his name on her lips made him weak inside. He wondered if this was what it felt like to love. If it was, it was both the best and the worst thing he'd ever experienced. He swung up behind her and rode out of town without looking to see if the preacher was following.

By the time they reached the arbor, word had spread through town that the Breed had come to get married. Most of the town, including the newlyweds, Alfonso and Sophie Worthy, came to bear witness. Sophie had a prance in her step and a smile on her face that hadn't been there since her dearly beloved Nardin had passed. Alfonso swaggered.

For Eulis, it would be his fourth illegal ceremony in a single day, not counting the two men that he and Letty had buried. For a drunk, it was a hell of a way to get a glow.

As he took his place at the pulpit, he realized he was beginning to enjoy the power with which his words were being received. He opened his book to the same place he'd used when marrying Alfonso and Sophie.

"Dearly beloved, we meet here beneath this roof to join these two people in the bonds of wedlock." Eulis couldn't bring himself to say the word, holy. He gazed out across the assembly with what he hoped was benign interest. "So we begin. Do you —"

Caitie interrupted. "I, Caitie, am takin' thee Joseph, as me lawfully wedded husband."

Caitie's words rang in Joe's ears. Her face slid in and out of focus as he stared down at the freckles and the upturned nose and wondered how anyone could have mistaken her for a boy.

"I'm promisin' everythin' to him, for always, and I'm gladly pledgin' meself to the only man I ever knew that didn't give up on me."

Joe didn't know if it was happening, but he felt as if he'd risen a good foot from the floor. Her words made him weak, but her love made him strong. When she slid that tiny hand into his palm, he knew he could have walked blind through a hailstorm and not been harmed.

Eulis cleared his throat. She'd said all there was to say and more. He felt awe in the presence of such faith, and a bit of shame that he was not a true man of the cloth to give credence to the love that was so obviously between them.

"So be it," he said. "And do you, Breed . . . I mean, Joe —"

Again he was lost. He didn't have to look to know that Letty was standing behind him. He could hear her hissing like a pissed-off goose. It wasn't his fault he kept getting this part wrong. He just didn't know what to call the man.

To his relief, Joe took over.

"I, Joseph Redhawk, promise in front of everyone here that I'll take care of and love

Caitlin O'Shea for as long as I live. I will protect her and see that she has all she needs. And I will always keep my word, so help me God."

Caitie beamed. It was done.

Eulis cleared his throat. "Then I pronounce you man and wife. Live long and prosper." He grinned when the congregation broke into a round of applause. It *had* sounded good, even to him.

Joe grinned at the woman who stood at his side.

"If you had a regret, girl, it's too late now."

She arched her eyebrows as he lifted her into his arms and headed for his horse.

"I'm havin' no regrets, Joe Redhawk, but I'm after thinkin' it's time ye stopped callin' me girl."

Joe set her in the saddle and then mounted behind her. To everyone's delight, he kissed her soundly.

"Hang on, Caitie girl. If you get tired, put your arms around me. I won't let you fall."

Caitie sighed. Five of the sweetest words she'd ever heard. *I won't let you fall.* Tears blurred her vision as she glanced at the evening sun. It was time to look ahead, not back. With Joe beside her, she would never be afraid again.

"Well now," Eulis said, as the towns-people watched them riding away. "That was a fine ending to an eventful day."

Letty chewed nervously on her lower lip. If this day were only over, she might rest easy. But there was still tonight, and the sermon. After that, she had to find a believable way to get the preacher out of town and Eulis back into character. Unfortunately, her ideas had gone dry. The only hope she had was that Eulis would come up with something on his own.

Unbeknownst to her, he already had. And if she'd had an inkling of his plans, he would have already been packing for an early escape. But she knew nothing except that people kept pouring into town like mice to a threshing. She'd not known there were this many people in the entire Territory.

THE RECKONING

The arbor sat on the hilltop like a hen roost. Nothing above the brushy roof but sky. Nothing below it but rows of boards atop borrowed kegs and boxes. Slipshod pews that slowly filled with a motley assortment of people as the day continued to die.

They'd been arriving for hours. Families in the Territory eager for the first hint of religion to come their way in years. They came on foot. By horseback. In wagons. But they came.

Thin-faced, ropey-skinned men tanned to a leathery red like the dirt beneath their feet. Windblown and harried women, old before their time with children scurrying around their skirt tails like little quail trying to get up the nerve to leave the covey. The slipshod pews slowly filled with a mingling of work-weary and weathered humanity.

Randall Howe would have been shocked to know that so many souls were thirsting for need of The Word. Eulis Potter was scared shitless that they expected it to come from him.

Chilled with nerves, despite the lingering heat of the dying day, Eulis clutched the Bible to his chest. He would rather it had been a bottle of Turkey Red whiskey, but all in all, he'd made it through in better shape than he would have imagined.

Letty Murphy was sick at heart. She hadn't thought it possible, but she felt worse than she had when her Jim had been killed. It had been, without doubt, the worst day of her life. She stared at Eulis with something akin to awe, unable to believe that he'd actually fooled so many, yet thankful that it had been done.

But the older the day got, the harder it became for her to separate Eulis the Preacher from Eulis the Drunk. The longer she looked at his clean-shaven face and neatly parted hair, the fine clothes and broad smile, the more believable he became.

June bugs began diving through the brushy rooftop, heading for the oil lanterns hanging beneath the rafters. Several hounds bayed from the settlers' wagons as coyotes howled on a nearby ridge.

Blue shadows crept across the prairie. Night moths danced dangerously close to the lamplight while the people laughed and talked, waiting for the services to begin.

When no one was looking, Eulis gave the part in his hair a final pat and then clutched the Bible even tighter, hoping that inspiration would transfer itself from it to his head. It was time. With a nod to Letty, Eulis started down the aisle between the pews, taking slow, measured steps that puffed dust onto the tips of his fine black shoes and gave him a trail-weary appearance the assembly could appreciate.

Letty headed for a seat down front. The urge to stay close to Eulis was still strong. She ignored the sly, sidelong glances the men gave her, as well as the indignant whispers from the good women of the area. She knew better than most how far she'd fallen. They just didn't understand that she felt obliged to sit as close to salvation as she could get.

And after the day that she'd had, her general store dress was much the worse for wear. Not only had the years of bright sunlight faded its front, but it had weakened the homespun fabric, as well. Her womanly charms were pushing their luck with each bounce of her step. The threads around the handworked buttonholes were fraying and stretching with each sway of her breasts. But Letty didn't see, and if she had, was past caring. She took a seat at the outside end of the first pew, sighing with relief as Eulis continued on with kingly aplomb.

Eulis nodded and smiled to everyone he passed, relishing the silence that accompanied his arrival into their midst. It was a power unlike any he'd ever known. Yet in the midst of that power, was a fear that matched it. Fear that he would fail. Fear that they would be found out. He wondered how long it took to die when hanged, then stepped behind the pulpit and turned to face the congregation.

Letty stared at him, wide-eyed and pale from her front row seat.

Seeing as he was now a man of God, Eulis tried not to stare at her body. But it was hard to look away. She appeared as if she'd been tamped and packed inside that two-tone dress like gunpowder down the barrel of a long rifle. Sweat beaded and ran out from under her brown curls like rainwater down a pane of glass. He looked away, unwilling to let her fear feed his own. His gaze slid from Letty to the rest of the congregation. Seventy-odd people stared back.

Unsmiling.

Unmoving.

It was a daunting and fearful sight.

Snickers came from the back benches. Another whisper from the front. His nervousness increased. The urge to look down and check his fly was overwhelming, but he was afraid that if he found it undone, he wouldn't have the courage to turn and fasten it up. Moisture ran down the inside of his pant legs, and he prayed for all he was worth that it was only sweat. A horse neighed. A child cried. And a hound bayed as a sliver of moon appeared in the night sky over the arbor. He took a deep breath. It was now or never.

The congregation shifted nervously. He felt them slipping away. His throat tightened. Where on earth did one start a sermon. Then it came to him. A song! They needed a song.

"You there." He pointed to Will the Bartender. "I'm told you have a fine singing voice, sir. Would you be so kind as to step forward and lead us in some songs?"

Will swaggered as he got up from his seat. To be called upon by such a man was an honor. He would have been shocked to know that it was Eulis who had asked. Nevertheless, he felt great pride that someone knew of his gift.

"I'd be honored," Will said, and turned to face the congregation. "First we'll sing

Nearer My God to Thee. After that, we'll do *Oh for a Thousand Tongues to Sing.* Then we'll finish out with a round of *Onward Christian Soldiers.* Will that be all right with you, Reverend Howe?"

Eulis nodded. At this point, anything was all right with him.

Will burst forth into song. His exuberance was such that even though some of the congregation didn't know the words, they still made a joyful noise unto the Lord.

Eulis said a prayer of his own while the people sang. There was no getting around the fact that when the songs were over, he would have to begin.

Letty was fidgeting in the seat below. Although Eulis refused to look directly at her, he could see that faded blue-white dress from the corner of his eye, fluttering like a moth to a flame. She hadn't been still a minute since he'd taken the pulpit, and he wondered if she just needed to pee. If she did, it would be simpler all around if she snuck out beyond the glow of lantern lights and took a leak behind one of the wagons. There wouldn't be anyone out there but a dog that might see her. Then he wondered why he cared who saw her bare behind. There were few men in the

Territory who hadn't seen all there was to see of Letty Murphy.

He set the Bible down on the pulpit and inhaled, then closed his eyes and counted to ten. Not because it was calming. It was just as far as he could count and not lose track. The Bible fell open to the middle with a plop. Eulis looked down at the jumble of words and knew that it would take him a month just to sound out the ones on the page before him.

Before he knew it, the singing was over and it was time to begin. As a child, Eulis had heard many sermons. And without fail, every preacher he'd ever heard had put the fear of God into him in such a way that he would crawl beneath the covers of his bed and hope he woke to see another day.

He looked at the people once more. They were waiting. He took a deep breath and leaned forward. Staring intently into their faces, he suddenly slapped the flat of his hand against the open pages of The Book.

"REPENT!"

Two women halfway down the aisle and three seats to the left shuddered in their seats, clutching their children to their bosoms.

"SINNERS ARE AMONG YOU!"

He pointed in random throughout the

congregation and succeeded in making several people give their neighbors a suspicious glance.

"WHISKEY IS THE DRINK OF THE DEVIL!"

Someone shouted, "Amen!" A woman wailed in agreement.

My God, Letty thought. *Has he lost his mind? He's talking about himself . . . and about me.*

"FORNICATION IS THE DOWN-FALL OF THE FAMILY!"

A man fidgeted in the back of the arbor as his woman glared him into next week. Eulis gloated. He was hitting home with some truths, he could feel it.

He leaned forward again. This time, his eyes were glowing with the fire of knowing he'd become a powerhouse onto himself. Letty buried her face in her hands, refusing to look at the monster she'd unwittingly created. Hearing these truths being uttered from his mouth was painful. It was almost as if he'd become the preacher he was pretending to be.

Then she looked up. With tears drying on her face, she saw Eulis Potter in a new and frightening light. Maybe he *was* a man of God! What if he'd *become* that which they'd buried? She gasped at the thought.

The way she saw it, there could be but one explanation. Either God had taken a hand in their misdeeds and decided to right the wrongs, or the ghost of the real Randall Howe had risen from his unhallowed grave and taken over the body of Eulis the Drunk.

Letty moaned, swaying where she sat. Several people nearby looked at her with renewed speculation. This was a powerful preacher indeed if he'd gotten the attention of a whore like Letty Murphy.

Eulis glanced toward Letty. She was turning paler by the minute. He feared the events of the day were finally getting to her, but he couldn't spare her more than a moment of thought. The congregation was in the palms of his hands and he had no intention of giving up his glory. This feeling was as strong as a stiff drink and he began to wonder if it was possible to substitute one for the other.

And all of a sudden, a pair of hounds that had been tied to a nearby wagon suddenly broke loose. They came running down the center of the aisle, baying and howling as the went. The momentary disturbance sent a round of giggles skittering across the assembly. Some young boys bolted, dashing after the dogs in a flurry of skinny arms and legs. Men on the aisle seats began doing their part by grabbing at the trailing ropes as the dogs ran past. But they missed, and the dogs continued toward a destination only they knew.

Eulis grinned. Nothing like a little action to liven up the place. While he was waiting for someone to curtail the animals, he happened to look up into the brushy arbor above his head. Within seconds, his heart skipped a beat. Two black, beady eyes were looking back. He stiffened with fear.

Dear Lord, it's the Devil!

He looked closer, and then relaxed. To the best of his knowledge, the Devil did not have a small, pointed nose or black, mask-like markings on his face. The urge to giggle with relief was overwhelming as he realized it was only a half-grown raccoon that had taken refuge in the brush arbor roof. That explained why the dogs had come running. They'd probably picked up the animal's scent.

But it would seem that the raccoon had enough of arbors and dogs. While everyone was involved in corralling the hounds, the raccoon leapt down from the roof, bouncing once at Eulis's feet and then running for the closest shelter, which happened to be underneath the skirts of Letty Murphy's store-bought dress.

"HELLSFIRE!"

Eulis hadn't mean to shout. But he was so startled by the raccoon's sudden descent that he jumped back in fright. It was only after he saw the varmit disappear that he realized he was the only one who'd seen him fall.

The congregation may have missed the animal's leap, but they hadn't missed hearing the preacher curse. All eyes turned away from the dogs to the front of the arbor in time to see Letty Murphy jump from her seat. With a shriek of pure terror, she commenced to tearing at her skirts, screaming and clawing in wild abandon.

Eulis stared in disbelief as her eyes rolled back in her head. It was then he realized that the raccoon had gone up her dress!

Letty beat at her clothes and commenced to tearing at her hair. "I'm possessed! Help me, Jesus! I'm possessed. The Devil is clawing at my legs, so help me God! Save me, Jesus, save me!"

Several people jumped to their feet as the hounds bolted past. But they couldn't catch them. They were after the raccoon that had, once again, escaped unseen.

Eulis was stunned by Letty's behavior, as well as her sudden attack of conscience. And right before his eyes, she suddenly fell to the floor; twitching and jerking like a woman in a fit.

Someone jumped up in back and shouted, "Hallelujah!"

The congregation was impressed that the preacher's words had been strong enough to sway a strumpet from the White Dove Saloon. And it was obvious she was swayed. She'd dropped to the floor before their eyes and now was crying and talking all crazy. Not a one of them understood a word that she said.

They began to mutter among themselves. This was powerful preaching indeed. The preacher hadn't been in the pulpit five minutes and already the town's worst sinner had gotten The Holy Ghost and was lying in the dirt and talking in tongues.

The raccoon was gone, but the spirit that it had delivered unto them was not.

"Praise the Lord and Reverend Howe," someone shouted.

It was followed by a chorus of "Amens" that stirred Eulis's very soul. For a moment, he was speechless, but he knew it was imperative to continue now that he had them firm in his grasp.

Letty was still writhing on the floor at his feet as he leaned forward. Piercing each and every one of them with a watery stare,

412

he pointed a finger slowly across the benches and shouted.

"REPENT YE OF LITTLE FAITH!"

Someone moaned. He turned to look. It was Letty.

In fascinated horror, he watched as the straining buttons down the front of her rotting, store-bought dress began to pop. And as they did, several pounds of blossoming bosom began to escape from the cloth. In places she seemed to explode from the bodice. In others, her breasts simply rolled, rippling out from behind the blue-white fabric in soft abandon. It was hard to say who was more stunned, Eulis or his congregation.

But before anyone could react to the sight, Letty bolted to her feet, holding up her arms to the rafters, and shouting the same thing over and over.

"I repent! I repent!"

As if that wasn't enough to stun the congregation, she began running up and down the aisle, her bare bosom bouncing with every leap.

"I am saved! I am saved. Praise the Lord, I am saved!"

Women wept. Men turned away from her nudity. If she was turning over a new leaf, it was no longer seemly to be staring at her womanly charms.

Eulis was in shock as Letty paused at the front of the arbor and lifted her skirts, baring even more of herself to the stunned observers.

"See here! The marks of the Devil are upon my flesh. He was about to take me under and the Good Lord has driven him away. Tonight I am a new woman."

Those nearest her spoke out in shock. "Yes, yes," they shouted, passing the news down the line. "The scratches are there like she said. The blood is fresh and running. Praise God!"

Along with joy, several groans of regret could be heard. Her change of heart now left the single men of Lizard Flats with no whore to ease their manly pains. With Truly Fine gone more than a year now and Letty changing before their very eyes, the last loose lady of Lizard Flats had turned herself into a sanctimonious saint.

"Preacher!"

Letty's shout reverberated upon the hill, echoing beyond the lantern light and into the night. Eulis broke out in sweat anew. What if she was about to confess *all* of her sins? Some of them included him.

"Preacher, I want to be cleansed."

Wild-eyed and on the verge of real panic,

he couldn't envision what it was she was asking? Surely she wasn't wanting that bath she was so fond of? Not now. Not when their lives were in jeopardy.

"She wants to be baptized!" someone shouted.

Another cried with joy. "Baptize the whore! Baptize the whore!"

The chant echoed beneath the roof until Eulis's ears were ringing with the noise. In the midst of the fervor, he caught himself repeating it, too, then made himself stop. This was getting out of hand.

"Then so be it," he shouted. "We'll wash her in the blood of Christ and take away her sins."

Anxious to get her energy channeled before she got them both arrested, he led the way down the aisle. On the way out of the arbor, he grabbed a lantern from a nearby pole and headed toward town with his head held high. They wanted to baptize the whore, then by God, he'd baptize the whore.

While it was a shame there was no river in which to perform the deed, Eulis had fond memories of Pete Samuels' watering trough. It had rid him of ants. It should do just fine on Letty Murphy's sins.

We Shall Gather at the River

or

A Reasonable Facsimile Thereof

Eulis led the way down the hill with Letty right beside him. From the waist up, she was nearly naked, yet she didn't seem to notice or care that with every bounce of her step, her right breast bobbed up while her left sort of tilted toward the center. Eulis thought it had something to do with the sway of her walk and tried not to stare.

Will the Bartender was well into the third chorus of *Onward Christian Soldiers* as the congregation turned the corner. Eulis felt like a general leading his army into battle. Out of the darkness, the stable suddenly came into view. He lifted his lantern higher, heading toward the watering trough with single-minded intent.

When they were there, Letty fell to her knees, trying to cover her bare breasts with her hands. She moaned. The Devil's scratches on her legs were stinging something fierce. She looked up at Eulis with wild-glazed eyes.

"Bless me Preacher for I have sinned."

Eulis groaned. *She's gonna say it! By God, she's gonna confess what we've done and they'll hang us both.*

Panic struck him weak. He hung the lantern on the fence and turned toward the congregation. They were waiting for the miracle to be finished, watching with fire in their eyes and expectation on their faces.

Eulis shuddered. Last time he'd seen a crowd look like this it had been a lynch mob. When they started moving forward, he held up his hands.

"Brothers and Sisters."

They inhaled as one, then paused.

"Step back and give this sinner room to grow." *Say! That sounded good, even to me,* Eulis thought.

They did as he bid, widening the space between themselves and the kneeling whore at the watering trough.

Eulis bent down. "Are you sure you know what you're doin'?" he whispered.

Letty looked up, her sweat-glazed face glistening in the dim, yellow light. Her eyes were glassy, her lips sagged. When she didn't answer, his stomach knotted. He'd lost her to the madness, and to the raccoon. Then she clutched at his pant legs.

"Have mercy on me, Preacher. Cleanse my soul."

He leaned closer so that only she could hear. "I'm not a preacher, you fool. Don't you remember nothin'?"

She buried her face in her arms and started to sob. Certain that it was only a matter of time before his identity started to unravel, his only hope was that a dip in the murky water of the trough might do her some good.

"She says she's ready," Eulis announced to the crowd, and sighed with relief at the pleased murmurs that he heard.

To the surprise of them all, Letty stood, then lifted her own skirts and stepped into the trough, lying back in the waters as if she were going to bed.

Bits of green moss scraped loose from the sides and floated to the top, sticking to her skin like a fungus. Her breasts, loose from their binding, moved with the ebb and flow of the water like two raw eggs in a pitcher of beer.

The congregation was behind him, waiting. Eulis didn't know what to do. He'd seen people baptized before but this required more than peach juice. He knew — sort of — what was supposed to occur, but he'd never heard the proper words being said.

"What the hell," he mumbled beneath his breath. "I been playin' by ear all day, anyway. What's one more incident gonna hurt?"

He grabbed Letty's hair and pushed her under.

"One for the money."

He yanked her up.

"Two for the show."

When he sent her back, green slime slid between the fingers of his hand.

"Three to make ready."

This time Letty was gasping for air as he shoved her back down in the trough.

"And four to go!"

Just before she passed out and drowned, he yanked her up the last time.

"Hallelujah, she is saved!"

Letty staggered to her feet, spitting moss and gasping for air while water ran out of her hair and into her eyes. Her clothes were plastered to her body like wet paper on a drinking glass, but there was a light in her eyes that had never been there before.

The congregation seemed stunned by what he'd done, and for a moment Eulis feared the worst. It was Letty who saved the day.

"I am a new woman," she announced, then bowed her head and covered her nudity with her hands.

A woman stepped out of the crowd and threw her shawl over Letty's chest. A sigh went up. The baptism might have been a little unorthodox, but the preacher *was* from back East. Maybe that's the way they did it there. And the whore knew shame. That meant it took.

Will the Bartender started singing again.

Eulis wanted a drink.

It was over.

Jubilant, he turned to face the crowd, only vaguely aware that three people on horseback were coming toward the livery. If they'd come for the baptizing, they were too late. He waved to Will the Bartender.

"Take them back to the hill," he said. "I'll be along as soon as I see to Miss Murphy's welfare."

The congregation marched back toward the arbor with Will in the lead. Eulis turned back to Letty. She was shivering.

"Maybe you should put on some dry clothes," he said.

She stared at him, as if seeing him for the first time. Her chin was quivering, her eyes glassy with shock. Eulis couldn't tell if it was from the chill, or from her emotional state.

"I'm a new woman . . . ain't I, Preacher?"

Eulis rolled his eyes and then lowered his voice. "Snap out of it, Letty. I ain't no preacher and you know it."

Letty blinked, then looked down at her dress and the lack thereof.

"What happened to my dress?"

"You come out of it like a pit poppin' out of a rotten peach. One minute you was all buttoned up and the next thing we knew, you was spillin' out all over."

"Oh Lord," she groaned, and pulled the shawl tighter around her. "I'll never be able to show my face in this town again."

Eulis snorted softly. "Hell, Letty, most of those men in that congregation has seen a whole lot more of you than your bare bosom."

She frowned. "That was the old me. I've been born again and that's a fact."

Eulis sighed. He didn't know how to talk to this Letty. In fact, the longer he thought about, the more convinced he became that he had liked the old Letty better.

They'd ridden at a gallop for miles. Their horses were lathered and heaving, and Charity wondered if she'd ever walk normal again. The closer they'd come to Lizard Flats, the quieter they'd all become.

All of a sudden, Charity felt her shame anew. She was anxious about facing Randall Howe again. Would he laugh at her? Would he deny what he'd done? So many questions were running through her mind that she was surprised when Wade James suddenly reined up.

"I reckon that'll be it," he said, pointing to the small nest of buildings lit up in the distance.

Her stomach knotted. "Should we wait until morning?"

Mehitable snorted. "Not from where I'm sittin'," she muttered. "He's ruined plenty of my sleep. I vote for ruinin' a little bit of his."

Wade James's expression hardened. "He ain't gonna have a need for sleep, or anything else."

Charity gave him a quick, nervous glance. "You have to promise me something, Wade James."

He turned then, his eyes piercing the

darkness to gaze upon her face. "If I can," he said softly.

"Don't do anything that will get you hung."

He turned away, staring at the sprinkling of lights in the distance.

"Let's ride," he said suddenly, and nudged his horse in the flanks.

The two women followed his descent into town. The fact was not lost upon either of them that Wade had promised Charity nothing.

At the edge of town, they slowed down to a trot.

"Something is going on at the other end of town," Charity said. "I see lanterns and people . . . a whole lot of people."

Mehitable's squint deepened. "Maybe we're too late. Maybe they done hanged the bastard."

Charity gasped. As badly as she wanted him to pay, she didn't think she could bear to see a man hanged.

A hundred yards away, Wade suddenly stopped. "Wait here," he said shortly, before riding on ahead.

Charity frowned. "What's he doing?" she asked.

Mehitable sighed. Sometimes her sister could be terribly dense.

"Just do what he says, Sister."

They sat silent in the saddle, watching Wade's every move. A few moments later, the crowd at the livery began to disperse. Charity wished for more light. She needed to see. To make sure that Wade James didn't get himself killed.

Suddenly, Mehitable gasped. Charity looked at her sister.

"What's wrong?"

"Look there!" Mehitable said, pointing to the tall, portly man in the preacher's dark robes.

In the darkness, in the distance, the small white band on the clerical collar of Randall Howe's shirt shone like a star.

"It's him!" Mehitable hissed. Her hand automatically went to her gun.

But Charity wasn't as convinced. There was something different — something that didn't ring true. The need to see his face moved her to ignore Wade James's order. She urged her horse closer.

Letty was thinking real hard on going to change her clothes when she happened to look up. A trio of riders was coming in. At first, she didn't pay them much mind. But then one separated himself from the group, and as he came closer, the skin on the back of her neck began to crawl. It was something about the way he was holding himself stiff. She'd seen enough men bent on vengeance before to know when to duck. She pointed.

"Uh . . . Preacher, I think . . ."

Eulis turned. More strangers. He sighed. Would this day never end?

The cowboy slid off his horse, letting the reins trail to the ground as he faced Eulis.

Eulis pointed toward the livery. "Pete Samuels is the owner, but he's up on the hill. Just put your horses inside for the night. He won't mind."

The cowboy took another step forward.

Letty took a step back.

"I ain't in need of a livery," Wade James said. "I'm looking for a preacher by the name of Randall Howe."

Eulis smiled. "That would be me. How can I help you, my son?"

Wade James drew his gun. "By bleedin' your sorry self out on this ground."

Eulis staggered backward, bumping into the lantern he'd hung earlier. It began to sway upon impact. The light pitched and rolled through the darkness like a ship on the seas.

"You came to kill me? But why? I've done you no harm."

Wade took aim. "It weren't me that you harmed. It was Charity Doone."

Letty screamed.

Eulis wanted to throw up.

Just when he thought his life was over, another rider suddenly came out of the darkness. A young woman leaped from her horse, shouting aloud as she ran.

"No, Wade, don't shoot! For God's sake, don't shoot! That's not the right preacher! That's not Randall Howe!"

Eulis sagged against the fence. It was over. They'd been found out. He looked at Letty. She was down on her knees in prayer. He frowned. Praying was good and all, but there was a time and a place for everything and right now he needed a gun and a horse to get out of town a lot worse than he needed a prayer.

Wade James froze, his finger just shy of pulling the trigger. Although Charity was tugging desperately on his arm, he wouldn't budge.

"What the hell do you mean, he ain't the one? I just asked him his name. He said it was Randall Howe."

Charity swayed, near exhaustion from their frantic ride. She looked to her sister, Mehitable, who was in the act of dismounting.

"Tell him, Hetty. Tell him it's so. I don't know who this man is, but he's not the man who came to our home. He's not the one who shamed me."

Eulis's mouth dropped. If he was understanding this right, the preacher they'd buried hadn't been that true blue. Somehow, just the knowing of that made their deception a little bit easier to bear.

Mehitable got down from her horse. She was dusty and tired and wanted a bath. But she wanted justice more. She stepped closer to the light, peering at Eulis with cold-eyed intent. Finally, she shook her head and stepped back.

"Sister's right," Mehitable said. "That ain't Randall Howe."

The tension slid out of Wade in one breath. "Then who the hell are you, mister? And what's yore game?"

Eulis's mouth was in gear, but his brain had yet to catch up. All he could manage was a flapping jaw.

It was Letty who saved the day. She'd given too much of herself and come too far today to lose it all now. She pulled herself up, mindful to keep the shawl over her state of undress.

"I don't know what your trouble is, mister, but you need to back off." Then she looked at Charity with a pitying gaze. "And I'm real sorry Miss, if you were lied to by some good-lookin' man. It wouldn't be the first time it's happened. But this man here *is* Reverend Randall Howe. Today he's preached four weddings, had a burying, given a boy a Christian name, and baptized a whore. And the night isn't over. Whoever did you wrong must have been an imposter."

Mehitable hissed through her teeth and threw her arms in the air. "I should'a knowed," she snarled. "He was too damned pretty for a preacher." When she realized what she'd just said, she added, "No offense, Reverend Howe."

Thinking how close he'd come to dying, Eulis shuddered. "None taken."

Wade went limp. All the fury he'd been saving had nowhere to go.

"Then I'll have to keep lookin'," he said coldly, and holstered his pistol.

Charity threw herself into his arms. "No, Wade, no," she cried. "No more. Wherever that man is, he can't hurt me anymore."

That's for sure, Eulis thought, but wisely kept his mouth shut.

Wade was torn between wanting to please Charity and the need for revenge. He wrapped his arms around her, his face bearing witness to his internal agony of having suffered a defeat.

"I don't know as how I can live with myself if I don't make that man pay."

Eulis cleared his throat. "Vengeance is mine, saith the Lord."

Mehitable's eyes squinted even more than usual as she considered Eulis's words.

"He's right, Wade James. We've all done our share of takin' Charity's side. Leave the rest of it to the Lord." She arched an eyebrow at the way Wade was holding her sister, and then back at the preacher. "From the looks of things, I'd say the trip wasn't altogether wasted."

Charity hugged Wade even tighter. The thought of losing him was more than she could bear.

Wade James crumbled. But it wasn't so much what Eulis said that changed his mind, as it was the feel of Charity's soft breasts pressed against his chest.

"Then that's that," he said softly, and laid his cheek against the crown of her hair.

Relieved that it was over, Mehitable shoved her hat to the back of her hair and frowned.

"While I ain't got no problem with you lovin' my sister, I'm tellin' you right now that I ain't ridin' all that way back with the two of you tryin' to spoon behind my back. There's a preacher. Get the words said now and ride back to the ranch man and wife."

Wade swallowed nervously as Charity smiled up at him. "I ain't got anythin' to offer her except me."

Mehitable butted in one last time. "It's true you ain't got much now, but marry my sister and I reckon you'll be ownin' the ranch one day."

Wade took a deep breath. "Then if you'll have me, Charity Doone, I'd be honored."

Charity hesitated. Her girlish dreams of a fancy wedding and a party to boot had ended in Randall Howe's bed. Mehitable was right. There was no time to waste. Not when a good-looking man like Wade James was willing to overlook what she'd done.

"As would I, Wade James." Then she whispered for his ears only. "You will always be my hero."

A sideways grin tilted the corner of his mouth. He nodded, then looked up at the man he'd almost killed.

"Uh, say, Preacher?"

"Yes?" Eulis asked.

"If there's no hard feelin's, I reckon I'll be askin' you to marry me and Charity, here."

Eulis managed a smile. "I'd be honored."

A short while later, the trio mounted up and rode away. Eulis was still shaking as he glanced toward the lantern-lit arbor. Faint strains of *Onward Christian Soldiers* drifted down the hill. Will didn't have much of a repertoire, but Eulis couldn't bring himself to worry about that now. He shook his head and then sat down in the dirt with a thump.

"You'll get your good clothes mussed," Letty muttered.

Eulis dropped his head between his knees. "Dirt is the last thing I'll be worryin' about tonight."

Letty thought about it for a minute and then sat down beside him. Her clothes still dripped. Where she was sitting would make mud. But right now, she had to agree. Getting dirty was nothing compared to what they'd endured.

Finally Eulis looked up. "I reckon I'd better get on up the hill and close out the service."

Letty gave him a hard look and decided she could trust him that far. "Considering my dress and all, I think I'll go on to bed."

Eulis sighed. "That sounds good to me. I won't be far behind."

Letty gave him a glare. "Just don't go

gettin' yourself drunk 'fore this is over."

He studied her face, trying to absorb the fact that she was no longer the whore at the White Dove Saloon. He looked away. Leticia Murphy wasn't the only one today who'd had a change of heart. He hadn't told her yet, but he was thinking of giving up drink altogether.

"Did you hear me?" she muttered.

"Yes, ma'am. I heard you loud and clear."

She dragged herself up then. "Well, that's that. I'll see you tomorrow?"

He got to his feet. "Bright and early."

She frowned. Bright and early? She didn't know as how she could manage that. She hadn't been up before daybreak in so long she wasn't sure what a sunrise looked like. And then she smiled to herself as she walked away. It might be nice to see a sunrise again.

A cock crowed, rudely calling Eulis from his sleep. He cracked an eyelid to test the air and groaned at the sight. Daylight. He rolled over and wiped at his face. His head hurt. His belly rolled. He wanted a drink and he needed to pee.

And then he sat up on the side of the bed, saw the suit of clothes and the bowler hat on the nearby chair and groaned. It hadn't been a dream after all. Yesterday he and Letty had pulled the biggest scam in the Kansas Territory and were still alive to tell the tale.

He shuddered.

Therein lay his fear. He didn't want the tale told. He liked his new identity. He didn't want to lose that acceptance. And with that thought, came another. The only person who could ruin it all was Letty herself!

He looked around the room, half expecting to see her standing in the corner, coated in green slime and pointing an accusing finger. Then he remembered she'd gone to bed in the room across the hall.

Alone.

Suddenly too pure to be in the presence of a man who was not her husband.

He thought of the promise she'd made him of free pokes for the rest of his life and sighed. It was the story of his life. Too little, too late. At that point, he got out of bed as the chamber pot beckoned.

Later, as he dug through the preacher's bag for a clean shirt, he began planning his next move. When he was dressed, he strode to the mirror, turning first one way, then the other, looking at his own reflection with a judgmental eye. He thought of that wanted poster under his bed over at the White Dove Saloon.

Dodge City wasn't all that far. He looked at himself in the mirror again. His eyes were bloodshot, his cheeks were red. He needed a drink in the worst way. His gaze slid back to his reflection. Baths and new clothes and another man's name might give him a new start, but before he could begin a new life, he needed to put the old one to rest. He'd have a little whiskey in his coffee. That should perk him up some. And he'd be weaning himself off the drink a little bit every day.

"I'll have to learn to read some better," he said aloud. "But it's a powerful long way between some towns out here. I can practice on the way."

He began to pack. "And I know there's a better way to baptize, but I'll watch one done before I try another."

With that promise made to himself, he checked Randall Howe's ticket for his next destination.

"I've always believed that a man should see what he can of the world a'fore he passes, but Sagebrush Pass will have to wait a bit until I get back from Dodge City." He frowned and rubbed his belly, ignoring the tremble in his hands. The need for drink was strong, but the urge to escape Lizard Flats was stronger. He laid Randall's Bible on the top of his clothes and then fastened the straps on the suitcase.

The more he talked to himself, the better it sounded. By the time he went down to get breakfast, the decision was firm in his mind.

Right in the middle of his bacon and eggs, Letty showed up wearing a dress he'd never seen before. Somewhere she'd found a new set of clothes to go with her new identity. He paused in mid-bite, wondering if this was where he ran like hell, or stood and offered her a chair.

"Preacher?" There was a question in her voice that he wasn't sure how to answer. Either she was asking for permission to sit down, or checking on his identity of the day.

She blinked and then smiled, so he swallowed his bite. It seemed it would be the chair.

"Miss Letty, won't you join me?"

She sat and when her food arrived, picked at it like a proper lady, afraid to show her appetite for anything, especially life. Her bites were dainty and she kept dabbing at the corners of her mouth with her napkin as if she'd suddenly sprung a leak.

"What are your plans?" she asked, then leaned forward and lowered her voice. "Will thinks Eulis left town with the last freight wagon. He's not too happy on having to sweep his own floors, and just so you know, I gave him notice that I'm leaving, too."

Eulis gawked. He couldn't get over the change in her. She was a different woman, right down to the way she ate.

"Where am I going? I'm going to Sagebrush Pass, by way of Dodge City," he said.

She nodded and used a bite of bread to sop the egg yolk from her plate.

"I can play the piano, when there's one to play," she offered. "And as you know, I sing. I can also count money and read real good. I got all the way through the first primer before Daddy died."

Eulis was beginning to sweat. What was she saying?

"That's fine. Real fine, Miss Letty."

"Leticia, if you don't mind," she amended, then batted her eyes like a vestal virgin.

Eulis choked on his swig of coffee and

mopped at his chin, hoping he hadn't splattered his clean shirt.

"Leticia. Of course, of course," he said. "Leticia it is."

She fixed him with a hard blue stare. "Then you'll be taking me with you. After all, you're gonna need to practice up on several things, includin' baptizin' your congregation."

It wasn't a question. It had been a demand. And he took instant offense to her criticism of the way he'd handled the situation last night.

"I don't know as how I was so far off. It seemed to do you a world of good," Eulis said, and tried not to frown. He didn't suppose preachers were supposed to glare.

Letty snorted. It was an unladylike noise from a woman who called herself Leticia, but it got his attention, nevertheless.

"One for the money, two for the show, my ass," Letty grumbled, then leaned across the table. "It goes: I baptize you in the name of the Father, and, uh, the Holy Ghost, and stuff like that."

Eulis leaned back in his chair and nervously slicked down the part in his hair. "I'll practice on it some."

"Not on me, you won't," Letty warned. "And not in no more horse troughs, neither. I was still blowing moss out of my nose this morning. I'll probably come down sick."

This time Eulis glared. Hard.

"You shoulda kept your mouth shut and your dress buttoned, and you wouldna' had no moss gettin' where it didn't belong. Besides, you was plumb out of your head. I asked you twice last night if you knowed what you was doin', and all you could say was you wanted to be saved. It wasn't me that was had by the Devil." He tried not to grin. "By the way, how are your legs?"

Her eyes narrowed at the mention of her body parts. Eulis got the message real fast. She'd become a proper lady, all right. In the old days when he helped his daddy farming and before he'd been a soldier and then a drunk, he seemed to remember that it wasn't seemly to mention limbs and such to a lady. He felt obliged to correct himself by adding, "The scratches! I meant, how are the scratches?"

She relaxed. "Oh! They're healing up just fine."

Something about the smirk on his face made her ask. "How did you do that?"

"Do what?"

"Make the Devil scratch at me."

His eyes widened. She still didn't know.

And something told him that the less she knew, the better off he was. After all, a man needed all the power he could get to save himself from a reformed whore.

"I don't know what you're talkin' about. I was as surprised as the next man to see you yank up your skirt tail and show them marks on your legs."

It wasn't a lie. Not really. He hadn't expected her to believe the Devil was up her dress. If she hadn't had such a guilty conscience, she would have known for certain that it had been a critter and not a demon that had taken refuge under her skirt.

A long moment of silence passed between them. Letty could still remember yesterday's panic and the knowledge that she'd committed an unforgivable sin. Somewhere between then and now she'd been given an unexpected opportunity.

While she suspected that Eulis wasn't telling her all that he knew, she didn't care enough to press the issue. She wasn't about to mess up her last chance to change her life.

Eulis dropped his napkin onto his plate and stood. "The wagon leaves in an hour, my dear."

Letty frowned. "I'm packed. And maybe you'd best not call me, 'dear'. People might get the wrong impression."

She flitted away to get her bag, leaving Eulis with a sinking feeling that while he was going to be in the company of a once-willing woman, she'd given up "willing" for "willful" and was going to conveniently forget about all those free pokes.

He went to get his bag and tried not to dwell on his disappointment regarding Miss Leticia Murphy, late of the White Dove Saloon, and now the new "assistant" to one traveling preacher on the amen trail.

A short while later, he stood outside, waiting for the Hollis Freight wagon to show up. "Get over it, Eulis," he muttered. "You been on dry tit before. Just because you lost a woman you never had and gave up sex you didn't get, don't mean you got to bawl about it."

Letty walked up behind him. "What was that you were saying?"

Eulis squinted against the glare of sun and the blast of dust that careened down the middle of the street.

"I was givin' myself a sermon."

Leticia grinned, and for a minute Eulis saw past her new facade to the old Letty beneath.

"Did it take?"

"I don't know," Eulis answered. "Only time will tell."

They smiled at each other and then turned to look at the freight wagon that was pulling into town. The first step to Dodge City. It was time to lay the past to rest.

Rest in Peace,

You Dirty Bastard

Dodge City was everything Eulis had imagined and more. He'd never seen so many people in one place in his entire life and it occurred to him as the stagecoach pulled to a halt in front of a grand hotel, that he might have been able to fool people back home, but these were of a different breed. They had culture and class and fine clothes and money. What if they saw through his act? Worse yet, what if somebody here knew the real Randall Howe? His gut drew as the passengers began to disembark.

Letty was as wide-eyed and anxious as Eulis, but not from anxiety. No one here knew her, except for Miles and Truly, who'd mentioned they might come this way. If she saw them, she'd take care to stay out of their sight because today was the beginning of her new life. She got up from her seat. Her foot was on the top step when the driver ran to give her a hand.

"Watch your step, there ma'am," he said lightly, and doffed his hat as her skirts hit the ground.

Letty blinked. So this was what propriety was like. She smoothed a hand down the front of her dress, taking pride in its plain color and simple style, and turned to wait for Eulis. Then she amended her thought. He wasn't Eulis anymore. She couldn't bring herself to call him Randall, or Reverend Howe, because that one had died in her bed. So she'd settled for Preacher, instead. It seemed to suit them both.

Eulis came out of the coach with less vigor than Letty. Fear had a good hold on him now and his need for a drink outweighed his desire to continue this mad escapade. And then he saw the expectation and the excitement on Letty's face and sighed. No drinks. At least not today.

"Here's your bags, Reverend Howe, and those of your sister."

Sister? Eulis turned. The driver was smiling at Letty. Eulis's mind shifted gears. Oh yes. The deception had taken on new depths.

"Yes, thank you," he said absently, and then pointed at the town. "Is it always this busy?"

The driver grinned. "Sometimes, like when the trail herds come through, or like now, when they're gonna have a hanging."

Eulis's heart skipped a beat. "Indeed?"

The driver nodded. "Yep. Tomorrow, I think. Ever heard of Kiowa Bill?"

The scent of smoke was suddenly up his nose. The thunder of hoof beats were loud in his ear. The sound of screams — and then silence.

"Yes, I've heard of Kiowa Bill."

"They're hanging him at dawn tomorrow." Then he eyed Eulis with new respect. "Say, I heard they were looking for a preacher to take the walk with him."

Eulis's panic subsided. He'd come to watch a hanging. Being a part of the ceremony was more than he'd hoped for.

"Then who might I see about such matters?" Eulis asked.

The driver pointed. "Sheriff's office is across the street and around the corner. I reckon you'd take it up with him."

Eulis nodded. "I thank you sir, for bringing my . . . uh, sister and I safely to our destination, and for your information as well."

Pleased by the preacher's praise, the driver beamed as he hurried away.

Eulis offered Letty his arm. "Sister

Murphy, let's go get our rooms. I'm sure you would like to rest before supper."

Letty beamed. Respect was a wonderful thing. "Why yes, Preacher, I believe that I would."

A short while later, secure in the knowledge that Letty was napping, Eulis locked the door to his room and headed downstairs. Five minutes later he was standing in the sheriff's office with his hat in hand.

The sheriff was writing at his desk. Eulis waited. There was plenty to occupy his mind, like that closed door behind the sheriff's desk that led to the jail.

He took a deep breath and then shivered. This was the closest he'd been to Kiowa Bill in more than twenty-five years. A part of him wanted to cry, just like that twelve-year old boy had done on the day everything died.

And then the sheriff looked up and Eulis made himself focus on the business at hand.

"Sheriff, my name is Reverend Randall Howe. I'm just passing through."

The sheriff stood. "Nice to meet you, Reverend. Name's Ben Wells. What can I do for you?"

Eulis took a deep breath. Everything he was hinged upon getting this right.

"I understand you are in need of a minister for the hanging tomorrow morning."

A smile shifted the spare contours of the sheriff's lips. "Would you be offering yourself for the job? It don't pay anything, you know."

Eulis waved away the idea of money as if it were filth. "That doesn't matter," he said. "I couldn't take money for this."

Sheriff Wells nodded. "I understand. Hangin' is a dirty business."

"But sometimes necessary," Eulis added.

Surprise showed on Ben Wells' face. Most preachers he'd known spouted that 'turn the other cheek' pap. Out here, if you didn't fight back, you were dead.

"You're right about that. Old Kiowa Bill has needed killin' for years. He has torn up his share of the Territory for far too long. It was only luck that we got him when we did."

Eulis added, "And maybe some of God's blessing."

Sheriff Wells grinned. "I reckon you can give God some of the credit at that, although the Marshall who brought him in might argue the point."

Eulis felt giddy. It was going to work after all. "So, I will see you here at first light."

Ben Wells shook Eulis's hand. "That's right. And thanks a lot, Preacher. Kiowa Bill has been a devil on earth, but I reckon he deserves his chance at redemption like everyone else."

Eulis made it outside without laughing, then all the way through supper without crying. By the time he'd seen 'Sister Murphy' to her door and gone to his own room, he was shaking. He came close to going after a bottle twice, but both times the image of his mother's face had stopped him at the door. Finally, he lay down on his bed and stared out the window. He'd been waiting for this moment most of his life and now that it was imminent, he didn't know how he felt other than hanging the man would be too swift for the justice he craved.

He never closed his eyes.

When shades of gray began to appear on the horizon, he got out of his bed, put on a fresh shirt, washed his face and combed his hair, taking care to get the part in the middle just right. Then he fastened the clerical collar around his neck and put on his coat. With the Bible in hand, he started out the door and then stopped, moved by the need to say more than a prayer.

He stood there in the silence of the room, remembering his mother's face and his father's laugh and that his little brother had not learned to walk before he'd been murdered. He remembered fear and then anger and the sound of the axe upon flesh. He reached for his hat, then walked out the door.

"I don't want no damned preacher at my heels," Kiowa Bill yelled, and threw his coffee cup full of coffee. Coffee splattered against the wall. The tin cup rattled to the floor.

Sheriff Wells shrugged. "It ain't about what you want any more."

The outlaw was still cursing as Sheriff Wells closed the door between the jail and his office. To his surprise, the preacher was standing by his desk.

"You're early," he said.

Eulis clutched the Bible close to his chest and then nodded.

"Want a cup of coffee?" the sheriff asked.

Eulis's jaw clenched. He made himself relax. "Don't mind if I do," he said.

The sheriff poured, then handed Eulis the cup. "It's black as hell and twice as strong." When he realized what he'd said, he grinned. "Sorry, Preacher. Didn't mean to say anything out of order."

Eulis shook his head. "It's nothing." Then he took a sip. "And I would say you were right."

Sheriff Wells grinned, then glanced at his watch. "Another five minutes and it'll be time to go."

Eulis turned to the window, gazing across the way to the scaffold that had been built, and then to the hanging noose. A ripple of satisfaction shifted some of his nervousness aside. Not a lot, but enough that he could finish his coffee without throwing up.

"People are gathering," he commented.

Sheriff Wells nodded. "Yeah. When it's over, they'll have themselves a party. See there." He pointed out the window. "Someone is already selling food in the street."

Eulis nodded. They were celebrating death in the same way that Kiowa Bill had taken lives, without guilt or thought of how their families might feel.

"It's time," Sheriff Wells said.

The empty coffee cup slipped from Eulis's fingers and onto the floor.

"Sorry," he said, and bent to pick it up.

Wells' gaze narrowed. So the man wasn't

as cool as he seemed. That was understandable.

"Wait here," he said shortly. "I'll be right back. When we walk out the door, you'll walk in front of us all the way up the steps. If old Bill asks for some particular scripture to be read, then you'll do it. You can pray over him if you're a mind to, as well, although I'll tell you now that he ain't none too happy you're here."

It was that bit of information that gave Eulis the strength he needed.

"That's all right," Eulis said. "He doesn't have all that much time left to be pissed off about anything."

Sheriff Wells grinned. Damned if he didn't like this preacher more with every minute. He disappeared into the back.

Eulis was shaking. His belly was rolling and he needed to throw up. But he wouldn't let himself or his family down. And when the door opened a few minutes later, he came face to face with the man who'd changed his world.

Kiowa Bill took one look at the man in the suit, and then the book he was holding and spit.

"I told you I didn't want no goddamned preacher," he muttered, and gave Eulis a hard, angry stare.

Eulis looked at the handcuffs on his wrists and the leg irons on his ankles, then straight at the scar. It separated one side of his face from the other in a long, puckering line. It was obvious to Eulis that he'd done Kiowa Bill great harm. If only he'd stayed and finished the job, a lot of people would still be alive today. Then he reminded himself that he'd only been twelve.

"What the hell are you starin' at?" Kiowa Bill asked.

Eulis heard the echo of his own childish voice. *I'll make you pay. I'll make you pay.* But he didn't trust himself to speak. Instead, he opened his Bible and started out the door with the lawman and the outlaw at his heels.

The sun was warm upon Eulis's face. Off to his left he heard a horse nicker. Somewhere in the crowd that had gathered, a baby cried. The sound carried over the chatter of voices, chilling Eulis's soul. His little brother had died crying. He wanted Kiowa Bill to die scared. He started to pray, loudly, fervently.

"The Lord is my shepherd, I shall not want."

Kiowa Bill cursed. "Damn it, Sheriff, shut him up. Ain't I got any say in the way that I die?"

Wells gave the outlaw a hard look. "I reckon you've got about as much say so comin' as what you gave to the people you murdered."

Kiowa Bill hunched his shoulders and kept on walking. No need to look up. There was nothing to see but the waiting noose. Eulis's voice soared above the quieting crowd.

"Yea, though I walk through the valley of the shadow of death . . ."

For the first time in his adult life, Kiowa Bill Handlin was helpless. The preacher's words rang loudly in his ears. Everything was suddenly acute.

The warmth of the sun upon his face.

The sound of his footsteps as he moved along the ground.

The jingle of the chains that bound his hands and feet.

The scent of his own sweat.

It smelled of salt and of fear.

"Watch your step," the sheriff said, and tightened his grip on the outlaw's arm as they started up the steps to the waiting noose.

Eulis's voice droned on. Persistently pushing every nerve Bill Handlin had.

"I will fear no evil, for Thou art with me. Thy rod and Thy staff, they comfort me . . ."

Kiowa Bill's eyes narrowed angrily. Fear no evil? Hell, he'd done evil all his life. He wasn't stupid. There wasn't a damn thing on this earth that could give him comfort. They were going to stretch a rope around his neck and then drop the floor from beneath his feet. He was going to kick and sway until his face turned purple and his neck finally broke. Comfort? Hell. He needed a gun and a fast horse.

Up two steps. Then three, then another and another until they were standing on the platform.

Eulis's voice rolled out across the crowd. The only passage he'd ever memorized from the Bible was standing him in good stead.

"Thou preparest a table before me in the presence of mine enemies . . ."

Kiowa Bill glared at the preacher. "Shut up," he muttered. "Shut the hell up."

Eulis turned. His face was pale. His eyes were red-rimmed and blazing with a fire that made the outlaw step back.

"Thou anointest my head with oil, my cup runneth over."

Kiowa Bill suddenly shuddered. Something was wrong here.

Eulis's nostrils flared as he met the outlaw's hard gaze without flinching.

"Surely goodness and mercy shall follow me all the days of my life,"

"I don't want no more prayer," he muttered.

Eulis's head was pounding. The rage in him was so strong he could taste it.

"and I will dwell in the house of the Lord forever."

Suddenly it was silent. Kiowa Bill flinched as if he'd been slapped. He looked to his right. A hangman stood waiting. The black hood over his face was an ominous sign to the outlaw of things to come.

Then the sheriff moved him backward until he was standing directly underneath the noose. He flinched when they slid it over his head and then down beneath his ears. The rope was new and stiff, and he knew that the only thing that would give when they pulled was his neck.

Then Sheriff Wells said his piece, as he had at every hanging he'd attended since he'd come into office.

"Kiowa Bill Handlin, for all the crimes you have committed over the past thirty years, you have been sentenced to hang by the neck until dead. May God have mercy on your soul."

The crowd was silent now. Watching. Waiting. Kiowa Bill hated them for the fact that when this was over, they would still be breathing and he would not. He stared at the preacher again. The rage on the man's face was impossible to ignore.

Sheriff Wells gave the noose a quick tug, just to make sure it was safely in place.

"Do you have any last words?" he asked.

Fear mingled with frustration as Kiowa Bill stared out across the crowd. Last words? What a joke. Then his gaze moved from the sheriff to the man with the Bible.

"Yeah. Yeah, I do." Fixing Eulis with a cold, angry stare, his voice lowered to little more than a whisper. "Who the hell are you?"

Eulis leaned forward, just enough so that his voice wouldn't carry.

"I'm the man who gave you that scar."

Kiowa Bill's eyes widened in shock. He stared at the pale, fleshy face of the preacher, trying to find the tow-headed kid who'd thrown an axe in his face. Then something thumped and the floor beneath his feet disappeared.

Bill Handlin's last sight on earth was the preacher's satisfied smile.

Letty woke up to find herself virtually alone in the hotel. Panicked that Eulis had somehow skipped out of town without her, it had been all she could do to get dressed. It wasn't until she'd come running out onto the sidewalk that she'd seen the crowd at the other end of the street. The hanging! They were having the hanging! In the distance, she thought she could see Eulis standing on the platform, his Bible held close to his chest. At that point, she started running.

Moments later, she was pushing her way through the crowd, and it was all she could do just to breathe. Only after she saw Eulis's face clearly, did she start to relax. He hadn't left her after all. He was just performing his Christian duties as a minister of the faith.

There was a sudden thump and then the floor fell out from beneath the outlaw's feet. He commenced to swaying and jerking like a chicken with its head wrung off. Letty looked at Eulis and frowned. He was smiling. She'd have to talk to him some about that. Preachers were supposed to stay solemn.

Satisfied that her shaky new world was still centered, she took out her handkerchief and dabbed at her eyes. Not because she cared a whit for the outlaw who had just peed his pants, but in relief that Eulis hadn't let her down.

Silence held sway over the crowd until the hangman cut the rope and Kiowa Bill Handlin's body dropped through the hole in the platform to the undertaker's wagon beneath. A collective cheer went up and a few moments later, people began to disperse.

Letty waited. Not because she was afraid any longer, but because it was her duty as the preacher's sister to stand at his side. And then Eulis was coming toward her.

"I see you're awake," he said. "Did you pass a good night?"

Letty stared. For a man who'd just witnessed a hanging up close, he was in an awful good mood.

"Uh . . . yes, yes I did."

"That's good," Eulis said, and offered her his arm. "How about some breakfast, Sister?"

She glanced back at the scaffold and then up at Eulis. "What was that all about?" she asked.

"Just fulfilling my duties."

She lowered her voice, anxious that no one overhear her berating a man of the cloth. "You should not have smiled."

Eulis frowned, as if considering her criticism. "You're probably right. If there's ever a next time, I'll take better care."

Satisfied that she'd done her sisterly duties, she took Eulis's arm. "About that breakfast you promised."

Eulis settled his hat a bit firmer on his head. "Then let's go. I'm a man who likes to keep promises."

The wind tore through the dust, lifting it into the air in a yellow-brown spiral. Eulis held onto his hat and Letty reached for her skirts.

It was going to be another hot day.

EPILOGUE

"Reverend Howe! I say . . . Reverend Howe!"

Eulis wiggled on the seat of the stagecoach and shifted his gaze from the bouncing bosom of Leticia Murphy, the sleeping whore turned preacher's helper, to the liquor salesman who was accompanying them in the coach.

"Yes?"

The salesman opened his case and offered Eulis one of the sample bottles. "It's a right dusty ride. If it isn't against your religion, I'd be proud to offer you a sample of my wares."

Eulis shook his head. "No, but thank you, my son. We'll be arriving in Denver before long and I need to be at my best."

The salesman nodded and closed his case.

It has to be said that Eulis did consider it. But several things prompted him to refuse.

One being the sharp kick on his shins

459

from the dainty toe of Sister Murphy, who obviously wasn't as sleepy as he'd assumed. Another was the slack-jawed expression of the little man who'd offered the drink. He looked as if he imbibed a bit too freely in what he sold, and to Eulis, it was like looking at a reflection of his old self — something he didn't want to regain. He was a man of the cloth now. Worldly pleasures were a part of his past.

But the benevolent smile stayed square on Eulis's face as the stagecoach continued to roll. Eulis was getting real good at those fatherly smiles and he knew it. He practiced on a daily basis.

Leticia Murphy had been fond of saying that practice makes perfect. Eulis figured she should know. She'd been the best whore in the Kansas Territory until a preacher had changed her life.

And while Eulis had a firmer grip on his life, he didn't know that last night Leticia Murphy had suffered a rendezvous with her past, or that she'd stood at her window until long after most of the town had gone to sleep, listening for the call of a small, brown bird.

It had been close to morning when she'd finally heard it, off in the distance, and almost too faint to be sure. At that moment, something happened that had never happened before. Right above her head, she'd heard an answering call. Startled, she had leaned so far out of the window that she'd almost fallen as she'd searched the night sky for a glimpse of the mate.

For a few moments, she'd seen nothing but the outline of rooftops and the faint glow of a lantern in the sheriff's office down the street. Then the call had come again, and this time when the second bird answered, she saw it take flight.

In that moment, her vision blurred and her voice started to shake.

"Oh, Mamma, I should have known you were right. It just took time and patience for me to understand."

Her hands were shaking as she went back to her bed, but her heart was light and ready for what the future held. Even before daybreak, she was up and packed, awaiting a new day. Now her life had purpose and her future was bright. Maybe one day she would find someone who would love her for who she was and not who she'd been, but until that day came, she was satisfied with what she'd become.

If she was ever blessed with children of her own, she was going to teach them to listen for the whippoorwill. She could picture it all now, cradled by darkness and safe within the shelter of her arms, they would sit on the front steps of their home and feel the warmth of the dirt between their toes, maybe even smell the dampness as dew settled on the grass.

And maybe, just maybe, while they were waiting for the bird to call, if they were quiet long enough and old enough to know the difference, they would be able to hear their own heartbeats and know the truth of their own minds before it was too late.